Sweet Surrender

Also by Deanna Lee

Games Girls Play

Exposing Casey

"Abundance" in *Sexy Beast IV*

Barenaked Jane

Undressing Mercy

Published by Kensington Publishing Corporation

Sweet Surrender

DEANNA LEE

APHRODISIA
KENSINGTON PUBLISHING CORP.
www.kensingtonbooks.com

APHRODISIA BOOKS are published by

Kensington Publishing Corp.
119 West 40th Street
New York, NY 10018

Copyright © 2011 by Deanna Lee

All rights reserved. No part of this book may be reproduced in any form or by any means without the prior written consent of the Publisher, excepting brief quotes used in reviews.

All Kensington titles, imprints, and distributed lines are available at special quantity discounts for bulk purchases for sales promotion, premiums, fund-raising, and educational, or institutional use.

Special book excerpts or customized printings can also be created to fit specific needs. For details, write or phone the office of the Kensington Special Sales Manager: Kensington Publishing Corp., 119 West 40th Street, New York, NY 10018. Attn. Special Sales Department. Phone: 1-800-221-2647.

Aphrodisia and the A logo Reg. U.S. Pat. & TM Off.

ISBN-13: 978-0-7582-3500-8
ISBN-10: 0-7582-3500-3

First Kensington Trade Paperback Printing: April 2011

10 9 8 7 6 5 4 3 2 1

Printed in the United States of America

1

Lauren Evans was so very, very late. The rush across Boston had left her flustered, and her once perfectly contained hair now flew all over her head. The job at Holman Academy was the chance she needed to change her life—to make the move to Boston permanent. The last thing she wanted to do was stay in San Diego.

She had one successful show under her belt, and she hoped that after years of work, it was enough to give her a change of scenery. Her stomach tightened as she shoved more money than was necessary at the cabdriver and hopped out of the car, putting on the shoes she'd pulled off as she'd gratefully hauled herself into it fifteen minutes before.

Lauren pulled out the hairpins that had managed to stay in and shook out the too-long mess as she pulled open one of the double glass doors that led into the Holman Gallery. As soon as Lauren entered, a slim, dark-haired woman stepped forward with a wide, friendly grin.

"Your pictures don't do you justice," she stated, and held out a hand. "I'm Jane Tilwell. Welcome to Holman Gallery.

Mercy sends her apologies for not being available today, but we've set up a lunch for you two tomorrow. You'll have to pardon the noise today—we have fifty fifth graders on the first floor breaking plates for an abstract mural we're going to put on the east wall of the building."

"That sounds great." Lauren allowed herself to be pulled through the gallery and up a set of stairs. "I've heard some great things about the student program the gallery runs with the city schools."

"It's my baby, so I'm proud of how well it's done. This session was supposed to be led by Lisa Brooks, but she's so very pregnant and her doctor put her on bed rest. So Shamus Montgomery is here today, and his idea of entertaining children involves safety goggles and throwing things." Jane cupped Lauren's elbow to guide her into a large office area. "Mr. Brooks, however, is on-site today, and we've set up a small conference room for a meeting. He's pretty excited to have you here, Ms. Evans. Your exhibit in LA was the talk of the art world for months, so, of course, we'd like to discuss a show at a later date."

Lauren managed to keep her mouth from dropping open. "I have fifteen paintings of a series I'm working on, but when my agent set up this appointment, I assumed it was an interview."

Jane paused and turned to her with a frown. "No, not an interview." She huffed out a breath. "I'm going to kill her."

"Kill who?"

"My ex-new assistant and probably Mr. Brooks, too. I had a great assistant—a fantastic assistant—but James Brooks kept bogarting her until finally he just kept her, and now I'm stuck with a series of twits from the university because it was my ultrabright idea to *mentor*."

Lauren bit her bottom lip to keep from laughing. "So, I'm not here for an interview."

"No, we"—she blushed—"we offered you a job, Ms. Evans. A two-year contract for the Holman Academy as the artist in residence and an opportunity to show once a year in the gallery."

The relief of that moment was so overwhelming that Lauren felt a little dizzy. "I . . . wow . . . really?"

Jane laughed. "Okay, let's go talk to Mr. Brooks, and we'll discuss the deal we thought we'd already made with you."

So, meeting James Brooks was sort of like what she thought meeting Thomas Crown would be like if he were real. All dark, hot, mean-looking, and *loaded*. What she knew about him made him even more attractive than his altogether too-pretty face. His dedication to charity work and his well-known love for his wife made James Brooks the kind of man she would love to work for.

"Twit the Fourth didn't send the job offer."

James Brooks raised an eyebrow. "It was your idea to mentor students, Ms. Tilwell."

"Obviously I can't be trusted to make such decisions in the future," Jane muttered as she flipped through several folders in front of her. "Okay, Lauren, as I said, we meant to send you a contract memo through your agent. Again, I apologize for the confusion."

"It's fine," Lauren murmured. "I think my interest must be clear, since I traveled across the country for what I thought was an interview." She blushed and took a deep breath. "I could use a change of scenery, to be honest."

Brooks offered an utterly charming smile, and Lauren couldn't help but smile, in return. "I think we can certainly arrange that. My wife finds your work inspiring, and what inspires her interests me greatly."

She really didn't know how his wife could even think when he was around, especially if he smiled at her like that. "I had the privilege of seeing part of the *Shattered* collection several years ago on display in San Diego. I'm honored that someone so talented as your wife would find inspiration in my work."

"Lisa is a student of the arts in all forms, but her sculpture is what draws the crowds these days. I think she'd eventually like to return to canvas work. One reason why we are so interested in having you at Holman is for your use of oils and watercolors. She finds your mixture of mediums stunning and complex. Our last long-term artist in residence was a sculptor. We believe you will offer the academy something new and exciting."

"And I would have show space in the gallery once a year?"

"Yes, we'll open a show for you once a year and house the collection for six months. We have a standard contract on the proceeds of such showings that would be separate from your employment at the academy. We would also arrange, through your agent, for the show to travel anywhere you'd like."

Jane Tilwell slid a contract across the table. "This is the contract that should have been sent to you through your agent. After this meeting, I'll send one her way for review and we can refine it any way she deems necessary. In the meantime, you can look it over and let us know if there are changes to be made."

It was a dream come true. A new city. A place where she wouldn't have to continue to look over her shoulder. Lauren pushed all thoughts of that situation aside and managed a smile for the other two people in the room.

"Sounds great."

Twenty minutes later, she found herself on a guided tour of the gallery with Jane Tilwell. The contract, clutched tight in her hand, was the most surreal lifeline ever. Her fingers compulsively curled around the rolled-up envelope as she viewed some of the most beautiful art in the country—including a few private collections that she knew hadn't been shown in public in over fifty years.

"It's amazing," Lauren confided. "It must be very rewarding to work in a place like this every day."

"The work we do here is beautiful both in reality and intent," Jane admitted. "I never thought I'd have a position so fulfilling." She led Lauren into a small room. "This is the special collections exhibit—it's where we'll house your show for half the year. It's probably the most coveted show space in the city, and you'll make yourself and the Foundation a great deal of money."

That idea appealed on several levels, but mostly it was appealing because it was one more step in separating herself from San Diego completely. A chill ran down her spine, and she pushed down a swarm of emotions that she could barely contain.

"There's my favorite lady."

They both turned at those words, and Lauren's eyes widened a little as an extremely good-looking black man strolled toward Jane with a predatory look.

Jane offered him a hand as soon as he got close. "Lauren Evans, this is my fiancé, Mathias Montgomery. He's the head of security for the Holman Foundation."

Lauren immediately offered her hand. "It's a pleasure, Mr. Montgomery."

His hand was warm, his grip firm without being unpleasant. "Ms. Evans, welcome to Boston. Mercy and Jane have been looking forward to your arrival for weeks."

Jane sighed. "You won't believe what Beverly did."

"Beverly?" Mathias frowned. "Was that the redhead who hung up on Lisa Brooks or the blonde who made a pass at Shamus?"

"Neither—Beverly will be known as the blonde who sent

Lauren Evans an invitation to be interviewed instead of the job offer."

Mathias laughed softly. "Wow, well, we are definitely pleased to see you in Boston, Ms. Evans."

"Lauren is fine." She glanced around the room and took in a few of the sculptures. "You're related to the artist?"

"Yes." Mathias nodded, and his gaze drifted to a sculpture of a couple carved in rosewood and ash. "I'm his older brother."

Lauren's gaze moved to the sculpture that Mathias still looked at. "He's lucky to have such beautiful and inspiring people in his life. I've noticed in the last few years that his work has taken a passionate and loving turn. The sexuality still punches you in the gut, but it's more settled now, beautiful and engaging all at the same time."

"I agree." Jane blushed. "But he'll never get me naked in his studio again."

They all laughed softly, and after a few minutes Mathias wandered away to take a phone call. Jane invited her to lunch, and Lauren found herself neatly maneuvered down the street to a small café.

"Since you didn't come prepared for a move as we expected..." Jane hesitated. "I can't believe I didn't call your agent to confirm the contract details before you arrived. It was a foolish mistake."

"No harm done," Lauren assured her. "I'm here and I'm very interested in the position. I'm sure that Rachel will find the contract in order, and we'll get everything settled quickly enough."

"Holman will take care of your moving expenses," Jane said. "We'll set up a company with your agent and get everything squared away. Do you own or were you renting?"

"I was subletting from a friend. All I'll need packed are my clothes. I'll be starting basically from scratch in Boston, but that's okay. I'm really ready for a change."

Jane set aside her water glass and frowned a little. "Just clothes? You were living in Los Angeles before the move to San Diego—were you subletting there as well?"

Lauren bit her bottom lip. "I was living with someone, but it didn't work out. I let him keep everything and just got the hell out of there. I've never been one to keep much of anything. My parents were both in the military, and we moved around a lot when I was younger. I don't get attached to things or places if I can help it."

"And the ex-boyfriend? Is he a problem?"

"Beyond putting a few dents in my credit, no. Scott is a user, and he found someone else to use not long after I hit the road. The last I heard, he'd married her. I almost sent her a condolence card but figured that might just be too cruel."

Jane laughed and shook her head. "Remind me sometime and I'll tell you about the last man I dated before Mathias."

"He's beautiful," Lauren said, and then her eyes widened. "I didn't mean to say that out loud."

Jane just grinned. "He is beautiful. He's gotten sexually propositioned by most of the artists who've shown at Holman, but so far he's only done that one project with his brother and only because it was for us both. The sculpture is actually an engagement present and isn't for sale. Though the gallery has been offered an obscene amount of money for it."

"I can imagine. It's easily the most intimate piece in the entire collection, and you both have great bodies." Lauren flushed. "Not that I was looking in some kind of perverted way."

Jane laughed again. "Oh, we know we're pretty."

The food came, giving Lauren a few minutes to censor her

tongue before she suffocated herself with her own foot. Jane Tilwell was nothing like what she'd imagined. Friendly, outgoing, and snarky just didn't mesh with the image she'd put together in her head for the assistant director of the Holman Gallery.

"Tell me about Mercy Montgomery."

"She's tall, redheaded, and built like a brick shit house. Honestly, I hated her on pure principle for the first three months I knew her. No woman should look like that and be smart and successful. It's just obscene." Jane grinned. "But she's also generous, funny, dedicated, and probably one of the best human beings I've ever met in my life. She loves life and sees beauty in the strangest things *and* people. You don't meet a lot of people like that in your life. I know I haven't. I count myself a very lucky person to work with her and be her friend. Really."

"Does she walk on water?"

"No, it might ruin her shoes." Jane wiggled an eyebrow as Lauren laughed. "Honestly, she's a great person. You're really going to like her a lot. Everyone does."

"Okay, I'll keep my automatic resentful period down to about a week," Lauren promised.

"You might need two weeks, considering she has a beautiful baby and a husband who thinks she's the reason the Earth continues to spin."

Lauren thought the relationships at the Holman Gallery seemed a little incestuous, but it wasn't uncommon in small working environments to see people come together and pair off. "Have you considered stealing your assistant back and letting Mr. Brooks do the mentoring for a while?"

"I don't hate those college kids that much," Jane confided. "I mean...don't get me wrong, I could cheerfully strangle all of the ones who made it into the internship program, but Lisa would leave those poor kids in shreds. She's furious to be on mandatory bed rest, and even I hesitate to pick up the phone when I see her on the caller ID. She was kind of mean before she got pregnant, but now it's like an extreme sport to take a phone call from her."

Lauren laughed. She'd heard enough about Lisa Brooks to believe that was true. Three years ago, she'd even found herself viewed a clip or two on the Internet of Lisa shooting trespassers with a paintball gun.

"Have you checked the town house personally?"

Connor Grant looked up from his laptop and raised one eyebrow at his boss. "No, I sent Mitchell and Bennett to take care of it. Has the new little diva had a problem?"

Mathias leaned against the door. "Ms. Evans hasn't moved into it, actually. She's staying at a hotel, but Jane will probably move her within the next few days. I just want to make sure everything is set with the security system."

"We had the entire place remodeled after Stein left two months ago. Jane handled the decorator, and Mitchell rekeyed all of the doors. The new security system was put in, complete with exterior cameras as planned." Connor closed his computer and sat forward a little. "Something wrong?"

"Just an itch I can't find to scratch," Mathias murmured. "I met her before Jane took her to lunch, and she looks skittish and on edge. Her background check didn't reveal anything shady—at least nothing that hit a law enforcement agency. She has a few credit issues, but they coincided with a loser exboyfriend. With the money she'll be hauling in here, it's not really an issue anymore."

"You think something is off about her?"

"She looks haunted," Mathias finally said. "And I've seen

women look like that before and I don't like it. I just want her to feel safe in the home that the Holman Foundation is providing."

Connor frowned and after a few seconds turned to his computer. He opened it and quickly found the security footage that showed Lauren Evans hopping barefooted out of a cab in front of the gallery. He smirked a little as she put on her shoes and shook out her hair in a way that instantly reminded him of sex.

Her ebony hair was falling down around her shoulders in a hopeless fall of curls as she entered the gallery. He switched to an interior view and watched as she met with Jane—confident but clearly a little rattled. Her face was beautiful, expressive. Her complexion honey brown, and her skin looked like silk even on the security footage. "Peaches and cream."

"What?" Mathias asked.

"My mum would say that about her," Connor murmured. "She looks like dessert."

"Hmm." Mathias leaned in and took a look. "Interested in taking a bite?"

Connor grimaced. "I don't mix with the artists. They're all insufferable."

"I'll be sure to tell Shame you said that." Mathias flicked a paperclip at him. "And Lisa Brooks."

"Lisa Brooks prides herself on being insufferable, and your brother is the biggest straight male diva I know. I like them both despite their faults, but I don't make exceptions for others."

Mathias's gaze flicked to the computer screen. "What? You don't like peaches and cream?"

"Fuck you," Connor muttered, and closed his laptop abruptly. "I don't like messy desserts."

Mathias stared at him for a few seconds and then started to laugh.

*　*　*

Lauren dropped the keycard to her hotel room on the carpet at her feet and looked around. The contents of her suitcase had been tossed around the room. The mattress was stripped bare, and all of the bed linens were on the floor.

She fumbled her cell phone out of her purse and then stared at it. She was absolutely alone in Boston and maybe even in the world, unless she counted her agent, which she really didn't. Friends had never been easy to make, and she'd learned as a child to never get attached to people because it wouldn't be long before her military parents would be reassigned.

Lauren clenched the cell phone in her hand and took a deep breath. She was absolutely not going to have a panic attack. It was stupid—she was thirty-one years old, which was too old to have a fit like a child because someone had made a mess of her hotel room.

"Jesus." She looked down at the phone and dialed the only person she really knew in Boston.

Thirty minutes later, Lauren decided that Jane Tilwell was a complete and total powerhouse. Lauren had been perched on the luggage rack in the room when Jane arrived with her fiancé and four intense men with guns.

One man with dark brown hair and startlingly blue eyes squatted down in front of her. Her eyes immediately dropped to the latex gloves he was wearing.

"I'm Connor Grant."

"Hi." *Hello, James Bond,* she thought, and then wondered how a British man ended up on Montgomery's security team. Lauren huffed out a breath. "Sorry to get you out in the middle of the night."

"Not a problem, Ms. Evans."

"Lauren."

"Lauren," Connor repeated. "I need a brief outline of your trip, starting in San Diego."

"Okay." She took a deep breath. "I left my apartment about two hours before my flight because airports sort of freak me out and I hate the extra security and I was afraid I would get pulled aside and you know *searched* and"—she blew out a breath—"I'm babbling."

"You are," he acknowledged. "Keep going."

"Okay, so I got on the plane."

"Did you sit next to anyone who seemed unduly interested in you?"

"No." She shook her head abruptly. "I purchased the ticket for the seat next to me, too. I didn't want..." She blushed. "It doesn't matter. There was no one beside me on the plane."

"The airport in Boston?"

"There was a limo there to pick me up. The driver had a sign with my name and produced identification to confirm his employment with Mr. Brooks. I made sure."

Connor nodded with a little frown. "And last night—after you checked in? Did you eat in your room or in the hotel bar?"

"A small café down the street. It wasn't very busy, but no one bothered me."

"Okay, so no one bothered you. Did you get approached by a man? Did someone offer to share his table with you? Walk you back to your hotel?"

"No, nothing like that. I'm pretty good at putting up no-trespassing signs." She blushed again as she said it, because every man in the room turned and looked at her, each wearing a small little frown like Connor's. She had no idea what that said about her, and maybe she didn't want to know.

"Did anyone knock on your door last night? Pay attention to you in the elevator?"

"No, why is this important?"

Connor sighed. "Because unless you're the kind of lass who doesn't own a stitch of underwear, all of yours has been taken."

Lauren's mouth dropped open. "Well, of course I wear panties. Who doesn't wear panties?"

Jane laughed and sat down beside her on the luggage rack. "Any high-end items?"

"Hmm. Well, yeah, I like to wear nice..." She hesitated. "Is that all that's missing?"

"Actually, no." Connor stood up from his place in front of her. "Come with me for a second."

She took the hand he offered and, with relief, curled her fingers against his nice, wide palm. Lauren forced herself to let go far sooner than she wanted and walked over to the suitcase with him. Inside it, her makeup bag lay empty, along with a few other things. She reached out but he stopped her.

"No touching, love. We have to let the police handle that part of things."

"Right." She huffed out a breath. "Okay, that's my makeup bag. Minimal stuff—powder, blush, lipstick, a few shades of eye shadow. It's all gone." The dark red leather bag that she'd hoped like hell airport security would let pass without comment was open and empty. "Jesus."

"Clear the room, gentlemen. Someone go downstairs to meet Detective Trainer in the lobby and get the manager of the hotel."

Lauren said nothing as everyone but Connor, Mathias, and Jane left without a word. She took a deep breath. "Are they all ex-military?"

"Yes," Connor answered.

"You?"

"Yes, plus some extra government-type work."

"This is why you asked about men?" Lauren demanded. "Because some pervert ransacked my room, taking all of my panties and makeup and my vibrator?"

"This was definitely not theft for profit. They didn't touch your computer or your jewelry."

Lauren nodded and glanced toward the small wooden box she'd left on the desk. "Can you open it so I can check?"

"Yeah." Connor flipped open the lid and glanced her way.

Lauren nodded. "That's . . . Nothing's missing. I was wearing everything I have that was *real*, anyway. This is mostly just crystal. I like the way it sparkles." Her voice broke a little. "I thought . . . I thought I was . . ."

"Getting away from this by leaving San Diego," Connor responded carefully.

"There was nothing like this," Lauren murmured. "It was just . . . a bad feeling and a few nightmares."

"Nightmares?" Connor asked.

"I felt like I was being watched, and sometimes that followed me into sleep. I haven't slept well in months because of it. The last few weeks I've been dreaming about a man breaking into my house. Several times he gets all the way into my bedroom before I wake up."

There was a knock on the door, and Jane let two men in. The one she called Shawn greeted Mathias warmly and then shared a look with Connor that was neither friendly nor hostile, and Lauren wondered about their history.

"What do we have, Grant?"

"No forced entry. No real financial bent to the theft. Just her undergarments, cosmetics, and a"—he glanced at her—"a sex toy."

Shawn raised an eyebrow and turned to the manager of the hotel. "Mr. Bernard, this is where you assure me and the pretty lady here that you don't have any convicted sex offenders on staff who would have access to her room."

The hotel manager shook his head. "We have a large staff, Detective Trainer, and the housekeeping staff aren't as thoroughly vetted as we'd like, due to high turnover. I no more than get a background check back on someone and they've already moved on to another job."

"So, what you're saying is that you stopped doing background checks because it was expensive and a waste of your time?" Connor asked, his voice carefully neutral.

"Administrative staff are checked. Housekeeping, maintenance, and janitorial not so much."

Lauren's stomach tightened at the man's flippant tone, but before she could respond, a cell phone started ringing.

Jane answered her phone, her gaze fixed on the hotel manager. She glared at him until he looked away and then stalked away to have a private conversation. Trainer and Grant were both still glaring at the hotel manager.

"I have a forensics tech waiting in the hallway. We'll take fingerprints, but considering the transitory nature of a hotel, I don't think we'll get anything on that front." Shawn shook his head.

Connor nodded and then both turned to look at Lauren. "You two haven't been introduced yet. Lauren, this is Detective Shawn Trainer, Boston PD. Shawn, this is Lauren Evans. She'll be working at Holman as the artist in residence. We'll be setting her up at the town house."

Shawn took the hand Lauren offered and looked over her drawn, pale features. "Are you up for a few questions?"

"I can try," Lauren whispered. She looked toward Connor and cleared her throat. "You'll..."

"I'm not going anywhere," Connor assured her, and

checked his watch. "Mr. Bernard, is there an empty room on this floor we can use while forensics handles this one?"

The manager nodded and pulled out his cell phone. "I'll find one."

Within a few minutes, Lauren found herself in a room nearly identical to hers. Grant was leaning against the wall near the window. Jane had settled in beside her on a small couch, and the cop, Shawn Trainer, was seated in front of her on a large ottoman. Her gaze flicked several times to the gun he wore, and then she concentrated on the floor.

"Okay," Shawn started. "Grant, anything to worry about here?"

"Loser ex-boyfriend she dumped last year. She has no criminal record—never even had a traffic ticket. She's never reported anything or anyone to the police for an incident like this, though she has had a few altercations with a neighbor in the last few months that resulted in a few patrol-car visits. No charges or warnings."

Lauren blushed and huffed out a breath. "He's an asshole."

"What kind of asshole?" Shawn asked. "The kind of asshole who watches you undress with a high-powered telescope or the kind of asshole who puts his garbage in your trash can?"

She laughed a little. "The kind of asshole who reports me to the police because I paint pornography and have naked men in my apartment at all hours. He tried to say I was hiring prostitutes."

Jane snickered but sobered when Lauren glared at her. "Not funny?"

"Well, maybe in a year or two. But you try explaining to a couple of uniformed cops that the nineteen-year-old college student you have tied up on a bondage cross *naked* is being paid for it and it's okay—that he's even getting college credit for it."

Jane's eyes widened a little. "Do you have pictures?"

"Of course." Lauren grinned. "But, the neighbor is more of a nuisance than a real problem. I don't even think the cops respond to his complaints anymore."

Shawn nodded. "I suppose Grant has already covered this with you, but who have you had contact with since you came to Boston?"

"Beyond hotel staff, the limo driver, a taxi driver, and the people at the gallery, no one really. I haven't had time. I've barely been in the city twenty-four hours. I don't know anyone here, that I'm aware of. I went to college at Washington State, and I went high school in a variety of locations because my father was in the army. I have no siblings, cousins, or living parents. The only person from San Diego who knows where I'm staying in Boston is my agent, Rachel Keller."

Connor Grant's phone rang, and he had a one-word conversation before closing it with a snap and returning it to its holster. "The loser ex-boyfriend had dinner with his wife an hour ago in San Diego, so he's not an issue."

Lauren frowned at him briefly and then looked at Trainer, who had a questioning look on his face. "He married her after he ruined my credit and I dumped him."

Shawn just quirked an eyebrow and nodded. "Did you have any money in the room? My wife tells me you're an up-and-coming star in the art world and had a very successful show in LA last year."

Lauren shook her head. "No, I used the money I made in LA to pay off the credit cards the loser ex-boyfriend went mad with while we lived together. I have a bit left over, but it's in savings. I rarely carry any serious amount of cash on me—I can use my debit card in most places, anyway." She tucked a lock of hair behind her ear. "Who's your wife?"

"Casey, the assistant Brooks stole from me," Jane explained.

"You didn't meet her—she's on maternity leave. Babies are contagious at Holman; it's in the water there, so be careful. And avoid the break room and any flat surface a fertile male has touched."

Lauren laughed before she could help herself. "Yeah, okay." But secretly she thought she wouldn't mind a flat surface and a man. It had been a while since she'd found herself occupied by a man in that fashion.

Connor pushed away from the wall and took a seat on the other side of her. "Okay, Lauren, talk to me. Tell me why you look like you haven't slept in weeks and why your nails have dug grooves into your palms. Explain why you bought two seats to fly solo to Boston and why you put out no-trespassing signs so men don't even think about trying to buy you a drink."

Lauren flushed. "I didn't want anyone to sit next to me on the plane."

"You're not sleeping," Jane whispered. "Come on, Lauren, I know it's hard to trust us because we're strangers, but we can't help you if we don't start somewhere."

"It's stupid." Lauren shook her head. "I keep waking up because I dream I'm not alone in the room. I wake up and there is no one there—there is never anyone there." Her voice broke a little, and she left the small couch abruptly. "My agent says I'm paranoid."

"Paranoid or not, someone broke into your hotel room and took intimate personal items from you," Shawn Trainer said evenly. "Not your computer or your costume jewelry—he took personal things. He even shook out your laundry bag and took the underwear you wore last night."

Lauren took a deep breath. "And a box of tampons. That's missing from my suitcase as well."

"It's rude to ask, but are you menstruating? Your bathroom

trash was emptied, the bag taken. Housekeeping would have left a bag."

"No, not currently. I expected an interview and a nerve-wracking experience here while I waited on Holman's decision, so I came prepared for that. I emptied the trash can personally this morning before I left the hotel. I dropped the bag in a maid cart in the hall on my way out." She shrugged when everyone but Connor Grant frowned at her. "I couldn't leave the trash there when I left."

"So you cleaned your own room this morning and told maid service not to bother?" Connor asked.

"I asked her to leave a supply of trash bags on the counter. I think she did," Lauren admitted.

"How advanced would you say your OCD is?" Connor asked dryly.

"I like things to be clean, orderly." Lauren frowned at him. "It's not abnormal to want that."

"Not at all, lass." Connor raised one eyebrow. "Do you have any repetitive behaviors? Because I haven't noticed anything."

"No, I just like things to be clean, and I don't like strangers to touch me much, and I don't like a mess. I grew up with an army general for a father—messy wasn't allowed. I was a late-in-life child for them both. They hadn't anticipated ever having kids."

"Surprise," Jane said brightly with a little smile on her generous mouth.

"Very much so—I'm just thrilled they didn't name me that. Though my father did call me Little Miss Oops for years." She laughed a little. "At any rate, yeah, I took out my own trash."

"Since you don't like strangers to touch you, you would have noticed if anyone had taken an interest in you," Shawn started. "Right?"

"I'm aware of men—the control and discipline of their bodies. As an artist, even in college, I always focused on the male body. I started drawing men in my teens—being surrounded by perfect bodies on a military base proved to be pretty inspiring."

"You've had a lot of men in your studio in the past year—you said you almost had a show ready." Jane raised an eyebrow. "Anyone want to stick around and get an *in-depth* session with you?"

"No, the models I work with know better than to ask for sex. If I want it, I make it clear but I rarely do. They aren't ... In some ways they aren't even sexual to me when I'm working." She grinned then. "Though there was this student six months back who I talked into posing for me. I handcuffed him to a stripper pole ... nice."

"Anything personal happen?" Shawn asked with a frown. "Handcuffs?"

"Well, fake ones. They had a release on them if he started to freak out. He proved to be an excellent model—lots of patience and strength. As for personal, yes, but it was mutually not serious." She shared a smirk with Jane, who laughed but swallowed it quickly when Mathias cleared his throat.

"How many models have you used in the past year? Have any of them tried to contact you without your encouragement after your professional relationship ended?" Shawn asked.

"Eight and no. They were mostly students, and they worked for college credit and an hourly wage. I paid well for the sessions, and I ended up with a large roster of young men willing to pose for the collection. In fact, I've finished with that section of the collection and need only one more model for the last five paintings."

"I can't wait to see it." Jane hopped off the couch with her phone. "I need to update Mercy. Be right back."

Lauren didn't protest as Jane walked to the small foyer in

the large room and then disappeared into the bathroom. "Couldn't this just be an employee at the hotel? Someone with a fetish for girl stuff and a rabbit vibrator?"

Connor choked briefly and Shawn laughed. Mathias just shook his head and walked to the front of the room. "Well, I think that's entirely possible, but there is the matter of you thinking someone is watching you while you sleep."

Lauren shivered before she could stop herself. "It's stupid. My apartment was always secure—no open windows, no broken locks on my doors."

"You'd be surprised how easy it is for someone to get a copy of your keys," Shawn said, and he exchanged a knowing look with Connor. "You never called the police?"

"And tell them what? I can't sleep because I keep dreaming there is some man sitting on the bed beside me?" Lauren rolled her eyes. "Come now, Detective Trainer, how well would that have been received?"

"Okay," Shawn sighed. "No phone calls? No letters? Nothing missing from your apartment in San Diego?"

"No, nothing. Just SWS."

"SWS?" Shawn asked with a frown.

"Single woman's syndrome," Lauren informed him with a wry grin. "Noises in the night, flat tire I don't want to change myself, et cetera, et cetera. I'll get a dog and become a member of Triple A. All fixed."

"Except for the part where some perv stole your panties, makeup, and vibrator," Jane shouted from the bathroom.

"Oh, honestly," Lauren said.

"He could be wearing your panties *right now*."

Lauren's mouth dropped open, and she glared at Jane, who came out of the bathroom tucking her phone away. "I didn't need that image."

"Makeup, too. Maybe he has a wig." Jane frowned. "And a

dress. Did you notice if any of your regular clothes were missing?"

"It appeared to be all be there. I only brought a couple of outfits. I didn't want to check my luggage on the plane, so I packed light."

"When I pack light, I usually leave the sex toys at home," Jane informed her with a wicked smile.

"Really?" Lauren asked sweetly. "So your fiancé doesn't mind being left at home?"

Mathias laughed and Jane shook her head. "It's good to know you haven't let the loss of all of your panties get you down."

"Panties can be replaced easily." Lauren dropped back down onto the couch beside Connor. "But that was my favorite vibrator. That's a personal crime of the first order. What man does that to a woman?"

"It could be a woman," Shawn informed her.

"No way would another woman take my vibrator." Lauren shook her head.

"Agreed," Jane said. "It's a complete and total violation of the Girl Code of Conduct. You don't take another woman's vibrator or her Prada bag."

"Prada should have come first on the list," Lauren informed her, and then let her head fall back on the couch. "So what comes next?"

"We'll need a formal statement." Shawn stood. "You can come down in the morning to take care of it. A list of items missing and estimated value will help determine the type of crime we're dealing with. I'll check the hotel employees for sex offenders, and we'll get a record of your door's electronic lock to see when this happened. I already have a uniformed officer asking your neighbors if they saw anyone or anything odd."

"And you're moving into the Holman town house tonight," Connor announced. "I have a man checking it out right now. We'll have a car pick you up in the morning—no more public transportation for you for a while. I'm sure Jane and Mercy will arrange a shopping trip to take care of any replacements that need to be made." He looked at Shawn. "I take it she can't have anything from her room?"

"We'll see what the crime scene guys think," Shawn answered. "If there are no prints but hers on her computer case, I'm comfortable giving that back to her. We don't like to take that kind of stuff into evidence unless it's necessary."

2

The town house Holman provided was clean and furnished very nicely. Lauren immediately felt at home in the space. Connor Grant had gone through the place while Jane had given her a two-cent tour. She'd watched him from the corner of her eye, checking windows, the placement of motion sensors, and even a few pressure plates under the carpet.

He showed her the security panel and entered a series of codes for her to use. The setup was way sci-fi and an extreme comfort. She couldn't even imagine what the system had cost and wondered what exactly made the people at Holman as paranoid as she was.

Jane took her down into the basement of the town house and showed her a safe room. Lauren blew out a breath. "And I thought I was paranoid. What the hell, Jane?"

Jane looked around the basement with a frown on her face. "Lisa Brooks has a crazy ex-husband. Casey Trainer was stalked. I'm sure you know Mercy Montgomery's past—it's hardly a secret to anyone. Two years ago, I had a pansy, mama's-boy-stalker-type follow me around. As a result, James

Brooks is a little security conscious, and he lets Mathias and Connor pretty much do whatever they want on that front. Additionally, since this will be your home and your work space, you'll have very valuable art here—the kind of art that people would like to steal. We estimate that we'll see upward of twenty million dollars from your first show at Holman. That kind of money brings out the freaks."

"A pansy mama's-boy stalker?"

"Yeah, I mean, I had to call his mother to make him stop." Jane blushed when Lauren laughed. "Total idiot. It was all I could do to keep Mathias from killing him, and we were just sleeping together at the time."

Lauren snorted. She had a feeling that Jane and Mathias had never been *just* anything. She envied the fire and the connection that burned between them.

Back up in the kitchen, Connor Grant was at a table cleaning a 9 mm.

Lauren sat down at the table. "Is that for me?"

"Yes. If you want, I'll have Trainer push through a license for you, and we'll have a weapon picked out for you. This is mine and is licensed in my name." Connor offered her the weapon, grip first, and nodded when she took it confidently. "I trust your father taught you how to handle a weapon?"

"Yes, several." Lauren checked the gun over confidently, her thumb grazing over the safety to make sure it was in place. "Do you think I need this?"

"I think the security in this house will keep out the garden-variety idiot, but we can't trust that whoever broke into your hotel room isn't someone more accomplished. Keep this within reach while you're here, but do not take it from the town house."

Lauren nodded. "Yes, of course. I'm not licensed to carry here."

"We'll fix that," Jane said.

Lauren took a deep breath. "You know, I really don't think there is anything to worry about."

"It's a mistake to ignore your instincts," Connor said as he stood and pulled on his jacket. "We'll get to the bottom of what is going on soon enough. In the meantime, pay attention and call me if you need anything. The alarm system in the house will notify me immediately of a problem, so no worries. I'm five minutes from here when I'm in no hurry at all."

Lauren took it for the reassurance it was and glanced briefly at the gun before nodding. "Thank you, Mr. Grant."

"Connor," he corrected. "Call me in the morning when you're ready to start your day."

Lauren watched him leave and then turned to Jane. "Are all the men who work at Holman pretty, or is it just a coincidence that I've met only the hot ones?"

Jane laughed. "I did say that Mercy likes to surround herself with beautiful things." She rubbed the back of her neck. "So, anything you want to tell me that you didn't tell them?"

Lauren sighed. "Beyond the fact that it was my *favorite* vibrator and it was purple? No, not really."

"No creepy guy at the airport who made your gut itch but didn't actually do anything weird?"

"My dad never pulled his punches about teaching me how to defend myself or when to concern myself with someone's interest with me. He knew I'd be alone in the world after he died, and my mother died when I was pretty young."

"The only child of only children," Jane murmured. "Your bio makes you sound tragic and worldly all at the same time. It plays well with the buyers."

"Rachel says the same thing," Lauren admitted with a wistful smile. "My dad died on what would have been my parents' fiftieth wedding anniversary. We had a great dinner and watched his favorite movie. Then he went to sleep and didn't wake up. He was seventy-two, and I really wasn't ready to let him go. Though, honestly I doubt I would have ever been ready to let him go."

Jane stood up abruptly and went to the fridge. She pulled out two bottles of beer and opened both. Without comment, she put one in front of Lauren and then took a long drink from her bottle. "Mine killed himself. He was a cop, and my mother shows up once or twice a year on my caller ID. Sometimes I answer and sometimes I don't. My brothers work every day to forgive her for abandoning us, but I can't make myself work on it—not after she left us all because she didn't want to be a wife and mother anymore."

"I don't blame you." Lauren turned the beer bottle between her hands and picked at the green and white label before taking a drink. "So, the place has good supplies?"

Jane laughed. "Security stocked it. So, beer, sandwich meat, bread, and an impressive collection of takeout menus are surely on hand. We can do a grocery order later and get it delivered for you. After tonight, Mr. Brooks and Mathias just wanted you in a location they know is safe. I imagine the manager of the hotel will be in James Brooks's crosshairs in the morning."

Lauren wasn't sure if she wanted the man to be verbally eviscerated for being cheap and lazy. But then she changed her mind when she thought about her room and missing panties. "You know something?" She frowned at her beer. "I packed all of my really great panties for this trip. Ten matching sets. Now some jackass has them all—well, except the ones I'm wearing." She peeked in her blouse to check the color of her bra. "The baby-blue ones."

"That bastard," Jane murmured. "We'll get you a whole bunch of new ones tomorrow. Better ones. It'll be okay."

"That's easy for you to say! You don't have some perv jerking off on your *date* panties on his head."

Jane sputtered and then laughed outright. "You're going to fit right in."

At four o'clock in the morning, Lauren stopped trying to pretend to sleep and ran on the treadmill for nearly an hour. Afterward, she dragged her ass into the shower and stayed there until she exhausted the hot water heater. By six she was dressed and sitting at the table in the kitchen where she'd shared a beer with Jane Tilwill. The gallery didn't open until nine, and she was at a loss as to what to do with herself. Finally, she picked up the phone and called Connor Grant.

"This is Grant."

Lauren cleared his throat. "Good morning, Mr. Grant. I hope I didn't wake you."

"No, I just finished my run. Did you need me?"

That was certainly a loaded question, Lauren thought, and huffed out a breath. "Actually, I did an hour on the treadmill and showered and now I'm sitting here and the gallery doesn't open until nine and I'm babbling again."

He laughed, soft and easy. Lauren's stomach did a little dance at the sound. It had been entirely too long since a man had made her feel that way. "You're actually kind of cute when you babble. Have you eaten?"

"No, there isn't much in the way of that kind of food here. I thought about a peanut butter sandwich, but that's not prime breakfast material in my book."

"I couldn't agree more. Give me twenty minutes to shower, and I'll swing by to pick you up. We can do breakfast and tuck away a bit of food in the town house before we take you downtown to the gallery."

"Sounds good." Lauren bit down on her lip. "But not exactly in your job description."

"Let me worry about that. I'll see you in a few minutes."

Lauren had just pulled her panties out of the clothes dryer and wiggled into them when the alarm panel told her she had a visitor. A quick check of the monitor revealed Connor, and she hurried to the front to let him in.

He was dressed in a pair of tailored black slacks, a white button-down shirt, and a tie. A leather jacket was thrown over his wide shoulder. When he moved past her to enter, she caught the glint of his gun in a holster under his arm.

"How did you sleep last night?"

Lauren shrugged. "Not as much as I should have, but I think that's more habit than anything else. I think I'll settle down quickly enough. No nightmares—just worked up from the break-in." She pulled her phone off the charger and dropped it into her purse as Connor grabbed her light coat from the rack. "So, breakfast?"

"I have a favorite place down the street—their menu is pure indulgence, but it's not a bad place to visit once or twice a month," Connor explained as he settled her coat on her shoulders. "I didn't take you for a runner."

"I usually do five miles in the morning every day," Lauren admitted. "It helps clear my head. Is the place close enough to walk?"

"Yes, just a block away." Connor took care of activating the security system as they left, and Lauren allowed herself to be tucked close to his side for the walk.

He kept his hand pressed against the small of her back and angled his body between hers and the street as they walked. "I'll set aside some time to handle the unpacking of your equipment and art once it arrives. Jane is coordinating with your agent this morning on setting up a bonded moving company to handle the packing of your studio unless you'd like to fly back and do it personally."

Lauren bit down on her lip, but the real fear she felt at the thought of returning home kept her from even thinking about going back. "I trust Rachel will take care of it."

"Good." Connor prodded her into a small restaurant with a tiny sign and absolutely no style.

Lauren fell in love with the place as soon as she opened the menu. After she ordered a breakfast large enough for a trucker, she settled back with a strong cup of coffee and watched Connor make a production with the teapot that had appeared on the table as soon as the waitress arrived.

"Just once or twice a month, huh?"

Connor laughed. "Well, maybe I come here more than that, but I'm on my feet enough that I work it off pretty easily. This place is about as close as I get to home on this side of the ocean. Their cook is from Ireland and knows just how I like my food."

"You're from Britain, right?"

"After a fashion," Connor hedged. "My mum is Irish, and my father was a surveyor for the British government. I was born in a London hospital shortly before my parents' very short marriage ended. I split my time between London and Belfast for years until I joined Her Majesty's armed forces. I did two tours in the Royal Marines and then was recruited for another government posting."

Lauren figured Interpol or Secret Intelligence Service, but she knew better than to ask. "Then you came here and went to work for an ex-FBI agent in private security?"

"I met Mathias on a joint operation when he was still with the Feds. We'd both burned out on what we were doing, and when he told me what he had planned, it interested me. I figure I've done my part in the service of my country." Connor

31

picked up the honey and poured it liberally into his tea. "Her Majesty is welcome to let me know if she doesn't agree."

Lauren laughed softly and looked out the window. "Boston wakes up fast."

"Most cities this large do," Connor murmured. "Mostly because they never really sleep. Everyone lives on espresso and ambition in a town like this."

Lauren nodded. "Yeah."

"So you said last night you almost have a show finished."

"Yeah, I've been working on it for over a year. Thankfully, my first show in LA did so well that I was able to pay off all of my bills and set aside enough money that I didn't have to pick up a job to eat. In fact, this is the first time I've ever been able to do that. It's like a dream come true to devote myself and all of my time to my craft."

"You'll be inviting models over to try out?" Connor asked.

Lauren nodded. "I usually get them from local colleges, but my agent already scoped out a few agencies that I can work with in the area."

"For security purposes, I'll want to vet the name of the model you choose so keep Jane in the loop on that front."

Lauren's eyes widened but she didn't respond immediately, as their food had arrived. After the waitress settled large plates in front of them both, she cleared her throat. "You want to do a background check on my model?"

"Yes, as long as you are in the employ of the Foundation, any model you hire will have to be vetted by Security. Additionally, we'll check out the men you date."

"Excuse me?" Lauren demanded in a fierce whisper.

"It's in your contract, Lauren. Read it before you get bent. You'll be working at the academy with children, and you'll have unfettered access to the gallery. I don't have to tell you how much the collections we have on display are worth. We've had people try to get close to employees in the past to gain access to the gallery. I know it sounds invasive, but it's the way Brooks operates, especially when it concerns the children at the academy."

Lauren huffed. "Is that really a problem?"

"We hired a dance instructor eighteen months ago—her live-in boyfriend turned out to be a convicted pedophile. She had no clue until the background check came back. Of course, she ran fast and hard from the man, but it was there. He'd gone to the academy several times to pick her up from work. Parents send their kids to Holman to follow their dreams—they should be safe while they do it."

"I agree," Lauren murmured. "You can't think that I don't. I just didn't realize that something like that was . . . Yeah, feel free to thoroughly investigate anyone who asks me out."

Connor laughed. "Just submit the name of anyone you get serious about. I don't care about men you meet for drinks or a single date, but if you find someone who seriously interests you, we need to know."

"Right." Lauren pulled a bottle of hand sanitizer out of her purse, pumped some into her palm, and then offered it to Connor. He took it with a smile that told her he was completely humoring her. She blushed and rubbed her hands vigorously. "Germs are bad, you know."

He laughed. "I know." He put the bottle aside with a grin and rubbed his own hands. "Have you tried the kind that foams? It's pretty nice."

"I had some, but the people at the airport confiscated it. I got this at a shop at the airport here before I met the car you sent." Lauren stabbed a piece of potato. "I would be a cow if I ate here every day."

"You can always work it off," Connor murmured, and glanced at her slyly. "What's an extra mile in the face of potatoes for breakfast?"

The police station was noisy and chaotic in a way that drove Connor batshit. He was a fan of neat and orderly himself, despite all the teasing he'd given Lauren since he'd picked her up in the early a.m. He hadn't expected that—the last artist/diva who had held the position before Lauren had been a prick who slept until eleven and then bitched when his driver wasn't immediately available to take him wherever he wanted to go.

By the end of breakfast, Lauren had made it clear that she wouldn't need a driver daily and was more than willing to take on a vehicle in Boston traffic. The academy would provide her with an SUV for equipment hauling, which she'd seemed pleased to learn about.

A suspect was being wrestled into a chair as they entered the Robbery/Homicide Division, where Shawn's office was. Connor didn't make it a habit to visit the husband of his ex-girlfriend, but he wasn't uncomfortable. The last year had done a lot to smooth out the rough edges between them, and he couldn't imagine begrudging either one of them the happiness and love they'd found together. Even though it had royally pissed him off at the time.

"Are these places always so noisy?"

"Yeah," Connor admitted, "pretty much. And the moon was full last night, which for some reason is always a bad time for the guys with badges in this town."

Lauren smiled, obviously amused, and tucked a lock of hair behind her ear as Connor prodded her into a chair outside of Trainer's office. They were a little early for their appointment, but Connor made eye contact with Trainer, who held up one finger and motioned toward the phone he was on.

"Just a minute or two," Connor told Lauren, and settled against the wall. His gaze flicked around the room and connected with two different guys in handcuffs. "The interview rooms must be packed."

A cop who did part-time work for the gallery entered and offered Connor a smile. "Hey, Grant, what'd you do now?"

"Not a thing," Connor promised, and jerked his head toward Lauren. "We have an appointment with Trainer."

His eyes lit on Lauren, and a wide grin emerged. "Ma'am."

Connor sighed. "Detective Anthony Vincent, meet Lauren Evans. She's new to the academy."

Lauren offered her hand as she stood. "Detective Vincent."

"Call me Tony." He took her hand in both of his. "Welcome to Boston."

Lauren quirked an eyebrow and extracted her hand with a laugh. "That get you far, Detective?"

"You'd be amazed," Tony said, and rocked back on his heels.

"I really wouldn't." Lauren shook her head and smiled. "My daddy warned me about men like you, you know."

Tony just laughed and strolled away. "As every good father should."

Connor rolled his eyes and relaxed again when Lauren sat. "He works for us part-time when we have big events. Good guy."

"Womanizer," Lauren murmured. "Nice body, though. I bet he'd take well to black-and-white photography."

Connor snorted. "Is that all men are good for with you? Getting naked to model?"

"Well," Lauren started with a grin when several detectives turned their way. "Naked has always worked for me."

Connor laughed and shook his head as Shawn appeared in the doorway of his office. "Trainer, good. A few more minutes out here and one of these guys will be putting cuffs on her on general principle."

Shawn laughed. "I'm glad to see her in a good mood after last night's upset. We have an update, actually, and a few more questions."

Lauren stood and soon found herself settled in a chair in the office. Connor remained standing and took a position near the closed door. She wondered if the man ever turned it off and why he felt the need to be so on his game in the middle of a police station.

She opened her purse and pulled out a flash drive. "I've typed up my statement and found pictures online for the"— Lauren sighed—"underwear."

Shawn took the drive with a nod and plugged it into his computer. "Thanks. I don't normally have witnesses who are so organized."

"I didn't want to take any more of your time than was necessary this morning," Lauren said. She messed with the closure of her purse and then tightened her fingers around the top of it to keep still.

Shawn printed out the statement and offered her a pen so she could sign it. "When you checked into the hotel, do you remember a conversation with the girl at the front desk?"

Lauren frowned. "I asked about local shopping, and she listed a few of the shops she liked."

"And while she checked you into the hotel, she made two copies of the keycard for your room. One she passed onto her boyfriend, who works in housekeeping," Shawn explained. "Now, she instructed him to take your computer, handbag, and the emerald ring you were wearing when you checked in—she especially liked that."

Lauren's brow scrunched in confusion. "But he . . ."

"Yeah, he has a problem that his girlfriend was totally unaware of. I don't even want to tell you how we found him when we arrested him at their apartment early this morning."

Lauren sputtered and sat back in the chair with a huff. "Oh, seriously?"

"Seriously," Shawn assured her. "You aren't even the first victim. The hotel has had several customer complaints, but the manager settled with each one—basically paying them off to avoid dealing with the police and the owner. He was quite unprepared for us to cut a path through his staff looking for sex offenders. By the way, he is one himself. The owner of the hotel has a formal apology for you, and of course you won't be charged for the night you spent in his establishment. He's also willing to issue you a check to replace the items you had taken from you if you'll provide a number."

Lauren pushed her statement across the desk. "I listed how much I spent on the items missing. I don't...want any of it back. I mean, really. Additionally, I'd rather not know what he did with it."

Shawn laughed. "I'm sure they'll plead out. I doubt he'll want to have this come out in court."

Connor was hiding out in his office when one of his bosses found him. On any given day, he had several bosses—from the man who ran the security company he worked for to the ultra-savvy and beautiful Mercy Rothell-Montgomery, the director of the Holman Gallery.

She leaned one hip on his desk and inclined her pretty head. "So, above and beyond the call of duty today. I understand from Lauren Evans that you're a mean grocery shopper, know great places to eat breakfast, and make visits to police stations absolutely painless."

Connor flushed. "I'm glad I could help."

Mercy grinned. "Oh, you did. She breezed through contracts this afternoon and signed off the moving company her agent set up without a single word of complaint or concern. It's like she wasn't even the victim of a hotel room break-in. That was a situation that could have gone very wrong for us, you know."

"Why are you so hot to get this woman on staff?"

Mercy shrugged. "I know art doesn't speak to you the way it does us, but when I look at her work, I see something amazing and startling. The same kind of thing I see in my husband's work. This gallery supports the dreams of hundreds of people—you see how much the money helps the academy and the shelter. We want to expand and offer more to the city, to our students."

"And she'll help with that?"

"She creates a stir with her work and will bring patrons to the gallery. Rich people like to spend their money, and provocative work like hers will make it easier for them to spend it. Additionally, she works in a wide range of mediums, which will be beneficial to the academy."

"Her private work makes the money, and her unique perspective gives the kids a different kind of educational experience?"

"Yes, exactly," Mercy agreed. "And it doesn't hurt that she is beautiful and worldly. Rich men in this city will fall all over themselves to meet her once we do a show with her."

Connor frowned at the idea of that but quickly cleared it when she smirked at him. "I'm sure it's good business."

She laughed, clearly delighted. "It's excellent business, and you did us a great service by making sure she was at ease with this choice."

"It was no problem," Connor murmured, but he was still stuck on the idea of Lauren surrounded by a bunch of rich assholes. She wasn't even his type, and she was an *artist*. So why the hell was he so fucking irritated?

"Mr. Brooks was relieved to hear that the problem at the hotel wasn't about her personally. Do you think we have anything to worry about?"

He thought briefly about the nightmares Lauren had mentioned and the haunted look in her eyes when she thought no one was looking. "I'll keep an eye on things to make sure." He frowned. "I made a mistake once on that front—I won't do it again."

"I don't think anyone blames you for the situation with Casey."

Connor looked down at his desk. "One of my men was stalking her, watching her sleep, watching her have sex. So, yes, I do blame myself. Nothing anyone says is going to change it. I saw that man every day and trusted him. It was my mistake, and I won't make it again."

Mercy nodded. "Alrighty, then. I wanted to let you know that Jane, Lauren, and I will be going to lunch this afternoon downtown, and then she'll be headed over to the academy to meet the dean. We'll be taking my car." She raised one eyebrow in her defiant little way and Connor sighed. "Seriously. My car."

"Are you sure you wouldn't like to take the limo? Aren't you supposed to be romancing her?"

"Nope, she signed a contract. Now she's an employee, and she can ride in my SUV like everyone else when I want to eat lunch at Romano's."

"Yes, but if you took the limo, you could drink silly girl drinks with umbrellas in them on your lunch."

"True." Mercy nodded. "But we're working and we plan on

coming back. Maybe dinner next week. I figured you'd want to let your guys know so they can stalk us across town."

He frowned at the term and sighed when the door to his office opened. He barely got the frown off his face before Lauren was fully into the room. "Hey."

"Hey." Lauren glanced the room. "Oh, cool, look at all the security cameras." Her gaze darted around all of the monitors. "You'd never know there were that many security cameras in this place."

"Sort of the point, lass," Connor responded with a small smile. "Did you need something from me?"

Mercy chuckled and Lauren blushed. "Well, beyond a ride home later. I don't think I know you well enough to ask for anything else." She offered him a grin that brightened her entire face and made his cock jump a little against the zipper of his slacks.

Connor straightened in his chair and cleared his throat. "Just let me know when you're ready to go home."

Mercy checked her watch and walked to the door. "We can go to lunch early if you're finished with your call."

"I am," Lauren confirmed. "Rachel was super pleased with the contract changes, and she's at my studio overseeing the packing." She leaned on the door. "And I have interviews for models later in the afternoon, so I need to set aside time to view naked men."

It was all he could do not to protest. "You're using an agency?"

"Yes, Shamus Montgomery referred me to the agency he uses." Lauren wiggled an eyebrow. "I did make a bid to get him naked, but he claimed not to have time."

Mercy laughed. "I keep him busy."

"I bet." Lauren bounced on her feet a little. "Did you want to come to lunch, Mr. Grant?"

Connor smirked at her formal use of his name and shook his head. "No, I try to avoid lunch out with Mercy and Jane—they attract trouble."

"I heard. I look forward to it."

Lauren settled into the backseat of Mercy Montgomery's SUV with a sigh. "I ate too much."

"I ate a whole cow," Jane moaned from the front seat. "Why didn't one of you stop me?"

Mercy laughed and put on her sunglasses. "That was a huge piece of meat, and you rarely order beef. You aren't pregnant, are you?"

Jane sat up from her slouch with a glare. "No, and how dare you ask such a vicious question."

Lauren grinned and sighed. "Well, you did say it was contagious."

"Yes, well, my designer wedding gown doesn't have enough material to be let out for a pregnant belly, so I'm totally not pregnant." Jane jerked on her seat belt. "Seriously. Totally not pregnant."

Lauren laughed. "Maybe we should visit the drugstore on the way back to the gallery."

"Stop with the evil conversation!" Jane exclaimed, and covered her ears.

Lauren shared a look with Mercy in the rearview mirror and then laughed. The ride back to the gallery was mostly Jane moaning about eating too much and Mercy teasing her about having cravings.

In the parking garage, Lauren leaned against the wall next to the elevator and raised an eyebrow. "You know, the horrible thing about being so thin is that if you were pregnant, you'd just be instant pregnant. I bet you'd start showing within three months."

"You mean little witch," Jane snapped, and stalked into the elevator. Mercy followed her with a laugh.

Lauren grinned and scooted into the elevator just before Jane stabbed the button to close the doors. By the time they were on the sidewalk in front of the gallery, Jane was chattering about a group of rich women she was trying to romance out of their money.

Once in the gallery, Mercy went upstairs and Jane dragged Lauren off to look at the on-site classroom space they used for special sessions. Lauren had allowed herself to be talked into doing one for a bunch of rich men's wives. Each woman in the class was going to write a check for the Foundation, so Lauren figured losing an afternoon to it was worth it.

It wouldn't be for a few weeks, so she had plenty of time to prepare for it. She'd been authorized to use the space to inter- view models since her space at the town house wasn't set up, and she wanted the situation to appear as professional as possi- ble.

Within an hour of lunch, she was ready and the agency had ten models waiting for her. She finished setting up the lights she needed. "Okay, I'm ready."

Jane raised an eyebrow. "And they are just going to take off all of their clothes for you?"

"Yep."

She huffed. "And you don't have to buy them dinner?"

Lauren laughed softly. "You can't stay, though, so find some place to go."

"Oh, I figured." Jane sighed and walked to the door. "I'll send the first one in."

The first model entered and shut the door. He was young— Lauren figured he might be twenty-five—and he had a profes- sional quality to him that spoke of experience that belied his years. He was also quite beautiful.

"Good afternoon." Lauren motioned for him to sit. "I'm Lauren Evans."

"Jayson Cord." He put a leather portfolio on the table. "I've done a few projects with Lisa Brooks and one with Shamus Montgomery."

Lauren nodded. "Are you in school?"

"Yes, I'm a business major. I model to pay the bills. It makes studying easier if I don't have to work thirty or forty hours a week."

Lauren understood that. "I did some modeling myself when I was younger. It's good and somewhat easy money if you can come by it." Lauren unzipped his portfolio and opened it. "The project I'm working on is not for the faint of heart. It will involve physical bondage and will be strenuous. I'm taking black-and-white photos as well as doing extensive line drawings. I will need you for studies for perhaps three weeks—daily."

"As long as you can work around my class schedule, I'm your man." Jayson offered a smile Lauren was sure got him much action.

"All right, then," Lauren sat back. "Do you play any sports?"

"No."

"Very good. I'll want you to keep your body as neat as possible during the time period I work with you if you're chosen. The means no bruises, meticulous shaving, and no significant changes like a piercing during the three-week period."

Ten perfect bodies later and she was no closer to choosing the model for the final piece. Disgruntled, she left the gallery and crossed the street to get a coffee. She spent a full thirty seconds ordering a single cup and winked at the man behind the counter when she didn't stumble over the jargon. Then as an afterthought, she ordered a tea for Connor, taking care to ask for it just the way she had heard him do it the day before. Both cups in hand, she started back across the street and wondered how she could pass off the tea without sounding like the anal-retentive freak she was. Who memorized how other people took their tea?

The security office was open, and as she peeked in, he motioned her forward, a phone tucked against his ear. She slid into the room, set the tea down, and darted out, completely okay with the fact that she wouldn't have to explain herself.

3

The beauty of an instant friend like Jane Tilwell was that she came with great accessories. Lauren glanced briefly at Mathias and Shamus Montgomery as they gamely manhandled open a shipping crate open. Beautiful, unavailable accessories. Mercy Montgomery sat cross-legged with her son in her lap while she stared at one of the biggest pieces in the collection. It was the first thing that Lauren had unpacked. The canvas was huge—easily the largest she'd ever worked with—and pictured a single man on his knees in a position of submission. The muscles in his body were tight, emphasizing his strength and the restraint he used to remain in the position he'd been posed.

Lauren sat down beside her. "His name is Stefan. I kept him in studio for nearly three months. The first five pieces of the collection are him." She glanced over her shoulder as Connor entered the town house's large third-story loft with the last crate. "He fucked like it was his *job*."

Jane laughed from her place across the room and shoved another handful of packing material in the trash bag she'd brought up with her. Lauren had discovered that Jane was pretty much as big a neat freak as she was. "I just bet. Look at him—he's, what, twenty?"

"Twenty-two," Lauren responded primly. "He's in law school at Harvard this year I think. I could barely stand to part with him."

"He's got great lines," Shamus said, and squatted down beside them. "I especially like the way you've posed him in the third portrait."

Lauren's gaze drifted to the third in the series. Stefan was on his back, arched on a piece of red silk, his face turned away. His cock lay on his thigh, semi-hard and slightly wet at the tip. It was probably the most explicit of all the pieces she'd done of that particular model. "I'm calling it *Postcoital*."

Shamus smirked. "Female artists get away with so much on that front."

"I doubt any of your models—male or female—would have ever told you no." Lauren shifted on her feet and looked at Mercy then. She wiggled one eyebrow. "You certainly didn't."

Mercy laughed. "He was very difficult to get into bed."

Shamus laughed and plucked his son from his wife's lap. The two-year-old giggled and looped his arms around his father's neck with a sigh. "Liar." He patted his son's back. "I figured we should head out. The rest of this collection is way too adult for these young eyes." He looked around the room. "But I would like to come back and see it later?"

"Of course." Lauren flushed with pleasure. "I'd be honored."

"The honor is definitely mine. I can't wait for this show to open—you'll have people flying in from all over the world to see it." Shamus offered his wife his hand, and Mercy took it with a smile. "I can definitely see why Lisa finds you so inspiring. Just seeing what I've seen tonight has my mind whirling around for a new project." He winked. "Hey, Jane, wanna get naked for me?"

"Absolutely not," Jane called back without even looking in his direction. "Posing for you is all foreplay and no payoff, because by the end of the night I was too exhausted to get laid."

Lauren laughed as Mercy tugged on her husband and waved good-bye with her free hand. Connor shrugged out of his jacket and dropped it on a stool near the door as he shut it.

"I signed off with the delivery company. I left the boxes downstairs for you. But all of the wood crates containing your art are here." Connor took the crowbar that Mathias offered and walked toward one of the larger crates.

"Thanks." Lauren went to the next painting and carefully turned it over. Her agent had wrapped each piece in expensive cotton sheets before packing. She planned to keep the sheets, so she was being careful not to tear or cut them. "Coffee? Tea?"

"Beer?" he countered.

"Beer," Jane agreed. "You know you should buy us pizza."

"I should," Lauren said with a laugh, and went looking for her phone and a menu. "Anyone opposed to as much meat as possible?" She grinned at the chorus of nos.

She had to go downstairs to find a number and was leaning against the counter in the kitchen when Connor entered. He pulled four beers out of the fridge and opened them all as she rattled off her address and placed an order for three large pizzas.

Lauren checked her watch as she hung up. "About an hour." She accepted the beer he offered. "Thanks, and thank you for handling the movers."

"Well, Jane ordered us all over here." Connor grinned when Lauren blushed. "And we all pretty much do what Jane says—it's easier and less painful."

Lauren laughed. "Really?"

"Well, yeah, she's kind of a hardass." Connor glanced at her. "She sent me down here to get beer and suggested I make a pass at you while I was at it."

Lauren grinned. "What kind of pass?"

"She left that up to me." Connor wet his bottom lip with the tip of his tongue. "The problem is that if I got started, I might have to kick those two out and spend the rest of the night doing something entirely filthy and morally reprehensible to you."

Lauren's toes curled against the cool tile of the kitchen floor, and she huffed out a breath. "If we kick them out, we'll have a lot of pizza to eat."

Connor just grinned, his dark blue eyes dancing with amusement. "We'd need the fuel because I'm pretty sure I could make fucking you a career."

Lauren laughed and jerked her head toward the door. "Let's go back up. I want to show you the rest of my collection, and we should get as much work out of them as we can before we kick them out."

Jane was leaning on Mathias, and they were staring at a newly revealed painting. It was of a couple bound together with ropes.

"Is he inside her?" Jane asked immediately. "And are you this big of a freak in the bedroom or just, you know, when you paint?"

"He's not inside her," Lauren answered with a laugh. "And, yes, I kind of am. That's Japanese rope bondage. I had a friend come in to my studio and tie them up for me." She tilted her head and looked at the portrait. "I kept them that way for three hours—took nearly one hundred pictures and he never even got hard."

"Gay?"

"Nope, he just hated her." Lauren smiled. "She wasn't too

fond of him. It made the pose perfect. I could have cut the hostility in the room with a knife."

Jane laughed. "What are you calling it?"

"*Thin Line.*" Lauren pulled a hair clasp out of her pocket and quickly put her hair up in a messy bun. "The first set is about male submission. The second set is about sex as a tool of domination in a modern society."

Connor snorted. "Do you honestly think sex is about domination?"

"Not all sex," Lauren acknowledged. "Just the good kind that makes it hard to walk the next day."

Jane choked on her beer and glared at Lauren as Mathias patted her on the back. She cleared her throat noisily. "You are evil."

Lauren just grinned. "You like me a lot. I know."

"What's the third set about?" Connor asked.

Lauren watched him set aside his beer and pick out a new crate to unpack. "The same as the first series, only with women."

"And what will you do for the last five in the collection?" Jane walked away from the bondage painting and started picking up the sheets that had been discarded.

"The focus will be male, but I'm not sure of the direction. I want power, strength, and dominance. Experience and sexuality without arrogance. Pride without artifice." She frowned as she spoke and then waved her hands. "I'll know it when I see it."

"So, in order to find this, you have to look at a bunch of naked men?" Jane questioned. "I have the *wrong* job." She only grinned when Mathias glared at her and went to join Connor opening the crate.

"She's not looking at men," Connor muttered. "She's looking at kids barely old enough to vote in this country."

Lauren frowned and started unwrapping the canvas that they pulled out. "Okay, so you're saying that the models the agency sent me are too young?"

"No." Connor shook his head. "Too soft. I've seen men in combat who had the kind of strength and personal power you are talking about, and they were barely old enough to serve."

"You think that what I want comes from going to war?"

Connor paused and then shrugged. "War is a man's business."

"Hmm." Lauren set the painting against the wall and tilted her head. "And women who serve?"

Connor grimaced. "Is it sexist to admit that I'd prefer that women not serve in combat?"

"It depends on why you think that," Jane said, hands on hips.

Connor sighed and looked at her. "Because the world is fucked up, and people do horrible things to each other. I've always believed that women deserved better than to see those things. They shouldn't have to be in war."

"So, not because you think we can't do it?"

"Not at all. In my experience, women are some of the most dedicated soldiers in the field. I've always found them to be level-headed during field operations that went to shit." Connor shared a glance with Mathias. "Unless they're at work and the place gets broken into and instead of calling the police they trot down to stop the big, bad thief by themselves. Then you know it becomes foreplay."

Jane was blushing furiously. "Shut up, Grant."

Mathias laughed softly. "Best moment of my life."

Lauren glanced between them. "What?"

Jane sighed. "I met Mathias when he was checking the security for the gallery by staging a break-in. I confronted him, and then we rolled around on the floor for a bit before he pretty much climbed on top of me and held me down."

Lauren grinned. "I never have days like that. I just get weirdos stealing my panties and doing deviant things with them."

"She had to call a man's mother to get him to leave her alone," Mathias offered. "That's pretty...lame."

"Agreed," Connor chuckled. "But it was either that or we were going to have to kick his ass."

"I could have kicked his ass myself, thank you very much," Jane snapped.

"Yeah, she could have," Mathias murmured. "But I think most people could kick his ass."

Lauren tilted her head as the doorbell rang. "Food."

"I'll get it," Connor said and walked toward the stairs.

"I have to go sign my credit card receipt."

Connor sighed but nodded.

Lauren laughed a little and followed after him. "You know I've been answering my door for a long time."

"I know."

"Is this one of those things I shouldn't have to do?" Lauren asked, amused.

"Something like that," he said as he punched a code into the control panel by the door and then did a cursory check through the peephole. Then he opened it with a little grunt of approval.

He kept himself centered in the doorway between the delivery guy and her. Connor reviewed the receipt and then offered it over his shoulder.

Lauren rolled her eyes but took the receipt and went to find her purse to get a pen. She passed it back after signing it, along with a ten for the tip. "Thanks!"

The pizza guy peeked around Connor and waved a little. "No problem, ma'am."

Lauren just laughed and took the pizzas as Connor shut the door on the kid. "You're horrible."

"He doesn't get paid to wave at his customers."

"Get us some more beer," Lauren ordered, and headed up the stairs with the pizza. "And napkins."

"At your service, lass."

I wish, Lauren thought. Connor Grant was nothing like her type and certainly not the kind of man she could control. Maybe it was time for a change—she certainly hadn't had any luck on the man front in a long time.

Lauren found herself alone at the end of the night, despite the teasing. She didn't take Connor Grant for the kind of man who took his time when he found a woman he wanted, so maybe his interest in her was more academic than anything else. Some men flirted on pure reflex alone. He was an attractive man, and she was allowed to indulge in a little harmless flirting. Maybe even a little harmless fucking if he proved interested.

She rolled onto her back and rubbed her stomach thoughtfully. Masturbation crossed her mind briefly, but her favorite toy was *gone,* and that reminded her that some pervy jerk had taken it and done deviant things with her panties, which ruined her mood.

Lauren rolled from the bed and threw on a pair of shorts and a T-shirt. She had nowhere to be the next day, so she could spend a few late hours in her studio. She wanted to start mixing paint for the final phase of her project, anyway.

It took her about ten minutes to get lost in the process, and before she knew it, it was nearly two in the morning. She took a quick shower and crawled back into bed.

A thump below made her sit up straight in the bed. She

barely had two seconds to think about what the sound was before the house alarm started going off. She scrambled out of bed and grabbed the gun Connor had left with her. The alarm noise was almost deafening. At least she never had to worry about sleeping through it.

There was no telling who was downstairs or what they wanted. She couldn't risk trying to reach the safe room, since she was pretty damn sure there was someone in the house with her.

The alarm noise ended abruptly.

"Lauren!"

She jerked at the sound of Connor's voice and lowered her gun as the door to the bedroom was thrown open.

He was wearing jeans, a pair of trainers, and a T-shirt—no coat. He lowered his own gun and motioned her to him. "What happened?"

Lauren shook her head. "I don't know. There was a noise from downstairs, and then the alarm went off. I didn't think I should risk trying to reach the safe room."

Connor reached out for her and cupped the back of her neck as he pulled her close. "Okay, we'll work on that. I can have one of the closets on each floor enforced with a lock from the inside. Not as secure as the safe room but something . . ."

Lauren rubbed her cheek against his T-shirt. "They were in the house before the alarm sounded."

"Whoever it was hit a pressure plate in the hallway by the stairs." Connor ran his free hand through her hair. "You're shaking."

"I've only ever had to shoot targets," Lauren admitted. "I was afraid someone was going to come through the door and I'd have to shoot them." Her grip tightened on her gun, and she shuddered against him. "That would have sucked."

"Aye, lass." Connor took a deep breath. He flinched as someone shouted "Boston PD!" "I'm not liking their response time at all."

"You got here *fast.*"

Connor's hand tightened briefly in her hair, and then he let her go. "As I said, I'm five minutes away when I'm in no hurry. You can trust that I was in a hurry." He went to the doorway and holstered his weapon. "Up here, Officers. My client is secure. I'd appreciate a thorough search of the place."

A uniformed cop appeared a few seconds later. "Your company called in an alarm. I need to see your ID to confirm that you're allowed on the premises, sir."

Connor pulled out his wallet and handed over his license. "I have people on the way as well, including someone who can check our system and let us know how far the intruder got and how he was able to get past the front door."

"The door was standing open when you arrived?" the cop asked.

"Yes, just as I reported to your dispatcher," Connor said. He glanced back at Lauren. "You'll want to get a detective on the scene."

The officer snorted. "Are you kidding? We have two detectives en route. James Brooks owns this place, right?" The officer glanced at Lauren and then back at Connor. "She should probably put on some clothes before you bring her downstairs. No need to show all of Boston's finest the new panties."

Lauren blushed furiously and tugged on the hem of her T-shirt. "How did you know?"

The officer laughed. "Well, the story made the rounds, Ms. Evans. That guy is a freak."

Connor heard James Brooks before he saw him. He had Lauren sequestered in the kitchen while the rest of the town house was searched. A brief survey of the security system confirmed that the intruder fled the moment he set off one of the pressure plates.

"Grant." Brooks's gaze flicked around the room and settled on Lauren. "Ms. Evans."

"Lauren," she whispered from behind her coffee cup. "Lauren is fine, Mr. Brooks. I'm okay—it was just a little scare. Connor was here before I could even decide where to hide."

Brooks nodded and pulled out a chair. "I don't feel like we're taking good care of you, Lauren."

Lauren's gaze widened fractionally. "It's not really your job to take care of me, Mr. Brooks, and it's hardly your fault that some pervert broke into my hotel room. I'm sure whatever happened here tonight wasn't...Whatever it was, I'm sure there is a perfectly reasonable explanation."

"I'm sure," James said dryly. "And call me James."

Connor smiled a little. He knew very few people who called James Brooks anything but "Mr. Brooks" no matter how often he told them otherwise.

James turned to him. "Tell me what you've got."

"I was in the front door two minutes and thirty-six seconds after the alarm was tripped. I would have been faster, but I had to put on shoes." Connor leaned against the counter. "She was in her bedroom when I arrived, and there was no sign of the intruder. I let the police search the place, and after they were finished, we checked her studio to make sure all of her work was accounted for. Then we came down here. Shawn Trainer is on scene—I requested him since he handled the break-in at the hotel. I have Derrick going through the digital records of the security system on-site."

James nodded and then focused on Lauren. "Anything I need to know from you?"

"No." Lauren shook her head.

"Nothing like this in San Diego?" James asked carefully. "I ask because you don't seem all that surprised or shaken up like I would expect."

Lauren blinked in surprise. "Well, if you want me to cry, I could probably muster up a few tears to satisfy your masculine desire to comfort me."

James snorted and sat back in his chair. "All right, point taken."

"I was raised by a military man, Mr. Brooks. I'm not some cowering little girl who is going to shake apart because someone breaks into my home."

"Good to hear," Shawn Trainer said from the doorway. "Grant, any word from your tech?"

"He's in the basement doing a hard connect with the system. We can only get basic information from the system externally. It's a security protocol." Connor checked his watch. "He said thirty minutes for a full system diagnostic. He has five minutes before I start thumping him on the back of the head for answers."

Lauren settled her gaze on her coffee and sighed. Connor watched her silently, taking in the set of her shoulders and the small lines of stress forming around her mouth. She wasn't taking the situation nearly as well as she would have them all believe, but he also didn't think she was going to shatter and get hysterical on him, either. He glanced up when Mathias appeared in the doorway. "I'm waiting on Derrick."

Mathias nodded and stepped aside to let Jane through. Jane dropped a duffel bag on the floor near the door and shrugged out of her jacket. "I thought I'd spend the night."

Lauren glanced toward the bag. "Well, it's practically morning."

"Right, we can eat some food and then go shopping. Then

we'll swing by Lisa's and show her all the stuff we bought. Then we can come back here and have dinner and a girl party."

"I don't need handling, Jane."

"Well, I want to handle you, so let me." She nudged her shoulder and then got up to pour herself some coffee.

Derrick entered at that point, a computer bag thumping against his leg and two laptops in hand. "We got hacked."

Mathias glared at him. "You said we couldn't get hacked."

"I said it was unlikely that anyone would hack my system because I'm really awesome," Derrick corrected. "It gets better—he hacked the system in about three minutes and killed the exterior cameras before he even came down the street. The good news is that he only hacked enough to get past the front door alarms. Because he didn't use a code, the pressure plates stayed engaged and of course went off when he stepped on one."

"Sure it was a he?" Jane asked.

"Well, either a he or a two-hundred-pound woman." Derrick shrugged. "The pressure plates recorded how much weight was on them when it went off. It's one of the ways the system determines a threat. The last guy who lived here had a cat, so we had to program the system to recognize the cat and not go off whenever it wandered across the plates or motion sensors."

Lauren frowned. "So a big guy?"

"Two hundred ten," Derrick answered promptly. "Based on motion sensor data, I'd put him over six feet."

Connor frowned. "Sure that wasn't me?"

"Positive, boss. I have your entry recorded three minutes and thirty-six seconds after his entry. Coming in at a respectable two hundred and one pounds and six foot three. I got the uniformed cops, too." Derrick put both computers down on the table and slid into a chair. He flipped one open. "Here, take a look at this."

Lauren watched in amusement as every man in the room moved around to huddle behind the younger man's computer like they were watching a football game or something. She got up and poured herself some coffee. Judging by the hmms and grunts coming from the men, she figured that Derrick had something pretty cool to show them.

Jane was on her cell phone when she came back to the table, obviously talking to Mercy Montgomery. More to the point, she was encouraging Mercy to stay home and promising to pick her up for shopping in two hours.

"So, if you're making me go shopping, I need some stuff." Lauren dropped down in the chair. "You know . . . *stuff*."

Jane grinned. "I love the *stuff* store. It's my favorite store."

Lauren huffed out a breath. "And I think I need a dress for that show you mentioned opening next week at the gallery. I don't think I have anything that will work, and I want to order some paint and some canvas, and I need a hardware store."

Jane nodded. "Yep, I can handle all of that. I could medal in shopping if it were in the Olympics, and Mercy, well, she'd have won the gold ten years running. We got all of that covered. Paint, new dress, more panties, sex toys, and power tools are no problem."

"I really don't need panties. I purchased some online and had them shipped overnight. But it might make me feel better about the panty loss to buy some really expensive and ridiculous ones that aren't even comfortable to wear unless I think I'm going to get laid." Lauren glanced up and found everyone staring at them. "What?"

"Nothing," James Brooks announced abruptly. "Mathias, do you think you have what you need to start working this problem?"

"We're already working this problem, sir." Mathias dropped a hand on Derrick's shoulder. "Jakes, head back to the office and get a leg up on tracing this guy's computer. See if you can't locate any similar activity and find out if he did this remotely or if he was physically in our system."

"I'll find his signature soon enough. It's art, and guys this talented are vain—he signed it. I just have to find it." Derrick Jakes stood and started packing away his computers. "Should I send Detective Trainer a copy of my report?"

Connor glanced from Mathias to Shawn Trainer, who had one eyebrow raised in question. "Yes, as long as you don't include any of information on our security protocols."

"Of course not, sir. Our patent is still pending." Derrick dropped his computer bag over his shoulder and left without another word.

Connor shrugged when Mathias looked at him hard. "He's brilliant but socially retarded. I think it kind of comes with the territory."

Lauren laughed a little and relaxed in her chair. "Cute, too."

Jane nodded. "He's kind of like the Energizer Bunny. It makes you wonder what it would take to wear him out."

"We could make a list for purely scientific purposes and then ask his boyfriend for confirmation." Lauren wiggled her eyebrows and Jane burst out laughing.

"How did you know he was gay?" Connor asked.

"I have great gaydar," Lauren announced. "It's a gift."

"Or a curse." Jane frowned. "I mean, you see a hot guy and you know immediately whether or not you should bother fantasizing about him."

"Or I see a hot guy and know he's gay and then spend half the afternoon imagining him having really hot gay sex with some equally hot guy," Lauren informed.

Jane wet her bottom lip and flushed a little. "You're filthy. I like you *so much*. Wait until you meet Lisa. It'll be great."

Lauren just laughed when she realized all of the men in the

room were staring at her, completely incredulous, *again.*
"What?"

"I . . ." Connor shook his head. "I don't even know, lass."

"Oh, come on, you're British," Lauren scoffed. "And ex-military. I bet you went to an all-boys private school. Nothing should shock you."

"I have to admit much has in my life." Connor rubbed the back of his neck. "Shawn, you want to walk this place with me and clear out the uniforms?"

"Not a problem." Shawn glanced briefly at Lauren. "I'll need a formal statement from you on Monday for the file on this break-in."

"Sure, should I come by your office?"

"No, I'll come to you. Half the guys I work with spent the afternoon trying to get your phone number the last time you came into my squad room." Shawn pulled out a card and put it on the table. "I'll get your schedule from Grant and put myself on it when I have time on Monday. In the meantime, keep the piece Grant gave you close when you're alone, don't answer your door for anyone you don't know, and keep the security engaged."

Lauren frowned at him. "How do you know he gave me a gun?"

"I saw it on your nightstand upstairs. It's one of the guns registered in his name."

Lauren ended up buying a dark blue silk dress that clung to everything she had. Currently they were trudging through Security so they could visit Lisa Brooks. She was only vaguely surprised not to get patted down by the guy in the lobby.

By mutual agreement, they'd left her new DeWALT in the car and carried only clothes up to show Lisa. Though, Lauren figured that Lisa might appreciate the multifunctional power tool with six speeds. She left the vibrator in the car, too.

The apartment was modern, beautifully decorated, but Lauren didn't have much time to glance around before a shout from the back bedroom had the three of them going down the hallway to find Lisa ensconced in a big bed. The personal nurse exited the room, giving them a look that could only be interpreted as relief.

Mercy laughed a little and sat down on the bed. "You're gonna run her off, too, if you aren't careful."

Lisa huffed. "She is paid an insane amount of money to put up with me, and I'm due in a week."

Lauren thought she looked overdue by *months,* but she sure as hell wasn't going to say anything. "Boy or girl?"

Lisa snorted. "Both. When I get them out, I'm going to kill that son of a bitch who fathered them and the doctor who supplied the fertility drugs. I'm too old to have twins. It's obscene." She held out her hand and wiggled fingers.

Lauren gamely took her hand and found herself pulled down onto the bed. "We bought you some stuff."

"And new panties for you?" she asked with a grin.

"Is there anyone in Boston who doesn't know my panties were stolen?" Lauren asked, and turned to glare at Jane.

"Well, I didn't take out an ad in the paper," Jane offered with a bright smile. "Though I was tempted to mention it for the social column."

Lisa laughed and unceremoniously dropped her feet into Jane's lap. "Rub my feet while you guys show off your purchases."

Jane rolled her eyes but gamely plucked off Lisa's socks. "Cute—does your husband know your toenails are painted Whorehouse Porch Light Red?"

"I think it was called Jungle Red," Lisa defended. "I thought it was cute." She wiggled her toes. "Besides, you don't think he gets to voice an opinion about such things, do you? He's lucky I still let him live here after what he's done to me."

Three hours later, Lauren was dropping her dress off to be cleaned and learning to live with the fact that she wasn't going to be able to ditch Jane. The woman only eyed her with cool amusement when Lauren had mentioned that she'd be okay on her own.

When they got back to the town house, Connor was chilling in the front room in front of the big-screen television, and there was a security crew mingling in the foyer. The control panel on the front door was in pieces. Jane helped Lauren haul her purchases upstairs with only a wave in Connor's direction.

In her bedroom, Jane dropped six shopping bags on the bed and quirked an eyebrow. "If you want to play helpless female to his superalpha male, just let me know. I can make myself scarce."

Lauren glared at her. "I'm not helpless, and if he wants that kind of girl, he needs to look elsewhere."

"Well, he does tend to go for those really soft, überfemale types. He dated Casey for a while until she started looking for something serious, and he wasn't game for it. I don't know all that happened between them, but since I've never seen Connor and Shawn come to blows, it must not have been too bad."

Lauren hadn't met Casey Trainer, and she really didn't want to now. The last thing she wanted was to compare herself to Connor's ex-girlfriend. "Soft, huh?"

"Yeah, like cake. All blond hair, curvy hips, and big breasts." Jane made an hourglass shape in the air. "She and Mercy are about the same size and shape when they aren't pregnant—you know that mouthwatering shape that make men run into things while they watch them walk."

Lauren frowned and sighed. She wasn't ever going to look like that. At five-nine and a hundred thirty pounds, she bordered on being overly slender and barely filled a C-cup. "So how long do I get to hate her?"

"I went a whole month," Jane confided with a grin. "But Casey is a sweetheart, and really you can't hate a woman who named her dog Harvey Wallbanger."

Lauren snorted with laughter and dropped back onto the bed. "No, you can't. I think I need a dog."

Jane checked her watch. "Probably hard to come by this time of the day. Did you want to rescue one, or do you want something professionally trained?"

Lauren bit down on her lip. "Well, I'd love to rescue, but practically I think I'd feel better if I had a dog trained to guard and protect when necessary."

"Breed preference?"

"My dad always liked shepherds, and I've always found them pretty cool to have around." Lauren started dumping out the bags. "We should let Connor know that I'm getting a delivery."

Jane stretched. "I'll let him know."

Lauren nodded and went in search of some scissors so she could take the tags off of her new collection of bras and panties. Jane and Mercy had helped pick out a lot of the colors—some pretty vivid stuff that Lauren would have probably never bought on her own. By the time Jane returned, Lauren had sorted everything for washing.

"Did you want to order in?" Jane asked with a raised eyebrow. "Mathias will be here in a few hours. I figured I would order him some food, but we can go out if you want."

"Thai would be good," Lauren murmured. "I really don't want to face another crowd. Lisa was pretty much exactly what I expected."

Jane grinned. "Yeah, she's pretty great. This bed-rest thing is getting on her last nerve, and she's fired six private nurses in the past month alone. Brooks just laughs and hires her another one. He's pretty much infatuated with her mean ass in every way possible." She hopped up. "Well, the washer and dryer are in the basement. We can look at the menus in the kitchen to see if they have Thai. The guys in Security are pretty varied, so I'm pretty sure we'll have one or two places to choose from."

"Get me some sweet and sour shrimp and some spring rolls." Lauren surveyed her piles and sighed. "Is there a laundry basket downstairs?"

"Yeah, I'm pretty sure, unless the last guy tossed it out. He was something of an asshole. Mr. Brooks ended up firing him, so things were a bit of a disaster in the town house after he left. He even put some holes in the walls. We had the entire place remodeled and decorated."

"Who was it?"

"Robert Stein—total asshole."

Lauren blinked in surprise. "I never heard that he worked for Holman."

"That's because he was hired and fired within the same month. The parting was not pleasant at all," Jane admitted. "But that's over and you're a much better fit for the organization and the kids at the academy." Jane waved a little over her shoulder as she exited the bedroom and went in search of menus.

Lauren stared at her piles and puzzled over the Stein matter for a few minutes before she went in search of a laundry basket. The basement was empty except for the washer and dryer and a few laundry baskets. The large steel door of the safe room was a bright and shiny reminder of the safety it could provide—if she could actually get to it. She sighed. She plucked up two baskets and trudged back upstairs.

Connor was in the hallway a few feet from the basement door when she came back up, and she raised an eyebrow in question. "Jane mentioned you wanted a dog for personal protection."

"And to run with," Lauren explained. "So nothing small. I was thinking a pit bull or a shepherd. I had a neighbor who had a pit in San Diego. I used to take him running with me."

Connor nodded. "Can't have a pit. Muzzle laws would make him ineffective if you were hassled on the street. I'll work on it, though. We know a guy who trained dogs for the U.S. Army. He's been retired for a few years and has his own training business. We haven't bought any dogs for work, but Mathias has been considering it."

Lauren's fingers tightened around the edges of the basket. "I'd be comfortable with that. I've seen military dogs in action. I wouldn't want a retired one, though—not one that had seen combat."

"Understood," Connor said. "Need help?" He motioned toward the laundry baskets.

Lauren grinned. "I think I can handle it."

4

_____

She was very tired of looking at naked men. That was so wrong on so many levels that it wasn't even funny. Lauren tossed aside her pencil but managed to gently order the model to get dressed. The model certainly didn't seem to notice her building ire. The agency she'd been working with had given her exactly what she asked for without exception, and not a single one of the thirty-six men she'd looked at even remotely inspired what she was looking for.

Lauren checked her watch and sighed. She had only twenty minutes before Shawn Trainer was due to arrive to pick up her statement and ask whatever questions he might have. She filled her coffee cup and made her way up to the Security floor where Connor's office was. The door was open, so she stuck her head in to let him know she was there.

He waved her in and shut his laptop. "How goes the cock search?"

Lauren grinned. "That's a rude thing to call it."

Connor smiled. "Should I apologize?"

"No." Lauren slid into a chair and dropped a thumb drive on his desk. "I wrote out my statement. I thought you could print it for me. I haven't set up my home office yet."

Connor nodded and grabbed the thumb drive. "So, should we discuss your very bad luck at some point?"

Lauren flushed. "I really...didn't have bad luck in San Diego."

"Really?" Connor asked. "Because you seemed eager to move here, and there's the problem of your nightmares."

"That's all they are," Lauren murmured. "Trust me when I say I searched for evidence to the contrary and never found any. There was nothing to find in my apartment."

A sharp knock on the door brought their attention to Shawn sliding into the room. "You guys busy?"

"No, not at all." Connor motioned him forward as he pulled a single sheet of paper from his printer. "Lauren already has her statement typed up for you." He put it on the desk in front of her and dropped a pen on top of it. "It's almost like she's done this a lot."

Shawn quirked an eyebrow. "Right, but we couldn't find any evidence of that."

Lauren flushed. "You're both assholes. I watch TV."

Connor snorted and rocked back in his chair. "I e-mailed my security report to you." He plucked up a manila envelope. "And my formal statement is here. I still have my guys working on how the front door was opened, but I'm not optimistic."

Shawn nodded. "I need you to consider the possibility of an inside job."

Lauren stiffened and frowned. "What? Really?"

Connor's expression was grim. "It wouldn't be the first time we've had a coworker get too interested in someone else on staff." He rocked back in his chair. "You can be assured that I'm looking at my men very carefully. That being said, they all know how close I am to the town house, and I don't have idiots working for me."

Lauren digested that information and wondered if the men and women who worked with Connor Grant had any clue how dangerous he was. She glanced at Shawn Trainer, who was slipping her statement into the envelope Connor had passed him.

The two of them had been so serious and concerned about both the hotel and town house break-ins that she felt like an asshole for not being up front with them.

Guilt pooled in her gut. "I made a mistake once."

Shawn walked to the door and shut it without saying anything. He locked it and pulled up a chair beside her, then straddled it casually. "Okay. We all make mistakes."

"It was a pretty big one."

"Did you get hurt?" Connor asked.

"No." Lauren ran her fingers through her hair. "But it could've gone that way."

"And you've been having nightmares about it?" Shawn asked, his tone so neutral that Lauren relaxed.

"It's been difficult to sleep since it happened. When I do sleep, I relive it. Sometimes the dreams are worse than what did happen."

"This mistake...have you seen him since?" Connor asked as he stood up and walked around to lean on the desk in front of her. "Has he called you? Tried to contact you?"

Lauren sighed. "No. It's not like that. I just don't want the two of you thinking I've got some mystery in my past that is intruding here. We met through a mutual friend and negotiated an arrangement. He abused my trust and left me a little freaked out. He never tried to contact me after the fact and even apologized to me through our mutual friend for taking the arrangement further than we agreed."

Lauren focused on the floor between her and Connor. She

really didn't want to admit more than that, but she figured neither of them were going to be satisfied with that vague explanation. "It was a sex game."

"He didn't honor your safe word?" Connor asked softly.

Lauren blushed. "We discussed several scenarios but not the one that really interested him. There was..." She sighed and rubbed her face. "He took me off the street and held me captive for an hour before he realized that I really wasn't playing—that I was really freaked the fuck out."

"You thought he was going to rape you," Shawn finally said. "He tied you up and..."

"Gagged me and then threw me into the back of a van he rented. I can only thank God his fantasy went more toward a *forced seduction* than a rape. He expected me to stop fighting, and when I didn't, he realized I wasn't into it. He released me."

"You didn't press charges?"

Lauren shook her head. "What would I have told them, Detective Trainer? That I planned a series of elaborate sex games with a man I barely knew and he took it too far?"

"It went so far that you've had nightmares about it for a while," Connor responded, his tone nowhere near as neutral and relaxing as Shawn's.

"I made a mistake," Lauren repeated. "And to be honest, he was just as freaked out as I was by the end of it. We were both playing at a game we were ill prepared for, and it was traumatic enough without involving the police." She sighed. "So that's why I was pretty eager to leave San Diego and come here. It's why I have nightmares."

"Because you made a mistake," Connor repeated. "It seems like he made the mistake, lass."

"I gave him the opening and made foolish choices." Lauren sat back in her chair and flicked her hair in frustration. "It's not something I want to talk about at length, but my string of bad luck here in Boston has got me on edge, as does the two of you looking at me like I'm keeping some deep, dark secret."

"How long ago?" Shawn asked, taking a notebook out of his jacket pocket. "Do you have any information on him?"

"His name is Anthony Davis. He's a corporate lawyer in San Diego. Blond hair, blue eyes, and around your size and weight. It was more than a year ago." She twisted her fingers together. "Are you going to contact him?"

"I'm going to check things out and make sure he's where he's supposed to be. If he's in Boston, I'll have a conversation with him," Shawn admitted. "How much would you estimate the work you have in the town house is worth?"

Lauren shrugged. "It really has no value until it's hit the show floor and people start talking, because I don't have much of a track record. I had a successful show in LA. I cleared a little over five million dollars after everyone got their cut."

"Mercy seems to think you'll make the Foundation a lot of money," Connor said.

"And maybe I will, but there are a lot of factors that go into determining how much the show will be worth. If the work was stolen before it was ever shown in public, I'd say it would be difficult to find a buyer."

"So, we're back to a personal motivation," Shawn admitted. "If the person who broke into the town house wasn't after your work, then he was there for you."

She hated the thought of that. "Check on Anthony, but he'll be in San Diego where he belongs. He's an insensitive prick, but he's not someone who would put aside his life to come across the country and break into my home."

"Not even to finish what he started?" Connor asked.

Lauren flinched but she shook her head. "He isn't a threat."

Connor reached out and cupped her cheek. He lifted her chin so he could meet her gaze. "You don't really believe that, lass, because if you did, you wouldn't have nightmares about him breaking into your home."

Lauren fought the urge to lean into his touch and took a deep breath. "It wasn't . . . a great experience."

"No, I can see that." Connor released her with a grimace.

Lauren stood abruptly. "I should go. I have three more models coming this afternoon."

Connor nodded and crossed his arms as she hurried from his office. "Sex game gone wrong?"

Shawn huffed out a breath. "A would-be rapist who lost his nerve if you ask me."

Connor's jaw clenched, and he glanced at the door Lauren had hurried out of as if her sweet little ass were on fire. "Your captain won't approve a visit for someone in your department. Not on your budget."

"No, he won't," Shawn acknowledged. "I could probably talk a local into questioning Davis. Or I can overlook the fact that you're going to send one of those one-man-wars you have walking around masquerading as security guards down there to check him out."

Connor laughed softly, but it wasn't a pleasant sound. "I'll keep you in the loop on what my guys find, and I'll have a background check done on him that will definitely resemble the Spanish Inquisition. You'll get a copy."

"You're a bit invested in this one," Shawn said. "Do I need to worry about you?"

"I don't know what you mean."

Shawn raised a dark eyebrow at him. "Look, things were tense with us when I first married Casey, and I realize you don't consider me a friend. I figure you'll never consider me more than a police contact who happens to be married to your ex-girlfriend. I get that. But give me some credit here. I'm fairly observant, and I know the look of man who is getting territorial about a woman."

"She works for the Foundation, and that makes her safety my concern."

"She's a beautiful woman who you touch *a lot,*" Shawn returned evenly. "I don't doubt for a second that you're doing your job. I just think you have some personal motivations."

"And if I do?"

"Casey will be thrilled." Shawn stood up and stretched. "And you're liable to endure untold amounts of teasing from the rest of the women in our lives."

Connor flushed and went back to his desk chair. "She's not even my type."

Shawn grinned. "They never are, man."

Connor slouched in his chair. "Get out of my office before I kick your ass. That will give all the women in our lives something to talk about."

"Keep me in the loop so I can at least pretend with my captain that I know what you're up to."

Lauren made it a point to never, ever frown at a man when he was naked. They were sensitive creatures and normally took the frown to mean something negative about their dick. "That'll be all, Cameron. Thank you for your time today."

"Not a problem, Ms. Evans." The twenty-three-year-old college student offered her a confident smile and walked to where he'd left his clothes. "You've got a lot of the guys at the agency talking about this gig. Do you know when you'll make a decision?"

Lauren shook her head. "No, I've got a few models left to see and some appointments next week. I do hope to make the choice by the end of the month, but it just depends."

He smirked a little. "Maybe you ought to tie a few of us up to see if that inspires you." He shot her a sly look as he pulled on his jeans but left them unbuttoned. "I could make myself available to you this evening for something a little more private."

She grinned. "You cheeky little bastard. You'd best go or you'll be late for that class you were talking about earlier."

He laughed. "Can't blame a man for trying."

She really couldn't. She closed the file she had on him and shooed him out of the room. "Off with you."

Thirty-nine cocks and counting. She sighed as the door shut behind him. The cock search was not going well.

"For a woman who has looked at as much man candy as you have today, you seem depressed."

Lauren glanced over at Jane. "Connor is calling it the 'cock search.'"

Jane sputtered and then bit down on her lip, her eyes dancing with amusement. "That's funny as hell."

"It's kind of funny," Lauren admitted with a sigh. "I kept thinking it during my last three interviews, so of course all I could look at was their dicks, which wasn't exactly professional."

Jane grinned. "Well, your work does focus on that a lot. I mean, you do seem to like dick a lot."

Lauren glared at her. "Most women like dick a lot, whether they want to admit it or not."

"I *love* cock," Jane declared. "It's practically my favorite thing on Earth." She jumped a little when a pair of arms suddenly snatched her from the doorway and then laughed when Mathias nuzzled her neck. "Hey."

"You've got to stop talking about cocks and sex toys in front of people," he declared.

Jane just grinned. "You're just a nosy man, and you shouldn't be listening to our conversations."

"It's my job to keep up with you, woman." He pressed a kiss against her temple, and Lauren felt a flash of jealousy at the ease of their relationship. "You'll always be in trouble otherwise."

Lauren chuckled. "He's got your number."

Jane leaned back against him. "Yeah, from day one but that's a story for another time. Wanna have dinner with us?"

Did she want to be a third wheel and watch two sexy, dynamic people be in love with each other? Since her masochism was mostly theoretical, she decided not to test it with a smug-engaged-couple charity date. "Nah, I think I'll be fine with some takeout."

Jane sighed. "Yeah, okay, just keep your alarm on."

Lauren just smiled. "You can't be my bodyguard, you know."

"I'd be a damned good bodyguard," Jane proclaimed. "I'm totally a lethal weapon."

"I heard all about your GI Jane way." Lauren wiggled her eyebrows. "Mercy caught me all up on your wallowing session with Mathias when we were shopping for my dress."

Jane blushed. "I do not wallow."

"Oh," Mathias laughed, "we might have wallowed a little bit."

Lauren braced her foot on the fourth step leading up to the town house and leaned forward into a full-bodied stretch. There was a park about three blocks away that she'd already scoped out for running. She was really looking forward to some scenery. Five days on a treadmill hadn't been inspiring at all.

She'd considered calling Connor to see if he wanted to run with her, but the man had been at or near her side for a solid week and she figured he needed some time off. She tightened her ponytail and tucked her earbuds in. She'd filled her iPod with enough '80s music to rival a Brat Pack film, so she figured she was ready to go.

She jogged the few blocks to the park and picked up her pace as she started up a well-maintained running path. There were plenty of people in the park, so it felt pretty safe.

Connor tossed aside his towel and reached for his cell phone. "This is Grant."

A man cleared his throat on the other end of the line. "Connor Grant?"

"Yeah, mate, who is this?" Connor frowned and hazarded a small glance at the screen of his phone.

"Look, man, I was jogging in the park, and I saw this man and woman in what looked like a fight. He was trying to drag her off the path." The man blew out a breath. "I interrupted them but she isn't talking to me except to say your name and your phone number. She said no when I asked if she wanted a cop."

"Where in the park?" Connor demanded as he went to his closet. "Black hair, blue eyes?"

"Yeah, beautiful lady you've got here, man, but she's in a *bad* way. You need to hurry up. We're on running path six, about three clicks in."

"Her name is Lauren. Tell her I'm coming and don't try to touch her."

"No, man, I won't."

There was a small crowd gathered, and a uniformed cop was squatting in front of her when Connor arrived. He could tell the man had been talking a while, because he was clearly getting frustrated by her lack of a response.

"Lauren."

Her head jerked up and she pulled away from the cop with a small wounded sound as she launched herself at him. Connor caught her tightly and glanced around the scene. "Where is the guy who called me?"

"Here, man." A tall man lifted a hand. "William Trent."

"You said you interrupted someone trying to take her off the path?" Connor asked, threading his fingers through her hair. She was shaking against him. "What did he look like?"

"About your height and weight, maybe a little heavier. He was in workout clothes, but he didn't look like he'd been doing any real running this morning, if you know what I mean. He was shouting at her about a code, and she was screaming for help."

Connor nodded and then looked at the cop. "Request Detective Shawn Trainer from dispatch, Officer."

The cop frowned at him. "I put in a call for a detective from Sex Crimes."

Lauren flinched in his arms.

"She knows Shawn Trainer, and he's working the investigation on her home invasion. Since the attacker was asking for a code, it stands to reason he wanted the security code to her home." Connor pressed a kiss against her temple. "You need to calm down, lass, and talk to me."

"Home," Lauren whispered. "Take me home, Connor. I can't...just take me home."

"Yeah, you got it." He reached into his pocket and pulled out a card. "I owe you a debt. Mr. Trent, give me a call if you ever need *anything*."

Trent took the card and glanced it over. "You work for Mathias Montgomery?"

"I'm his second in command for Montgomery Securities," Connor said, and turned on the path. "Officer, tell Detective

Trainer that I've taken Ms. Evans home. He'll know where to find us."

"I can't let you take the victim from the scene."

Connor glared at him, and the man took a step back. "If Trainer has a problem with it, he can talk to me about it later. She's not staying here. You need to mark this area off for Forensics and start taking witness statements. I'm sure they taught you how to do all of that when they gave you that badge."

"I have to shower," Lauren murmured as he prodded her into the town house.

"Not yet, lass." Connor took her to the couch and urged her to sit. "Did you scratch him?" He tilted her face and frowned over the bruise spreading over her cheek. "How many hits did he get to this beautiful head of yours?"

"He backhanded me across the face," Lauren whispered. "Just the one time." She rubbed at dried blood on the corner of her mouth. "I didn't know you were second in command at Montgomery Securities. I thought you just worked at the gallery."

Connor raised an eyebrow at her abrupt change of subject. "I own thirty percent of Montgomery Securities, lass. I work out of the gallery because it's our biggest contract in Boston. I was in New York until Mathias signed the contract for Holman. We have operations in New York and here in Boston. Our third partner is still in New York—Alasdair McBain. He's an ex-Navy SEAL and one truly vicious son of a bitch."

"Alasdair," Lauren repeated. "Lovely name."

"Most everyone who knows him calls him Dare," Connor said as he slid onto the couch beside her and pulled her close. "So we're going to sit here until you want to talk or alternately until Shawn tracks us down and berates me for bullying a uniformed cop."

Lauren laughed softly, but it ended in a little sob. She turned her face against him and dug her fingers into his side as she started to cry in earnest.

He glanced down at her hands and found them both scraped up and bruised. It looked like she'd gotten a few blows in herself, but he wasn't really surprised—after all, she was a military man's only child. No real man could raise a woman as beautiful as Lauren and fail to show her how to protect herself.

He lifted his gun when he heard the front door open and only relaxed a little when someone put a code in. He had the weapon leveled at the entryway of the living room when Mathias Montgomery and Shawn Trainer appeared there. Connor lowered the gun to the couch beside him and started to rub a circle against Lauren's back to try to calm her.

Mathias looked her over, taking in the shaking and the gut-wrenching sobs that hadn't diminished at all since she'd started. "Jesus. Fuck."

Connor couldn't have agreed more. "A witness on the scene said the guy was shouting at her about a code." He glanced around the town house. "What the fuck could he want in this place that would make him risk taking a woman off a well-traveled running path in a public park in *prime* hours? The park is never empty this time of the day."

Mathias's jaw clenched and he shook his head. "This isn't about art upstairs, is it?"

"No, it's not," Shawn murmured. "Do you know if she needs a paramedic?"

"He hit her in the face, and she's got some scrapes and bruises. I think some of this blood is most definitely his." Connor shared a glance with Mathias. "We can get someone to run the DNA for us—faster than anything the locals could do."

Shawn sighed. "Don't talk about that kind of stuff in front of me. Let me get a tech in here for *my* investigation, and if you're going to call the FBI, let me know in advance so I can warn my captain."

"A woman, Trainer. Make sure it's a woman."

"Yeah," Shawn agreed. "Not a problem."

Lauren shoved away her ruined workout clothes with one foot and gratefully slid into the shower stall. Her brain was on lockdown; it was the only explanation she had for letting Jane Tilwell strip her down with only a token protest. "I can handle this."

"Yeah, don't make me get in there with you," Jane warned. "Every man in the place will have wet dreams about us for *years* if I come out of this bathroom with wet hair, too." The crime scene tech exited the bathroom with an evidence bag full of clothes.

Lauren laughed before she could help herself. "I slept with a girl in college."

"Oh, yeah?" Jane asked with a grin, and leaned back against the counter. "Was she as hot as me?"

Lauren glanced over at her through the glass door of the shower. "Nah, not nearly, but she was pretty enough. She climbed all over me one night when we were supposed to be studying, and I let her." She reached for the shampoo. "How about you?"

"Hmm, actually, there was this woman once in a bar. She followed me into a bathroom stall—and shoved her tongue in my mouth and her hand down my pants. I didn't have the heart or the right amount of sobriety to tell her I was straight, so I returned the favor."

"You're making that up," Lauren accused.

Jane grinned. "Not at all. It was pretty hot, now that I think about it. She wanted me *bad*. And really, look at me—who could blame her?"

Lauren laughed and leaned against the wall. "It was a nightmare come true, you know."

"I see that," Jane murmured. "And certainly not the first time a man has gotten physical with you. Do you want to talk about it?"

"Not really," Lauren sighed. "But I will. Just not right now, okay?"

Mercy Montgomery was so upset her fingers were trembling slightly as she sat at the kitchen table in the town house. Connor really hated seeing her that way. He figured he wasn't the only one, because her husband was standing near her chair, completely furious.

"I want her to have twenty-four / seven security until this is figured out," Mercy whispered. "I want background checks done on every single man who has crossed her path since she got to Boston. Start with that pervert with the panties and the hotel manager. This is intolerable, Mathias."

"I know, Mercy." Mathias set a cup of coffee in front of her. "I'm working on this. Until this is figured out, she won't even get her mail without security watching. My word on it." He took a deep breath. "When you and Jane had this place remodeled, did you keep anything, or did you throw out all of the furniture and start fresh?"

"I don't know," Mercy admitted. "I mean, Jane handled most of that, as you know. I was still so pissed about Stein that I couldn't even come over here. You remember how much damage was left. He kicked holes into the walls, broke windows. He was an utter bastard. I should've filed charges against him for vandalism, but he was already gone when I found the damage."

"What if he didn't do it?" Connor asked. "What if it was done after he left?"

Mercy frowned. "Well, the security was damaged as well, you know. The alarm system was old, and most of the control panels were broken. That's why you guys put in the new system. Do you think this has something to do with him?"

"I don't know. I'm just wondering if it has anything to do with Lauren besides the fact that she's living here," Connor admitted. "The guy who attacked her wanted the alarm codes for this place—and I can assume he would've prevented her from calling for help, but none of her injuries...His interest wasn't sexual, and he wasn't prepared for her to fight back. He thought he could get her off the path before anyone noticed and get what he needed from her." He paused and turned to Mathias. "Do you know a William Trent?"

Mathias raised an eyebrow. "Six-four with shoulders like a professional linebacker? Blond hair, blue eyes?"

"Yeah." Connor nodded.

"Yeah, army ranger." Mathias set his cup of coffee down in front of him. "Why?"

"He was in the park today—he's the one who interrupted the attack."

"Hmm." Mathias leaned on the counter. "I wonder if he's out. We could use another man here on the ground who is comfortable with wet work." He paused and glanced briefly at Mercy. She apparently hadn't gotten the reference, because she was staring intently at her coffee.

"You mean someone who can kill?" Mercy asked softly.

Mathias winced and sent his brother an apologetic look. "Just someone who has seen combat."

Mercy glanced at him and lifted an eyebrow. "Yeah, okay." She ran both hands through her hair and let her head rest on the back of the seat. She clearly didn't buy the explanation. "Connor."

"Yeah?"

82

"She can't stay here."

"No, I agree." Connor stared into his coffee. "I could take her out to Brooks's country house. It has a studio, so she can work, and the security is a step up from what's here."

Mercy nodded. "Let me call James and see what he thinks." She pulled her cell phone out of her purse.

Connor waited until she left the room and then turned to Shawn. "I checked out Anthony Davis. What did you get on him?"

"No criminal record but there have been two uniformed visits to his home because of noise reported by the neighbors. Nothing domestic—both were parties that were out of hand. You?" Shawn raised an eyebrow.

"He hasn't left San Diego in over a year as far as Deacon could find. We confirmed his location for the break-in attempt, and he's engaged to be married. It's his second engagement in three years. She bears a striking resemblance to Lauren," Connor admitted.

"You'll stay with her. She obviously trusts you," Mathias said. "We'll move her work to the safe in the gallery to secure it. If it's her work he's really after, he'll have to come at us from that direction."

"You don't think it's the work."

"No," Mathias admitted. "You need to go pack a bag."

Connor nodded and stood up.

"You're leaving me?"

They turned and found Lauren hovering in the doorway. She was dressed in a pair of jeans and a T-shirt, no bra, and her hair fell damp on her shoulders.

Connor shook his head. "No, lass, I'm not going anywhere without you. Go upstairs and pack enough for a week. We'll settle the rest later."

"Yeah, okay." Lauren turned abruptly and left the doorway.

Shawn sighed. "Christ, Grant, you are in so much trouble."

"You're not telling me anything I don't know," Connor muttered, and ran his fingers through his hair. "I'll take her with me to my apartment, pack my own bag then. My building doesn't have the kind of security I'd prefer for her to stay there, so if Brooks would rather she not—"

Mercy entered the room then, closing her cell phone. "He says yes, of course. We can expect a meeting because he is not a happy camper. Connor is exempt, of course, but I imagine James will be visiting with you and Lauren before the day is over." She dropped her cell phone in her pocket.

Connor wasn't a happy camper, either, but that was another matter altogether. By the time he went upstairs to check on Lauren, she was all the way on the third floor, packing a second suitcase. He watched silently as she settled several cases of pencils, charcoal, and drawing pads in the case.

"You won't need anything else?"

Lauren shook her head. "I never paint until I've done over a hundred line drawings on a project. I still haven't found a model, so it could be weeks before I'm ready to paint." She flushed. "I'm sorry I put you on the spot down there. I would be fine with anyone you assigned . . ."

"No, lass, I never intended to leave you in anyone else's care." Connor picked up the case before she could. "Did you get all the clothes you'll need?"

"Yes." She looked around the studio. "My work?"

"I'm going to put a security team in here until we can move your finished work into the large safe at the gallery. You have to know we don't think this had anything to do with your work."

"I don't have anything of serious value beyond my work."

"I know." Connor sighed. "Do me a favor and put a shirt on over this one. It's see-through."

Lauren bit down on her lip and glanced down. "Sorry, I didn't pay attention when I got dressed."

Connor laughed softly. "I'm not complaining. I'd just rather you not show off your assets to the rest of the men in this house."

Lauren blushed. "I was starting to think you weren't interested." She moved to walk past him to the stairs, and he grabbed her arm. Lauren took a deep breath as he pulled her around. "What?"

Connor put the suitcase down, slid his hand into her still-damp hair, and pulled her close. "I'm very interested." He looked over her face, frowning at the bruise on her cheek. Then he moved in and covered her mouth with his.

Lauren shuddered and just surrendered to him. He'd never had a woman just melt against him, all soft and languid like she'd been waiting forever for him to kiss her. Connor groaned softly in shock and slid his tongue into her mouth. She tasted better than she looked, and that was saying so much.

Little hands with elegant, knowledgeable fingers curled against his back as she wrapped around him. Small, firm, hard-tipped breasts pressed against his chest, and his cock hardened against her. Her tongue drifted against his, and she made a soft sound against him that tripped his trigger so hard he had to pull his mouth from hers and take a breath to calm down.

"Okay, then," Jane Tilwell said from the doorway. "I'll just let Mathias know you guys will be ready to leave in a few minutes."

Lauren blushed but didn't move as Connor looked over her face. "Sounds great, Jane."

Jane laughed and left, her footsteps thumping loudly on the stairs.

"I didn't hear her," Lauren said.

Connor flushed. He hadn't, either, and that said more about

85

his state than anything else. He blew out a breath and slowly let her go. "Neither did I."

Lauren grinned. "Really?"

"Really." Connor sighed and glanced her over again, taking in her dark, hard-tipped nipples, plainly visible through the thin T-shirt. "Now you definitely need a sweatshirt or something."

She glanced down and blushed. "Yes, well." Lauren crossed her arms over her breasts.

"I'm going to take you to bed and do really nasty, probably illegal things to you," Connor promised casually. He picked up the case and walked toward the stairs. "You'll be down in a few minutes?"

"Yeah."

Connor forced himself down the stairs and set the case next to her bedroom door before going into a small bathroom. He shut it and turned on the water. "Jesus."

Mentally, he ran through all the horrible erection-killing mental images he could think of, starting with Sister Mary Kathleen and ending with Ann Coulter. As always, it worked like a charm. He washed his hands briskly and then turned the water off.

5

Connor Grant's place was almost exactly like she imagined. Neat, organized, and completely without personal information, but that just confirmed what she already suspected about the former military man. He hadn't really settled into Boston, which said a lot about his previous relationship with Casey Trainer.

He came out of his bedroom with a suitcase. "You could sit, lass."

Lauren glanced over at him and moved away from the bookcase. "I didn't take you for a fan of Ben Bova or even really a science-fiction fan at all."

"Reality blows," Connor admitted as he walked to a locked gun case. He opened it and pulled out a case, which he then set on the coffee table and flipped open. It held two 9 mm pistols and six magazines.

Lauren watched him check both guns over and put them back in the case. "Necessary?"

He looked up at her. "How can you ask that question?"

She laughed and shook her head. "It's pretty easy to forget

there is anything out there to be afraid of when I'm around you."

"You don't have to fear anything," Connor said. He locked the case. "I'm not leaving you alone again until this is resolved."

She nodded and glanced around. "No pictures."

Connor frowned. "Ah, no, I didn't bring anything over. I have a flat in London that my little brother is using—probably poorly and with little respect."

Lauren laughed abruptly. "Well, at least you're prepared for the sight of it."

Connor shrugged. "I was twenty-five once. I just don't remember it well."

Lauren picked up the gun case as he stood. "I can handle this."

"Thanks." Connor did a cursory check of his apartment as he picked up his suitcase.

"Pack your toothbrush?"

"Yes," Connor laughed. "I never forget my toothbrush." He hooked one arm around her waist and pulled her close. Gently, he brushed his mouth over hers. "Did it bother you that Jane caught us?"

"Not at all," Lauren murmured, and shifted up on her toes for another kiss. "She's probably just relieved you made that pass at me like she ordered."

"Perhaps," Connor admitted, amused. He curled his hand around her hip and kissed her again. "You're lovely, but we should go before Trainer comes up to investigate why it's taking so long."

"Is he going to follow us out to the Brooks farm?"

"Yes." Connor released her reluctantly. "His captain insisted, probably because Brooks is throwing his weight around with the police commissioner. He has a lot of powerful friends, and he makes no bones about it."

"I wouldn't want Shawn to get in trouble over what happened today. It's no one's fault...but maybe my own."

Connor sighed. "It isn't your fault at all. You shouldn't have to worry about being attacked in the park while you run, for fuck's sake."

Lauren found herself quickly settled in the front seat of a black SUV. Before they were even out of Boston, she spotted both of the Montgomery Security vehicles, which she pointed out to Connor.

"Yeah," Connor admitted ruefully. He glanced her way. "Mercy is upset. She doesn't handle violence against women well...at all. You getting attacked in the park has upset her more than she's going to admit aloud."

Lauren nodded. "I thought...when he first grabbed me... that he was going to...until he started demanding the security codes."

"Did he specify the town house, or did he ask if you had codes to get into the gallery?"

"No, he just kept asking for the code and saying my name." She took a deep breath. "He said, '*Give me the code, Lauren.*' Over and over again. It was insane." She rubbed her arms briskly. "I didn't like him saying my name."

"He was just trying to get in your head, you know that." Connor reached out and touched her knee and smiled when she settled her hand on top of his. Her small fingers curled around the side of his hands. "You've very small, soft hands."

"Is that a problem?"

He laughed. "No, it's just most of the female artists I've met tend to have large or rough hands. It's just a surprise." Connor turned her hand over in his and brought it to his mouth for a kiss. "A pleasant surprise."

"You know your men saw that."

Connor snorted. "If they don't know how much I want you already, then I'm going to fire them for being supremely stupid."

She laughed and blushed. "You think you're that obvious?"

"I think I have a lot of observant people working for me," Connor explained. He released her hand and pulled his cell phone from his pocket. He dialed quickly and glanced into his rearview mirror as he did. "Samuels, drop back behind us and get a license plate on the tan Ford."

He closed the phone and dropped it back in his pocket. "So, you've more interviews on Monday?"

"Yeah, I decided to try a different agency."

Connor nodded and pulled his phone out of his pocket again when it started to ring. "Grant." He frowned and glanced toward Lauren. "Yeah, Shawn, I see it. I'm going to get on the interstate in a few minutes and see if he follows." He closed the phone and reached out to take her hand. "Relax. He's not going to pick a fight with me."

Lauren bit down on her bottom lip and then checked the passenger side mirror. "I wouldn't want you to get hurt."

"I won't," Connor murmured, and rubbed his thumb over her hand. "And he won't touch you again."

"But you will?" she asked with a little grin.

"Yeah, I sure will," Connor responded with a small laugh. "You tempt me beyond reason. You know that, right?"

"I find the idea of tempting you very thrilling," she whispered, and then leaned in to brush a soft kiss on his cheek. "There, now they have something extra to talk about."

Connor laughed. "You probably need to be spanked for that."

She used her thumb to wipe off the trace of lipstick she'd left on his cheek. "And if I said that sounded like fun?"

Connor glanced her way and smirked. "You and I are going to have so much fun."

* * *

The Brooks farm had defenses like a maximum-security prison. Lauren had watched Connor move through the secured gate and then through two different security panels. Shawn Trainer and two security guards followed them in to go through the house.

Lauren dropped onto the couch, pushed her shoes off, and pulled her legs up against her chest while she watched the men move around the large two-hundred-year-old farmhouse. "This does not look like a country house that a man like James Brooks would buy."

"It's actually Lisa Brooks's home. She was living here when he finally managed to wrangle her into marriage." Connor sat down on the coffee table in front of her. "I'm going to have my team walk the fence to make sure everything is as it should be, and then they'll get us some groceries. If you could make a list of things that appeal to you . . ."

"Yeah, sure." Lauren nodded and reached for her purse. She pulled out a small drawing pad and dug around for a pen. "Did you want anything?"

He nodded and looked at her purse. "Make sure to get lots of stuff for sandwiches. I prefer a multigrain bread."

"Yeah, not a problem." Lauren focused on her busy work and mentally planned the evening meal while she was at it. It gave her something to think about, something to focus on besides her very crappy-ass morning.

Shawn Trainer sat down in front of her and cleared his throat. "At this point, I've been ordered to offer you police protection."

Lauren wrinkled her nose. "Wow, you're ready to go around with Connor over that?"

Shawn laughed. "Yes, if you want it, I'll go more than one round with Grant."

"Would you be insulted if I said I preferred Connor and his private army to police protection?" Lauren asked with a raised eyebrow.

Shawn grinned. "No, actually, I wouldn't. I'll be sure to convey your wishes to my captain." He paused then and took a deep breath. "However, if another incident happens, we'll be having this discussion again. I won't lie to you—I'm very concerned. I have confirmed that the pervy guy at the hotel still hasn't made bail."

"So it's not related to him?" Lauren sighed. "There goes the thought that he wanted my new panties."

Shawn laughed softly. "Yeah, no, I think your new panties are safe from him."

Lauren looked down at her grocery list and sighed. "So is it time to talk about what happened?"

"That would be good," Shawn admitted. He pulled out a digital recorder. "So, let's talk about your morning."

"Okay," Lauren started, and set aside the pad and pen. "So, there is a treadmill in the town house, and I was pretty tired of it. I'm not used to . . . In San Diego I did a lot of outdoor running. I prefer it." She glanced toward the doorway and relaxed when she saw Connor leaning there. "I stretched inside and then left the town house. I jogged the three blocks to the park and then picked out a running trail. I'd never been there, so I didn't know which one would have the most traffic. It was well maintained and it felt safe."

Shawn nodded. "I know that park. It's beautiful and popular. I can see how you'd feel safe there."

"Right. Lots of great trees." Lauren took a deep breath. "So, I'm hitting my stride. I can do a six-minute mile, and I was probably in that range. It felt great to stretch my legs." She focused on her toes and wiggled them. "I need to paint my toenails."

Shawn grinned. "You could put some polish on your grocery list and make Security buy you some."

"I think I will," Lauren said loftily. "I bet they'd pick great colors. They do really well with sandwich meat and beer." She sighed. "Okay, so he came out of nowhere. I took my iPod, but I didn't have the earbuds in. The park sounds were nice, you know? I didn't hear anything on the path behind me at all. No breathing, no footfalls, so he was lying in wait on the trail for me to pass him. He came at me pretty hard." She rubbed her shoulder at the memory. "And we hit the ground. I know I took some skin off his neck and face. I hit him in the face a few times with my fist, kneed him a couple of times in the side, so he might have a cracked rib. I tried my damnedest to break a rib or two."

Shawn raised an eyebrow. "Was he speaking to you?"

"He kept telling me to give him the code and saying my name. He said my name a lot and asking for the code. I was screaming."

"What were you screaming?"

"A lot of very foul language," Lauren admitted, and blushed when they both laughed. "Well, I was raised by an army man. I'm pretty sure I called him a motherfucker and maybe a son of a bitch when I was screaming at him to let me go."

"Good for you, lass," Connor murmured.

"And he didn't deviate from his demand?" Sean asked.

"No, he was completely focused on getting the code. Then there was this man shouting at him to get off of me." Lauren huffed out a breath. "Then he was gone—the man who interrupted chose to stay with me rather than run after him."

"Yes, I got Mr. Trent's contact information when I took his statement," Shawn explained. "He was able to offer a lot of details. Tell me about the man who grabbed you. What do you remember about him?"

"Much bigger than me." Lauren hugged her knees and rocked a little. "Six foot three, maybe four. Over two hundred pounds but *very* fit. He was unprepared for me to fight, so he probably uses his size to intimidate everyone he crosses paths with. Short blond hair, brown eyes, square jaw. Not military trained by any stretch of the imagination. A thug and probably not much of a fighter."

"Why do you say that?" Shawn asked.

"Because I'm five-nine and weigh a hundred and thirty pounds. Granted, I wasn't winning the fight, but a trained man would have been able to subdue and control me. Also, he should've taken me farther off the trail. He was rather unprofessional about the whole thing." She waved a hand as she finished.

Shawn turned off the recorder. "So, my guys and I took a poll and we voted you the woman with the worst luck in all of Boston."

Lauren glared at him halfheartedly. "Well, I haven't broken my leg yet. I think you should redo the poll."

Shawn stood up. "I'm going to leave you to get settled for the day. Give yourself some time to process this and acknowledge the fact that something fucked up happened. If you try to ignore it, you'll just suffer for it later."

"It could've been worse."

"Yes, it could've," Shawn acknowledged.

"I want to come in on Monday and start the paperwork I need to carry a weapon."

"If you insist."

"I do." Lauren's jaw clenched briefly. "I really do."

Connor set aside the bottle of nail polish he'd found in the bottom of the grocery bag. "Looks like Jake thought you'd like red."

Lauren laughed and plucked up the bottle. "He did great. Did you want help with this?"

"No, why don't you go get settled in a room upstairs and maybe take a bath? You've probably got bruises rising as we stand here. There is a large, girl-fantasy tub upstairs in the master bedroom. Jets and everything."

"Sounds good." She pushed the bottle of nail polish into her front pocket and ran her finger along the edge of the counter. "You know, I'm okay."

He glanced up from the apples he was inspecting more thoroughly than was necessary. "Yeah, lass, I know."

She blew out a breath. "Then why are you barely looking at me? You've been avoiding looking at me since everyone else left."

He carefully set aside the fruit and looked at her. "Because I'm trying to give you some space."

"Space is really overrated."

Connor looked her over and then snatched her up. She didn't hesitate to wrap her arms around his neck as his mouth covered hers. Lauren groaned softly into his mouth as she opened for him. His tongue slid like silk into her mouth and she shuddered.

He picked her up effortlessly, and Lauren wrapped her legs around his waist as he pressed her against the wall. Connor pulled his mouth from hers with a sigh and then trailed several kisses along her jaw.

Heat slid down her back, straight into her pussy, and her nipples tightened. "Jesus."

"Not even close, lass." His teeth grazed her pulse point and then he clenched them briefly. The pain was exquisite and perfect. "Is this what you want?"

"Please," Lauren whispered with a shudder.

"Do you want me to fuck you?"

Lauren's eyes closed involuntarily. "Yeah, I really do. I want all of those filthy, dirty things you promised me."

He hummed against her neck and she shivered. Connor lifted them away from the wall and carried her down a short hallway to a small sparse bedroom, where he spread her out on a full-size bed covered with an old-fashioned quilt.

He caught her mouth in a heated kiss as he slid one hand down between them and undid her jeans with practiced ease. Lauren lifted her hips eagerly, and he groaned into her mouth. He tugged on her bottom lip briefly with his teeth and then released it.

"You think this is what you need," Connor murmured against her throat. "You think if I fuck you long enough you'll forget what it felt like to have him touching you."

She sucked in a deep breath. "Do you always provide psychoanalysis with your cock?"

Connor lifted away and knelt between her spread legs. "I like to provide a full service."

She pressed her foot against his thigh and rubbed against his jeans. "Do you think you can do it?"

He quirked an eyebrow and unzipped her jeans. Connor rubbed her stomach and slid his thumb under the edge of her panties. "Sweetheart, I'm going to make you forget your name."

Lauren lifted her hips in demand and groaned when a beep sounded loudly throughout the house. "What is that?"

"That's probably your boss," Connor said with a sigh, and slid off the bed. "Stay back here until I make sure."

Lauren sighed in frustration and mild fury. "Who knew James Brooks would be a cockblock?"

Connor sputtered with laughter as he pulled his gun. "God, lass, I think you could be more than I can handle."

"I'm sure Her Majesty had you thoroughly trained for any

contingency," Lauren called after him as she dropped back on the bed and zipped up with a frown. She was still playing with the metal button of her jeans when Connor called her name. She buttoned up and rolled off the bed to go see her boss.

James Brooks was installed at the kitchen table with a lit cigarette in his mouth. He took a long drag as she entered. "Does this bother you?"

"No, not at all." Lauren sat down across from him.

"Good, I quit ten years ago." He glanced over her face. "Between you and my wife…frankly I'm surprised I've not smoked the whole pack since I bought it." He stubbed it out in the saucer Connor slid in front of him. "Who is Anthony Davis, Connor?"

"A man in San Diego who took a sex game too far with Lauren and scared the crap out of her. He hasn't taken a piss in the last three days that I didn't get a report on." Connor leaned against the counter near the coffeepot that was brewing. "I have Deacon down there doing an admirable job of stalking him."

James nodded and focused on Lauren. She blushed under his scrutiny. "Did anyone approach you and ask you questions about the job we offered you?"

Lauren blinked in surprise and took a deep breath. "Not here."

"But in San Diego?"

"I was offered a teaching position at a college around the same time I was contacted about an interview here in Boston. Because of the situation with Davis and because I hadn't slept well in months, Boston appealed. When I turned down their offer, they asked me who'd had the better offer and I mentioned the artist in residence position at Holman I was interviewing for."

"Were they pissed?"

"No, Claudia Murphy, the dean at the college, was thrilled

for me. She laughed and said it would be pretty hard for anyone to compete with you and the Holman Foundation."

"Claudia?" James relaxed in his chair. "Good to know she finds me tempting. I'll be opening a new gallery in New York within the next year, and I plan to offer her the directorship. Mercy and I have been head-hunting for a while—she's at the top of our list." James reached into his pocket for his cigarettes, but Lauren took them from his hand.

"You won't be keeping up with twins if you can't catch your breath because you smoke a pack a day." She tossed the package to Connor. "How is your wife?"

"Furious that I won't let her out of bed and berating anyone who gets near her for the fact that she believes she resembles a beached whale," James admitted, and looked mournfully at his cigarettes. "Just one more?"

"I'll tell your wife," Lauren responded sweetly.

Connor laughed and poured James some coffee. "Maybe you should start putting a clause in your contract forbidding your employees from tattling on you to your wife."

James took the coffee with a frown. "I think you're right." He sighed. "So, do you have everything you need out here?"

"Yeah. We're good," Connor answered. "I had the men do some grocery shopping for us, and I'll bring her back into town for the show tomorrow night."

James nodded. "I know you normally prefer to work the back side of security during shows, but I'll want you on the floor with her all evening. I want twice the security you had planned and metal detectors on the front entrance. I don't care what anyone has to say about it. If they refuse, they don't get in the door. This isn't an invitation-only event, so *anyone* could walk through the door."

"Mathias is already reworking the security plan," Connor admitted. "We'll do strip searches if you want it."

James smirked. "Christ, that would amuse the hell out of me, but Lisa would be pissed to have missed it, so we'll stick with a metal detector." He paused and frowned. "Lauren, I'd like to speak with Connor privately."

Lauren stood. "Of course. I'll just go upstairs and take a swim in the girl tub."

James grinned. "My wife says it's the best thing I bought for this place."

Connor sat down at the table when the kitchen door swung closed and they both listened to her walk up the stairs. He took a deep breath. "I should've been with her. I don't even know what to say."

"It's not your fault," James said and glanced at his cigarettes on the counter and sighed. "You think she's keeping anything else to herself?"

"No, she's baffled by the situation, and this guy Davis is just what she said he was—a guy with some serious sexual kinks who went too far. Deacon talked to his ex-fiancée and learned there was no violence in their relationship. She wanted kids and he decided he didn't. It's concerning that both women he's dated since Lauren look enough like her to be her sisters, but he might just have a very definite type."

James nodded. "Some men do." He smirked. "You don't."

"I really like women, sir. In all their various shapes, forms, and colors. I suppose Mercy told you?"

"Mathias mentioned that he thought you were personally invested in her. I don't have a problem with it as long as it's mutual, and from what I heard it is."

Connor blew out a breath. "I never crossed the line with Casey."

"Oh, I know. She made that clear to me on more than one occasion. She never once thought that you were a threat to her." James quirked an eyebrow. "Women are eager to trust you."

"I'm British," Connor offered with a sly grin. "They mostly all think I'm a real-live James Bond. It works in my favor *a lot.*"

James laughed and sat back in his chair. "Well, keep a close eye on this one. I don't want... I really don't want anyone to get hurt here, Connor, and things are escalating. Even if we don't count the hotel thing."

"I think the hotel thing was just really bad luck."

"For more than just her," James muttered darkly. "I bought it and fired most of the people working here."

Connor's mouth dropped open. "Excuse me?"

"Yeah, I sent a memo to Mathias. I'll have to expand my account with you guys to cover the hotel. I'll want you guys to supply the security after I finish with renovations. I've closed reservations and shuffled most of the guests and bookings to different properties around the city. I'm going to have the whole thing gutted and restored. It'll keep me busy for a while while I finalize the plans for the New York gallery. Dare seems pretty pleased with the building and security system you guys are building in."

Connor nodded. "Yeah, he sent a report to Mathias and me last week about it. I think we'll be on schedule for a spring opening if you get the staff in place on your schedule."

A part of him wasn't even surprised that Brooks had bought the hotel. It was certainly the kind of thing he'd done in the past. "I won't let anything happen to Lauren."

James nodded. "I get that. Try not to break her heart while you're at it."

Connor flushed. "I've never once set out to break a woman's heart."

"Most men don't," James returned dryly. "It still happens a lot more often than it should. We need to find out what this man wants. Also, I told Mathias that I want to have a discussion with Stein. I figure he owes me twenty thousand dollars in damages, and maybe it's time he cut me a check."

Lauren set aside her hairbrush and wiggled her toes. The red nail polish looked awesome if she did say so herself. Every woman should wear red toenail polish; it made everything seem better.

She glanced toward the doorway and found Connor leaning there watching her. "Hey."

"Hey." He shrugged out of his gun holster and put his weapon on the nightstand as he looked over. "Enjoy the tub?"

"It was great," she admitted, and propped one leg up. Her bathrobe slid down her thigh and fell open to her bare hip. "Is he mad about today?"

"He's concerned about today," Connor corrected as he pulled his shirt out of his jeans and jerked it over his head. "We're all concerned. We've been down this road before, and the last time, it ended with a man pointing a gun at Casey Trainer."

Lauren frowned. "This isn't about me—not really. This is about the town house."

Connor nodded reluctantly. "Yeah, I agree. We're going to pack up the rest of your things and bring them out here. You'll stay here until things are resolved or until the next semester starts. James is considering buying another property closer to the academy for your position, anyway."

Lauren blew out a breath. "He's going to own half of Boston before he's done."

Connor grinned and unbuckled his belt. "Yeah, probably. He's something of a collector, but at least he uses his money for good. Unless he's buying an entire hotel and firing all of the people who pissed him off."

She grinned and untied the belt of her robe. It slid away like good, heavy silk always does, revealing high, firm, hard-tipped breasts; a sleekly muscled stomach; and the bare flesh of her pussy.

Connor blew out a breath and shoved off his shoes. "We're probably going to kill each other."

"What a way to go." She spread her legs wide and planted both feet firmly on the bed. "I'm not fragile, so don't treat me like I am."

He laughed softly as he got rid of his socks and then worked off his jeans and boxers in one maneuver. He pulled a strip of condoms from the front pocket of his jeans and tossed it on the bed beside her.

"Lass, treating you like you're made of glass is the least of my plans." He grabbed both of her ankles firmly as he slid onto the bed and spread her wide.

Lauren shuddered at the exposure and bit down on her bottom lip as Connor lowered his head and licked her from hole to clit in one broad, wet swipe. She arched against the bed, her body sliding on the silk underneath her as much as he would allow her.

His grip on her ankles tightened briefly as he gently nipped the plump flesh of her bare mound. She lifted her hips, helpless and needy against the assault of his mouth. Words failed her as he slid downward and probed lazily between her labia with his tongue, flicking over her clit in a torturous way.

Connor's hand drifted away from her ankle and up under her legs, all the way to her ass. He repeatedly dipped one thumb into the clenched opening of her pussy until her body allowed him entry, and then he retreated.

She would have shouted her dissatisfaction at that if he hadn't slid that thumb right into her ass. Instead she shouted his name and came so hard her vision darkened. The orgasm was completely unexpected and so intense that she shook all over with it.

He lifted his head and pressed his thumb more firmly into her ass. "You know I'm going to fuck you here."

She blinked. "Yeah, God, anything you want."

"And I'm going to fuck your mouth," Connor said as he placed a soft kiss on her belly button. "Your pussy is mine, too. I'm going to ride you long and hard, Lauren. Then when you don't think you can take any more, I'm going to slide my dick into this pretty pink hole of yours and fuck your ass until you give up everything you have to me."

She was sure she should say something to all of that, but she just nodded as he latched on to one nipple and removed his thumb from her asshole. He didn't give her a chance to feel empty for long, because he reached for a condom, deftly tore open the wrapper, and rolled the latex onto his cock while he licked, sucked, and eventually bit her nipples.

Connor cupped her ass in both hands as he pushed his cock into her with one sure, hard thrust. She moaned against his neck and clenched her hands on his back as he settled his weight on her.

"Ah, goddamn it." Lauren arched under him and wrapped her legs high around his waist. "Fuck me."

He laughed softly against her jaw and shifted them as he let go of her ass and put both hands on the bed on either side of her head. He met her gaze. "Put your feet flat on the bed and spread your legs wide."

Lauren flushed under his scrutiny without a single word of complaint but did as he ordered. He shifted his weight and settled so deeply inside of her that her breath caught at the pain of it.

"Hurt?" Connor asked, his voice silky and all too knowing.

"Yes." Lauren relaxed into it, and pain burned into intense pleasure.

"Is this what you want from me?" Connor asked softly. "Is this what you need?"

"God, fuck yes." She arched under him and moaned when he started to move. "Make it hurt."

He set up a punishing and relentless pace. Their skin smacked together, lewd and harsh in the silence of the room. She clutched at him briefly, but he grabbed her hands and pinned them under his own to hold her still.

"Shhh," Connor whispered. "Just take it, Lauren. Just relax and take my cock." She clenched briefly and then just melted under him. "That's it, sweetheart, let me give you exactly what you want."

He thrust deep and hard into her pussy until she was sobbing with a second orgasm. Her whole body started to shake with it. Connor released her hands and gently slid one hand into her hair.

She moaned into his mouth as he kissed her, and she gave herself over to him, letting him stroke his tongue over hers at the same, now-languid pace as his cock.

He lifted his mouth from hers. "Come again." Connor slid his cock in deep and then ground against her. "That's it, lass, come on my cock."

"Ah, God, Connor," Lauren gasped. Her body tightened under his, and she clenched around his penetrating cock so hard that he arched away from her and came long before he intended.

"Fuck," he whispered as he relaxed against her and thrust into her lazily a half dozen times before going still. "Don't even think that I'm done with you," he warned as he pulled out, careful to take the condom with him.

She laughed softly. "I'm really looking forward to it."

6

Connor Grant, bathed in moonlight, was the stuff of an artist's dreams. He was power, strength, dominance, and absolutely everything she'd been looking for for the final series of her project. It was a little disheartening, because she knew she didn't have a snowball's chance in hell of getting him to agree to pose.

He rolled suddenly and pinned her effectively to the bed. "You know, I've been around enough artists in the past two years to know exactly what you're thinking."

She grinned and quirked one eyebrow at him. "You're beautiful."

Connor huffed and rolled onto his back. "No man wants to be called beautiful, lass. It really messes with my badassness."

"That's not a word," Lauren protested.

"Yes, it is, and being called beautiful messes with it." He shifted onto his side and propped his head up on his hand. "What do you want?"

"I have a list," Lauren confided. "Of sex acts, positions, and locations—it could take a while to complete."

Connor grinned. "I'm game, but that's not what I meant and you know it."

"You'll just say no, so I'd rather not ask and then I can fantasize about it for a while." She bit down on her bottom lip and then focused on the ceiling. "I think I'm about to pout."

"Oh, I think you're already pouting," Connor pointed out. "Shamus Montgomery asked me to sit for him; so has Lisa Brooks."

"It's no wonder," Lauren muttered. "Why did you tell them no?"

"Because..." Connor sighed. "It's sort of ridiculous, isn't it? I'm thirty-six years old, and that means I'm way too old to do a job that twenty-year-olds line up for."

She laughed softly. "Oh, come on, don't play the age card on me—you're physically perfect. You're gorgeous all over. Even your scars are...more interesting than anything else. I certainly wouldn't consider them flaws." Lauren ran a finger down his chest, over the chiseled muscles of his stomach, all the way to his cock. She wrapped her fingers around his cock and hummed under her breath when the flesh immediately began to harden in her hand. "Just perfect, really."

Connor shifted under her attention and sighed softly when she slid down to take the head of his cock into her mouth. "If you think sucking my dick is going to get a yes out of me"—he paused and gasped as she took him deep into her mouth—"you could be on to something."

Lauren prodded him onto his back, and Connor obligingly spread his legs for her. She took him deep into her throat and swallowed around the head of his cock as she considered just what he would let her do to him. She pulled away from his cock with an audible pop and surveyed him with a raised eyebrow.

"If you leave me like this, lass, I'll be forced to show you the true depth of my badassness," Connor warned, his eyes dark with arousal.

"Oh, I'm not going to leave you like this. I just need some supplies," she announced blithely, and slid off the bed before he could respond. "Don't move."

"Wouldn't dream of it," Connor murmured as he watched her walk to the small bag full of bathroom essentials she'd packed.

She was gratified to notice that he didn't even blink when she came back to the bed with lube. Lauren crawled back to her position between his legs. "Wanna call anything off-limits?"

"No," he murmured, and shifted so that he could rest the foot of his left leg flat on the bed. "I'll just have to punish you if you do something I don't like."

"Oh, yeah?" Lauren grinned. "This could be dangerous, then." She trailed her fingers down his thigh and over his balls. "You look dangerous right now—barely leashed and ready to jump me at any second."

"You like that?" he asked as he spread his legs a little more for her.

"I love it," Lauren admitted. "I mean, I really love it."

She lowered her head as she slid back, then flipped open the tube of lube and ran the flat of her tongue over the head of his cock. She slicked up two fingers and closed the lube before tossing it aside. Lauren chanced one glance up at his face before she slid his cock back into her mouth.

Connor shuddered and cursed softly under his breath as she slipped her slick fingers over his asshole. "Christ, Lauren."

Since it didn't sound remotely like a protest, she rubbed over the wrinkled flesh until he relaxed under the attention. Lauren paused to press her fingers there and worked his cock carefully with her free hand, sucking the head strongly until precum slid over her tongue.

Then she pressed her fingers firmly into his hole. He clenched around the invasion and shuddered when she knowingly rubbed across his prostate.

He arched into her mouth and groaned, his voice harsh with shocked pleasure. "Fuck."

She hummed, pleased with his reaction, and started to suck his cock with the same rhythm she was using to fuck his ass with her fingers. He was moving under her administrations, restrained but so close to just losing it that she could feel his skin getting hot.

"Ah, God, Lauren you're going to make me come if you don't..." He shuddered when she took his cock deep and swallowed around the head. "Fuck!"

Lauren slowly pulled away from his cock, stopping to suck and lick the cum from the head while he shook and groaned beneath her. Finally, she pulled her fingers from his ass and lifted her head. She had all of thirty seconds to look him over before she found herself flat on her back with him on top of her.

His mouth was hard, punishing on hers—his tongue pierced into her mouth like a weapon, and she just *knew* he was going to fuck the shit out of her as soon as he got hard again.

Connor released her mouth and distributed a series of kisses along her jaw before moving lower. He caught one hard nipple between his teeth and worried the flesh roughly, flicking his tongue over the abused skin as he worked it.

His teeth grazed across her ribs, fingers dug into her thighs, nails scored the skin with just the right amount of pressure, the right amount of sting. She was demanding more by the time he reached her cunt. Lauren spread her legs brazenly and lifted her hips.

"Eat me," she whispered, fisting her hands into the sheets. "Lick my pussy, Connor."

He glanced over her, his blue eyes dark with pleasure and arousal. "I think you could be perfect."

He dipped his tongue into her hole and groaned softly. He fucked his tongue into her repeatedly and clenched his hands on her hips to keep her still.

Finally, he moved up and sucked strongly on her clit while he sent one hand questing through the sheets for a condom. He found the strip easily but fumbled with it until she took it from him with a growl and tore one off.

Connor laughed a little as he lifted his head. He took the packet and ripped it open. "Turn over and grab the headboard."

She curled her fingers around two bars in the old cast-iron headboard as she assumed the position he wanted and rocked on the bed as he rolled the condom on. He slapped her ass, which made her hiss and then laugh a little.

"Be still."

"Make me."

He scooted up on the bed and smacked her ass again. "Cheeky little wench, I think I will turn you over my knee later. Spread your legs for me."

She did as instructed, and her breath hitched slightly as he pressed his thumb against her ass. "The lube is—"

"Not tonight," Connor murmured. "We have a busy day tomorrow, and I don't want people speculating why you can't sit."

She laughed softly and let her head fall backward as he shifted her around and then pressed his cock right into her. "I might have a hard time sitting, anyway."

"Not the same at all," Connor said. "You feel so good on my cock." He curved his hand around one of her shoulders and wrapped the other around her hip to brace her. "Perfect."

He pushed his cock into her, quick and hard. She choked on air and clenched down on him. "Yes."

"I'm going to tie you up," Connor muttered. "So you can't move. Then I'll just fuck you—your mouth, your pussy, your ass—anytime I want. I might leave you tied up all night."

"Ah, God, Connor." Lauren let her head fall forward, and her hands tightened on the headboard. "Please, please."

"I know what you want," he whispered. "I'll give it all to you."

He set a hard, punishing pace, taking her deep with each thrust until their bodies were smacking together so hard that it felt lewd and filthy. She was so relaxed and into it that it was easy to pull her upright and arrange her in his lap.

Connor covered her pussy with one hand and ground the heel of it into her clit as she started to rock his hips against her ass, pushing his cock in deep at the perfect angle to hit her G-spot. She shuddered and shattered against him, her fingers digging into his thighs for purchase as she screamed out her release.

Lauren winced as she slid down into the big bathtub. "Walking is overrated, anyway."

Connor laughed and leaned on the counter, wrapped in a small towel. "Think you'll be all right for a few minutes? I need to get dressed and make some calls."

"Yeah, I'm cool. I won't fall asleep and drown." She ran her fingers over the surface of the bubbling water. "I want to go back to the town house and pack my own stuff. Is that possible?"

Connor frowned but then nodded. "I won't leave you alone, though, so don't even bother asking."

"Not a problem. I'd just like to handle the packing of my paint and supplies myself. It's all new . . ." She blushed. "And I like things to be done a certain way. Also, I'd rather your guys not handle my new panties."

He laughed and exited the bathroom. "Relax, sweetheart. No one is handling your panties but me for the foreseeable future."

Forty-five minutes later, he was buzzing Mathias Montgomery through the front gate, and Mathias wasn't alone. Connor frowned from his place on the front porch as he watched Alasdair McBain exit the passenger side of Mathias's SUV.

"Something happen?"

Mathias glanced around the property. "Not yet. I thought it might be a good idea to bring in a few heavy hitters, and there is nothing much up with the accounts in New York at present. I pulled Deacon out of San Diego and hired a local PI firm to tail Davis for the duration."

Connor offered his hand to Dare as soon as the man reached the porch. "Good to see you, mate."

"Mathias tells me you've got your hands full."

Connor flushed. "Well, he never could keep his mouth shut when it would serve him best."

Dare laughed and then quirked an eyebrow over Connor's shoulder. "Ma'am."

Connor glanced back over his shoulder and found Lauren in the doorway, her eyes dark with questions. She was dressed in a pair of shorts that were too short and a T-shirt that wasn't see-through but so damn tight it didn't matter. Written across it in bold black letters were the words *An erection doesn't count as personal growth.*

Connor sputtered, Dare snickered, Mathias laughed, and Lauren smirked. She held out her hand. "Lauren Evans."

"Alasdair McBain. Most call me Dare." He took her hand in his. "Heard you had a hard time lately."

"Oh, yeah," Lauren agreed, and rocked back on her heels. "Real hard." She grinned when he laughed again. "Coffee?"

"I could use some coffee."

"Great," Lauren responded brightly, and tugged him into the house. "Say, you don't model, do you?"

"Lauren," Connor started, and then sighed. "You're going to come out here and find me dead—just so you know."

Mathias laughed softly and slapped him on the back. "Let's get some coffee before she talks him out of his clothes."

Dare was already ensconced at the table with a cup of coffee by the time they arrived, and Lauren was digging around in the refrigerator for breakfast.

"Brooks is on edge about the show tonight?" Connor asked. "He laid out a few things for me last night while he was here."

Mathias nodded and accepted the coffee that Connor offered and sat down. "Reason number two I brought Dare in. With you on the floor with Lauren, I need someone on the top level running the show behind the scenes. The guys we have are good but"—he shrugged—"I've never been hip-deep in bodies with any of them." He winced and glanced toward Lauren. "I have no self-editor on my mouth lately."

Lauren emerged from the fridge with a carton of eggs and a package of bacon. "I grew up on army bases, Mathias. I know what men like you do and see when you serve. You don't have to censor yourself around me." She pulled an elastic band out of her pocket and whipped her hair up into a bun in a series of maneuvers that left all three men baffled. "I should cut this mess."

"You really shouldn't," Connor countered with a frown. "Really."

"Pfft," Lauren responded with a flick of her hand. "Men don't know what kind of work long hair calls for. If you did, you'd never ever tell us we should have long hair."

"How are your bruises?" Mathias asked, looking her over critically.

"Oddly enough, I have some scrapes but only a few bruises.

I need a manicure before the show tonight. I've never worn my nails long, but the forensics lady cut them all really short." She frowned at her legs. "My shoulder is a little sore, but my dress will cover up the bruise. I didn't go backless, so that's a relief— I have a few contact bruises there." She pressed on her shoulder. "Not much hurts. I hope he can't say the same."

"Connor mentioned that you wanted to do your own packing?"

"I'd prefer it," she admitted as she searched through the cabinets for a bowl to scramble her eggs in. "But I won't have a big screaming diva fit if that's not possible." She looked toward Connor. "I like to save those up for really important stuff."

"Good to know," he returned dryly. He frowned then. "What would you consider really important?"

She shrugged. "A sale at Macy's?" She grinned when he snorted. "I called the agency and canceled those model appointments I had for today. I think I need a break from the"— he waved a hand—" 'cock search.' "

Dare choked on his coffee and glared when Mathias and Connor laughed. "What?"

Connor passed him a paper towel. "That's what I've been calling Lauren's model search, since she makes them all strip naked for the interview." He glanced her way. "She's yet to offer a good reason for the naked thing."

"Well, I'll be posing them naked," Lauren started. "And a man can have a great body, perfect really, and then just have truly fucked-up junk." She waved a hand. "An ugly cock can be uninspiring." She hummed and began cracking eggs. "Though not as uninspiring as a small one. Some models body build and beef up with steroids to get the great body, but it ruins them for nude modeling." She glanced back at them and saw they were all staring at her. "Should I find my self-censor?"

Mathias laughed. "Nah, I think we'll be okay. I hesitate to

ask, but if I don't, I'll have to ask Jane later—what would make a cock ugly?"

"Hmmm, well, if it hangs wrong, that's a turnoff—you know, if soft tissues are damaged, it can be crooked." She wrinkled her nose. "Which can be worked around when it comes to sex but not for art. An ugly dick just ruins the whole package. Same goes for women—if their stuff isn't trimmed and neat, I can't work with them. I actually prefer my female models to wax. It's just easier."

Dare chuckled. "I like you a lot. Wanna come to New York with me?"

She glanced at him over her shoulder and then at Connor. "Do you poke snakes, too?"

He grinned. "Sometimes."

"Well, now that I know what your I-got-laid face looks like..." Jane trailed off and raised an eyebrow.

Lauren sighed. "I didn't get laid."

"Oh, yeah?" Jane questioned.

"*Laid* doesn't really cover it. I got..." She waved her free hand and glanced around the salon. Two security guards were outside the shop where Mercy had specifically told them to stand, looking menacing and very much like they were guarding the president instead of three smart-assed women. "*Shagged.*"

Jane sputtered and then started to laugh.

Lauren waited until she stopped laughing and then said, "Four times and I haven't even got all of the filthy, dirty things he promised me." Half the women in the salon turned and stared. "What? A man has to be held accountable for the things he promises a woman or else we'll have anarchy."

The doors opened and a beautiful blonde came in, shrugging out of a stylish coat. "Sorry I'm late. I had to take Aidan all the way across town. Shawn's mother is keeping him for the weekend, and then I had to find a shirt I could get my breasts into. Who said breastfeeding was a good idea? Really? The breast pump is the devil and I'm exhausted."

With what she hoped was a friendly expression, Lauren stared at Connor's ex-girlfriend, who was a younger and more beautiful Brigitte Bardot clone.

"You must be Lauren. I heard all about you and the panties from Jane." She offered her hand. "Sorry about the vibrator—that's the stuff of nightmares."

Lauren laughed before she could help herself and took Casey's hand with her free one. "Hi, so you're the assistant who James Brooks hijacked?"

"Yeah, and he totally regrets it!" Casey dropped down into a free chair and shoved off her shoes. "I micromanage him to within an inch of his life, and I spy shamelessly for his wife. He has horrible eating habits."

Lauren shifted her hand into a bowl the manicurist offered. "I took a pack of cigarettes away from him last night."

"Oh, he's in so much trouble." Casey got out her Black-Berry and started writing a text message. She glanced up as she did so. "So, you're sleeping with Connor."

Lauren flushed and focused on her hands. "So, you've a new baby?"

Casey laughed. "Yeah, he's great. I'll bring him around the gallery on Monday and you can meet him. I think I'm about to die of boredom on maternity leave. If I'd known six weeks would feel like this, I wouldn't have taken so much." She sighed. "Shawn's mother is a *saint,* and I love her more than my luggage and my new purse combined."

"You'll get used to it," Mercy offered from her place across the aisle. "I had a huge adjustment period, and it took me forever to get used to the idea of leaving him with anyone. At least you have family nearby. I had Mathias conduct the Spanish Inquisition to find a nanny, and I still have my entire house wired for audio and video. It took Julian about three weeks to find the cameras. He waves at them all the time."

"Your *manny* is an ex-Marine," Jane said dryly. "You picked him because he had the best spread in target practice."

Mercy sniffed delicately. "That's so not true. Connor had the best spread on the range, but Mathias wouldn't let me have him and we *all* agreed that Julian needed security as well as child care."

He figured he was going to kill someone before the night was over, and it was going to be all Lauren's fault. The *dress* that he'd heard about but not seen until she'd strolled out of the employee lounge was dark blue and clung to her lithe body in such a way that his tongue got dry every time he glanced at her.

Her hair was falling over her shoulders and down her back in soft, ebony curls. She was wearing four-inch heels, an interesting choice for a tall woman. It put her just at six feet, and the way she moved on those heels should've been illegal. The show was in full swing, and Lauren had made a huge effort to turn any attention she received toward the young artist being shown. He liked her more for it—she had no ego in the mix beyond her obvious self-assurance. The woman knew she was beautiful, and she worked the room like a pro.

The man she was talking to moved in close to her and put his hand on her hip. Half the security assets in the room shifted to respond, but she casually took a hold of his hand and dug her thumbnail into his palm in such a way that Connor winced in sympathy. The man's eyes widened and he took a step back.

"The artwork is for sale, Mr. Williams. I am not." Lauren released him and smiled. "Now, if you are interested in purchasing this painting, you can place a silent bid with Chelsea." She put her hand on his elbow and prodded him toward the young woman in question.

She parted ways with him and strolled back to Connor with a smile. "If looks could kill, he would be on the floor. Stop glaring at people."

"I'll glare at anyone I like," Connor muttered under his breath.

She laughed softly and looked down at the champagne glass she'd held most of the evening but had not even sipped from. "There are about ten men in this room I can't handle, and you're one of them. The others work for you or with you." She inclined her head. "Or does this fall into that elusive shouldn't-have-to category you have for women?"

"Something like that," Connor admitted roughly. "You look good—I hate this dress. You can't ever wear it again."

She laughed, clearly delighted, and people all around them turned to look. He couldn't blame any of them for that. There was something so genuine and striking about Lauren in that moment that he wanted to kiss the hell out of her right then and there.

"You're Lauren Evans, the artist."

Connor turned and watched Henry Wallace III offer his hand to Lauren in that self-entitled way that he knew well and completely hated.

She took his hand with a smile, but her nose scrunched up just enough to let her distaste be known. "Yes, and you are?"

"Henry Wallace the third of Wallace, Redding, Bisson and Associates."

Lauren raised an eyebrow and pulled her hand free of his. "Lawyer?"

"Yes, of course." He pulled out a card and offered it. "Corporate."

Lauren glanced at the card and then down at her dress. "Forgive me, but I seem to have left my pockets at home." She smiled when he laughed nervously. He put his card away.

"You're new to Boston," Wallace offered.

"Yes, but Mr. Brooks and his people are taking excellent care of me. I don't want for a single thing." She glanced around the room and then offered him a bright smile. "You'll excuse us. Mr. Grant promised me some air."

Connor led her toward the balcony doors. "You realize you just brushed off a millionaire."

"Nowhere in my contract did it say I had to let rich, weak bastards look down my dress and hit on me awkwardly," Lauren returned evenly.

Connor winced when half his men snickered in his ear. "Just so you know, my guys can hear you when we're this close."

"Oh, you know what? I want my own earpiece before the next event. I'm positive I'm missing out on some great conversations." She leaned on the balcony railing and looked out over the small parking lot behind the gallery. "They should dig that up and plant a pretty garden. It would be a better view."

Connor frowned. "Give up parking spaces in downtown Boston for a *garden*?"

She nudged him. "Don't be such a man. It would be pretty."

"Yeah, for five months out of the year and then it would be dead," Connor returned.

"Yeah, but we could plant evergreens and decorate them with white lights in the winter." She turned and leaned back on the railing. "So, you hate my dress?"

He made a show of turning off the mic on his cuff and looked her over. "You look good enough to eat, lass, and yeah, I pretty much hate it. It'll look great on the floor later, though."

She grinned and let him prod her back into the room. He turned his mic back on and gave a few brief instructions to several men in the room and asked for an update from the security office. Dare gave a concise rundown on the entire building, including a current head count, before signing off.

Lauren had taken a cue from Mercy and joined the featured artist in a group conversation. Connor didn't like the guy. In fact, he didn't know anyone who did like the guy. He was arrogant, but Mercy said he was good money for the Foundation, and everyone tried to do their best to put up with assholes if it made money for the kids.

His real name was Donald Greenway, but he made everyone call him Don G., which Connor thought was the lamest thing ever, but he kept that to himself. When Donald introduced himself the first time, Mathias had turned to Connor and they'd shared a look that said everything they were never going to say about the artist also known as Donald Greenway.

Three hours later, the show was over and Lauren was artfully and demurely sprawled on a small couch on the second level. In one hand, she had the BlackBerry Jane had gifted her, and was industrially texting away. Connor had a feeling she was chatting back and forth with Jane or Mercy.

"You like her a lot."

Connor glanced to his left and found Casey Trainer leaning in the doorway of the hallway that led to the security offices. "Yeah, I do."

"Good," Casey said with a grin. "I like her a lot, too. She's fun and not at all like that last woman you dated."

"I wasn't dating Julia."

"Yeah, whatever you were doing with her, she was evil. I think if I'd cut her, she might have dripped acid all over the place like those creatures in the alien movies." Casey jerked her head in Lauren's direction. "She's talented, beautiful, snarky, and full of sunshine—quite a heady combination."

"Yeah," Connor admitted roughly, and then sighed when Don G. strolled across the room and slid onto the couch with Lauren. "Great, should we let her maim him or what?"

"Oh." Casey glanced over her shoulder. "Jane."

Jane Tilwell came out of the security office and joined them. "What?"

"Should we let Don lose a limb or rescue him from himself?" Casey jerked her head toward Lauren and Don, who was doing that leaning thing that practically had him bending over her.

Lauren, for her part, was staring at him over her BlackBerry with that cool-eyed look that Connor had already learned meant she was about to go on the offensive. There was something about the way her eyes narrowed and her mouth slanted just a little in displeasure that really turned him on. He figured he was a little pervy for it.

She stood up abruptly and then leaned down to say something to Donald. Connor had no idea what she said, but Donald backed up so quickly that he hit his head on the wall behind the couch.

Lauren patted his cheek gently and then smoothed down her dress as she walked away. "Have a good evening, Donald." She walked purposefully to Connor and stopped in front of him. With one hand on her hip, she tilted her head at him. "For future reference," she started, and jerked her thumb over her shoulder, "he's one of those things I feel I shouldn't have to deal with."

Connor laughed softly. "Understood. You ready to go?"

"Yeah, I'm totally starving." She slipped her hand into the inside of his jacket, tucking her BlackBerry into his interior pocket.

"Let me check in with Dare and I'll be back in a few minutes." He glanced back at the couch and found Don G. missing. "Watch out for that guy—he has ten hands."

"If I cut a couple off, will he grow them back or bleed out?" Lauren asked with a raised eyebrow.

Connor laughed and kissed her right on the mouth. "Let me know."

She huffed out a breath as he strolled down the hall. "He's lucky he's so pretty."

Jane chuckled. "I've always thought his face was his best weapon. If he were just decent-looking, I'm sure some woman would've cheerfully strangled him years ago."

Lauren nodded in agreement and glanced at Casey. It was always disconcerting to see *knowledge* written on another woman's face. "What?"

Casey looked at Jane. "When is the last time you saw Connor kiss a woman?"

"Besides Lauren?" Jane frowned and thought about it. "I don't think I ever saw him kiss even you."

"Right, he doesn't *do* public displays of affection," Casey said with a wiggle of her eyebrows.

"Except for when he does," Jane responded, and glanced at Lauren. "I think it's cute."

"He hates my dress," Lauren said with a frown.

"I think he hates the attention you got in that dress," Casey corrected with a small smile. "It looks great on you—really brings out your body and long legs. I just wish I could pull something like that off."

"I'd trade two inches of height for bigger breasts," Lauren confided.

"You can buy breasts," Casey offered. "But you're quite perfect the way you are. I can just wish for two more inches of height."

Lauren flushed and glanced down. "I always thought fake ones would look weird on me."

This statement made Casey and Jane both seriously consider the thought, which meant that when Connor returned, all three women were staring at Lauren's breasts.

"I don't even want to know," he proclaimed.

Lauren smirked at him. "Don't even, Grant. You've probably got some weird vision of a lesbian threesome flitting about in your head involving Catholic schoolgirl uniforms and riding crops."

Connor just laughed and pulled her close. "How did you know I went to Catholic school?"

"I know a person who is afraid of nuns when I see one," Lauren responded primly. "We recognize our own."

"I thought I escaped long before I was marked for life." He manuevered her toward the stairs, and Lauren gave Jane and Casey a little wave as she gamely went along.

7

_____

"So, how does it look?" Lauren asked softly, and glanced down at the dress pooled around her shoes.

Connor leaned back on his hands and looked her over, taking in the blue lacy panties and the matching bra. "I love that dress, and the panties are made of complete and total _win_."

Lauren grinned as he clasped her hips with both hands and pulled her toward the bed. "Yeah?"

"Yeah," Connor murmured, and then took a deep breath. "Lady, you really do it for me." He slid his hands up her back and unhooked her bra with nimble fingers. "And for the record, your breasts are perfect—the last thing you need are fake ones."

Lauren laughed. "I'm sort of used to them. I wouldn't really get surgery."

"Good to know." He pushed the straps down her arms and let the bra drop away. With a sigh, he nuzzled between her breasts and cupped her ass with both hands.

She crawled astride his thighs and wrapped her arms around his neck as he caught one nipple in his mouth. He worried the soft flesh with his teeth and tongue until it was hard. Connor released her nipple with an audible pop.

"Lovely," he whispered softly before he shifted and sucked her neglected nipple into his mouth. She was squirming in his lap and moaning by the time he released the hardened flesh. "I like you like this." He ran his fingers over one nipple. "Hard and wet from my mouth." Connor pinched the nipple and chuckled when she moaned. "When this is all over and we have time for some serious play, I'd like to tie you up and figure out just how far your little kink for pain goes."

She relaxed in his lap and then ran her fingers through his short dark hair. "I'd let you."

"Yeah?" Connor asked softly, pulling her closer.

"I trust you," Lauren admitted. "You remind me of the men I grew up around—strong and honorable. I feel so safe with you, and I haven't felt that in a while." She exhaled sharply as his fingers slid along the edge of her panties. "We rushed into this physical thing."

"Yeah, we did." Connor pulled her closer. "But you can't think I'm going to give up my spot in your bed without a serious amount of discussion."

She grinned. "I'm not even interested in having that kind of discussion. I just don't want you to feel cornered or pressured to offer me more than you already have. The people you work with—that *we* work with—will have expectations that are really not theirs to have."

"Yeah," Connor admitted with a sigh. "I shouldn't have kissed you in front of Casey and Jane. I'd just wanted to kiss you *all night*. I couldn't resist."

"I didn't mind," Lauren said. "It's nice to know I tempt you that way." She leaned in and brushed her mouth against his and sighed when his cell phone started to ring. "Seriously?"

He laughed and pulled it out of the holster on his belt to answer it. "This is Grant."

"We have a body."

Connor shifted Lauren off his lap with an apologetic half smile and cleared his throat. "I'm sorry, Dare, can you repeat that?"

Dare McBain snorted. "I said we have a body. As far as I know, our guys didn't actually make the mess, but we've got a big one."

"Where?" Connor asked.

"Behind the town house," Dare said shortly. "Based on his height and body weight—I'd say it's the guy who broke in before and tried to take Lauren in the park."

"Great," Connor said. "How long do you think?"

"We pulled the security team here after we removed all of her finished work from the studio upstairs. I haven't touched him, so no clue on body temp or rigor. I figured I would stay here—kill two birds with one stone, so to speak. I hate hotels, you know."

"Yeah," Connor acknowledged, and looked toward Lauren who had left the bed and pulled on an old T-shirt that said *Gore got hosed and the rest of us got screwed.* He bit down on his lip to keep from laughing. "Have you called the police?"

"I followed procedure. Cops first, Mathias second. He told me to call you and tell you to keep Lauren on the farm. He doesn't want either of you near this scene, because he figures the Boston PD might try to blame you. They certainly aren't going to let Trainer investigate the murder. He has too many personal connections for it not to be a conflict of interest."

"Yeah," Connor agreed. "I would certainly be my prime suspect if I didn't know I didn't do it." He focused on Lauren, who was staring at him wide-eyed. "Okay, I have to go, Dare.

Try to keep me in the loop as much as possible, and snap a picture of this guy's face. I want to see if Lauren recognizes him." He closed his phone and cleared his throat. "Okay, so Dare went to stay at the town house and found a body."

Lauren's mouth dropped open. "The guy who attacked me?"

"Yeah, probably. Hopefully he died while we were all at the gallery for the show. That would alibi pretty much everyone on staff." Connor glanced at his phone when it beeped and then with obvious reluctance opened it. "Can you look at a picture for me?"

Lauren grimaced. "Is there blood visible?"

He shook his head. "No, not at all. I wouldn't ask you to look if it were that kind of scene." He offered her the phone and she frowned. "Not familiar?"

"Actually, the exact opposite. When he grabbed me in the park, I had this niggle in the back of my mind telling me he was familiar and that I should know who he is, but I didn't and still don't."

"But this is the guy who grabbed you?"

"Yeah," she huffed. "I mean, I scratched him up pretty good. The cops are going to want to talk to me, right?"

"Definitely, but I won't leave you unless I'm given no choice. They certainly won't question you without a lawyer present."

"What about you?" Lauren asked softly. "You said you'll be considered a serious suspect?"

"I'm sleeping with the woman he attacked," Connor said as he pulled his shirt from his slacks and started to unbutton it. "I'm the obvious suspect. In addition, all of the men and women at Montgomery Security will be scrutinized because they might try to say I ordered someone at the company to kill the guy."

"Oh, that sucks."

"Yeah, it really does." He tossed his shirt aside and then jerked his undershirt over his head and threw it in the chair with his shirt. "You need to put on something comfortable. Good shoes, something warm, because police stations can get kind of cold. Layer with a sweater—that's the best. They won't send a patrol car after us, but we'll both be requested."

"And after you were attacked in the park, what happened?"
Lauren rubbed her face with both hands and resisted the urge to bang her head on the table in front of her. "You're recording this, right? Why don't you just go in the other room and rewind the video and watch one of the six different times I've told you?"

"Ms. Evans, it's in your best interest to cooperate."

"Detective March, I find your attitude irritating." James Brooks relaxed in his chair and draped his arm along the back of Lauren's chair. "Lauren has been open and very honest with you. She's revealed intimate details of her personal relationships and given you a complete and consistent timeline for the day in question. This is turning into harassment."

"She isn't telling us the truth," March returned evenly. "And I find that irritating."

"No, I'm just not telling you what you want to hear," Lauren countered. "We can go over the events a hundred times if you want, but my story won't change. I don't have anything to lie about or hide."

"You expect me to believe that you were sexually assaulted in the park in the early morning and then spent the evening in bed with a man you claim to have met only a week ago?" Ron March asked snidely.

"What the hell are you talking about? I wasn't sexually assaulted. I was tackled by a guy twice my size and held down while he tried to get the security code for my front door. He never touched me in a sexual manner and didn't even threaten to hurt me that way. In fact, the only thing he demanded of me was the security code. The entire attack lasted less than two minutes because he was interrupted." She sat back in the chair and glared at him.

"The uniformed officer who responded in the park requested a sex crimes detective."

"He didn't even ask me what happened. He just kept *telling* me what happened."

James Brooks frowned. "What do you mean he kept telling you what happened?"

"He said. 'Ma'am, you were sexually assaulted. Ma'am, I need to call an ambulance because you've been sexually assaulted'." Lauren sighed. "Then Connor was there and I asked him to take me home. I don't know what that cop wrote down, but it wasn't anything I said to him. I gave my statement to Detective Trainer later."

"So you weren't sexually assaulted?" March asked.

"No. Jesus, he didn't even grab my ass. He tackled me and demanded the security code while he tried to prevent me from scratching his face off." Lauren blew out a breath. "As for your nasty little insinuation that I'm promiscuous because I'm sleeping with a man I've known only a week, you can keep that sexist, backward, chauvinistic bullshit to yourself or I'll be suing you and this police department for defamation of character."

James Brooks laughed briefly and then coughed.

Connor slouched in his chair and drank deeply from the bottle of water he'd been given. "Detective Silven, I'm not your man. I don't leave bodies behind. My government taught me to always clean up my messes. I won't insult your intelligence and tell you that I'm not capable of killing, but you're looking in the wrong direction for this one."

"It is your statement that you took Lauren Evans to bed around six p.m., shortly after Mr. Brooks left the farmhouse, and you stayed there for a little over six hours. Then the two of you showered, had a meal, and went to sleep," Silven said with a raised eyebrow. "Six hours?"

Connor sighed and glanced at Mathias and then at their lawyer. "She had a difficult morning—I gave her something different to think about."

Silven snorted. "Six hours of it."

"We're both healthy, athletic adults. I'm not giving you a detailed account of the time I spent in bed with a woman. It's inappropriate, but I imagine you could go sit in on her interview if you have a hard-on for the details. She's probably getting a little irritated at this point and will probably spill all of the naughty details soon enough."

"Sarcasm isn't going to help your case."

"I don't have a case, because I didn't do this. I certainly wouldn't have left a body for my business partner and friend to find. Additionally, if he'd thought I did it, he wouldn't have called the body in. This guy is dead, and that really doesn't serve me, because I have no idea what he wanted from the town house and if it had anything to do with Lauren." Connor plucked his phone off his belt when it vibrated and sighed when he viewed the text message. "Great, you ran a check on me?"

Silven shrugged. "Sure. We requested your records. I have a source in the FBI."

Connor exchanged a look with Mathias, who pulled out his phone and left the room with a frown. "I spent ten years in the Royal Marines and did four years in the service of the Crown."

"Doing what?"

Connor frowned at him. "It's classified, Detective."

"Classified?" Silven repeated dryly. "Really, Mr. Grant, this secret agent stuff is amusing for some people around here but not for me. What did you do for your government?"

"I served ten years in the Royal Marines and was recruited for government work directly after I was discharged. I did a variety of things for Her Majesty, the details of which are between me and my government. I'm not endeavoring to be mysterious or whatever you might think. I am simply unable to say."

"You think I won't arrest you?"

Connor's phone vibrated again and he checked it. "In about three minutes, your captain is going to be in here apologizing to me for wasting my time, and you're going to be told to go sit in a corner and think about your actions. Don't take it personally—you're just doing your job, and I'm sincerely sorry that your captain is going to pass the buck to you to avoid getting his own ass reamed by the chief of police."

Lauren leaned into Connor as he pressed his hand against the small of her back and guided her toward the elevator. "Did you do something in your interview? 'Cause they're all looking at you like did *something*."

Connor laughed. "I didn't do anything but sit in a chair and answer a few questions, love."

Lauren raised one eyebrow at him but said nothing as she was prodded into the back of the elevator behind Brooks and Mathias. "Yeah, right."

The elevator doors closed and Mathias cleared his throat. *"Six hours?"*

Connor sighed. "Shut it before I forget you're like a brother to me."

"She threatened to sue the entire department," James offered over his shoulder.

Lauren blushed and looked at the ceiling of the elevator. "So, is he like the brother who is currently trashing your apartment in London?"

"Nope," Mathias answered before Connor could. "I'm the brother who tore down a whole building to save his ass. I'd tell you all about it but it's classified."

"Does that 'classified' stuff get you laid a lot?" Lauren asked with a raised eyebrow in Connor's direction.

"I've never once used it to get laid," Connor promised. "However, I do not make any assertions about the past behavior of anyone else in this elevator."

Lauren laughed softly and said nothing as she was maneuvered out of the elevator and through the maze of hallways that led them out to the street. She waited until Connor had her fastened into the front seat of the SUV, then said, "Six hours and forty-two minutes—roughly."

Connor laughed softly and kissed her mouth. "Very roughly." He shut her door and rounded the vehicle. Once he was in the driver's seat, he turned to her. "Okay, so the crime scene is actually in the alley behind the town house, so we can go in and pack up the rest of your stuff. I can have a team onsite to handle the actual moving part."

Lauren frowned. "Do I have to move out now? I mean, the guy is dead."

"Yeah, lass, because someone murdered him ten feet from your back door." Connor looked at her with a frown. "Seriously?"

Lauren scrunched down in the seat and sighed. "Yeah, okay. It's a pretty cool farm."

"It is," Connor acknowledged. "And there are no neighbors to hear you scream."

She grinned. He'd made her scream a few times. "There is

that," she murmured. Lauren relaxed against the seat and closed her eyes. "Those cops totally ruined all of the hot sex I was planning on getting tonight."

"I'll make it up to you," Connor murmured, and picked up her hand. He threaded their fingers together. "Want me to have my guys pack your stuff?"

Lauren sighed. "Yeah, whatever. Just make them be careful with my paints and tools. I don't want to go shopping again."

"I'll take care of everything."

She turned her head on the seat and looked at him. "I know."

Detective Ron March was one very persistent bastard. Lauren ignored him as she entered the coffee shop, but the security guard who had trailed along behind her from the gallery gave him an evil look.

She went to the counter and ordered herself the most complicated coffee she could think of and a tea for Connor. Lauren glanced back at the cop. "Would you like something, Detective March?"

He glared at her and shook his head abruptly. "You know when I get the evidence I need, you'll be an accessory for covering for him."

Lauren glanced at him and took both cups she was offered. "I certainly won't look good in prison orange. That being said, I don't have anything to worry about."

He followed her doggedly across the street, ignoring how the security guard was giving a terse report of the situation. "You think so? I will *find* the evidence I need, and I will charge him with murder."

Lauren turned and stared at the cop as the front doors of the gallery opened behind her. "I'm sorry, Detective March, did you just imply that you will manufacture evidence against us to make your case?"

March's mouth dropped open. "No, God, of course not. I'm just trying to do my job here, lady!"

"What you're doing looks an awful lot like harassment to me," Jane Tilwell said dryly. "Lauren?"

Lauren turned and let herself be taken into the gallery. Jane was on her cell phone before they even reached the stairs where Connor was standing. Lauren offered him his tea and he frowned at her. "What? I took a security guard."

Connor huffed, which made him look vexed and entirely too sexy for his own good. He took the offered cup. "What did March say to you?"

"He threatened to charge me as an accessory to murder," Lauren said with a sigh. "You know, I'm too cute to go to prison, and I'm pretty sure I have too much attitude for it."

"No, I agree," Connor said sagely. "You have way too much attitude for prison." He looked her over and walked away. "But you'd probably have quite a following with the other ladies."

Lauren grinned and walked off toward the back of the gallery. She'd been roped into sketching out the design for the wall project that Shamus Montgomery had broken a ton of glass for. She was pretty sure she'd gotten the crappy end of the deal, all things considered. Breaking a whole bunch of plates and ugly vases had a lot of appeal.

She'd rolled out paper on the classroom floor—one-third scale of the wall and it still covered most of the room. The butcher paper wasn't the best medium, but it would do for a rough draft of the project.

Lauren pulled off her sandals and walked across the paper as she mentally mapped out what she'd been asked to do. Mercy

and Jane both had been pretty adamant that it should be a land-
scape like a park with children playing. Lighthearted, fun, and,
above all, bright.

She went back to her worktable and pulled on her knee
pads. It wasn't a hot look, but it would certainly keep her knees
in good shape so she could have a better time later. She grinned
at the thought and picked up the tray she was using to hold her
supplies.

Connor leaned against the doorway and watched Lauren
shift down the large impromptu canvas she'd had a few of his
guys help her roll out and tape. She was flat on her stomach, her
legs up and crossed. Her hair was up in a high, bouncy ponytail. She looked all of sixteen years old, and he figured it was
really bad how much he wanted her in that moment. He took a
deep breath, which caught her attention.

She glanced over her shoulder. "Hey, there." She lifted off
the floor to her hands and knees, and Connor swallowed hard.
"Wanna see?"

Connor nodded and casually toed his shoes off. He walked
carefully across the blank paper to the section where she was
working. "I was really surprised when you agreed to do this."

"Busy work," Lauren offered with a smile. "I think Mercy
and Jane are the kind of people who like to fill up their day
with lots of things to keep them busy when things are upset-
ting."

Connor nodded and glanced over the work she'd already
done. It was simple and beautiful. "So what are you going to
do?"

"I'm going to put a park in the background with lots of trees
and grass." She waved a hand. "And then I'm going to put three
children playing in the front. Of course, it won't look exactly
like this. We'll make panels and use the glass pieces like a puz-

zle to make each section. After that, we'll throw a layer of glaze over the entire lot and fire them to seal the work so it'll hold up under the weather." She patted the floor beside her. "You can sit down. Just be careful not to tear it."

Connor sat down cross-legged and rested back on his hands. "You skipped lunch—don't think I didn't notice."

Lauren nodded. "I was busy." She glanced at him and selected a piece of charcoal from her tray. "I figured you'd take me out for dinner."

"Oh, yeah?" Connor smiled. "Maybe I will. Do you have a preference?"

"Italian," Lauren murmured as she focused on her work. "The real stuff—not some chain place."

"Not a problem," Connor said. He pulled out his phone and started to scroll through the address book. "How much longer on this?"

"An hour," Lauren said. "Not too formal since I can't change clothes before we go." She cut her eyes at him. "Your guys did take all of my stuff out to the farm, right?"

"Yep." Connor tilted his head. "Why don't I order something—we'll pick it up and go home."

"That sounds like a plan." She smiled and then glanced his way. "And maybe a nice bottle of wine."

He leaned forward and kissed her. "Yeah, sounds good. I'll take care of it. Have a preference on a dish?"

"Chicken, and I hate mushrooms." She licked her bottom lip and then shifted toward him. "Lots of bread."

He brushed his mouth over hers again. "I think I can manage that."

Lauren hummed and moved closer. "We're at work."

"I'm off duty," Connor responded with a grin. He leaned closer and kissed her again. "You're so lovely."

"Go away and order our food before we get naked in here.

There are too many cameras." She bit down on his bottom lip and shifted away with a grin.

"As you wish, lass." Connor rolled to his feet carefully and walked off the paper. "An hour."

"Agreed," Lauren called after him.

Connor paused in the doorway to watch her and sighed. She was *not* in his ten-year plan and neither was Boston. Chicago had been on his horizon for over a year—since he'd followed Mathias to Boston, actually.

"We're going to have to rethink our business plan, I think."

He turned and found Mathias Montgomery standing there. "What makes you say that?"

Mathias laughed and walked away from the doorway. Connor reluctantly followed his oldest friend to the security office. He dropped down in his chair and rubbed his hand over his face.

"I want you to seriously think about what you want six months from now, because Dare and I were pretty sure you were going to be game for Chicago at that point."

Connor groaned. "And if I'm not?"

Mathias raised an eyebrow. "Is it that serious?"

"I don't know," Connor admitted. "It's consuming...and I can't even pinpoint when it happened. I've never..." He couldn't talk about it. "Can we not discuss this?"

Mathias laughed softly and nodded. "Yeah, okay. Just know that Dare and I want what you want. If Chicago isn't on the table anymore, we're okay with it. The offices we have in New York and here in Boston are serving us all very well. We can find a different way to expand—a way that doesn't require you to leave anyone important behind to accomplish it."

Connor nodded abruptly. "Appreciated."

Lauren rushed through the door then, a little breathless. "I know who he is."

"What?" Connor asked with a frown.

Lauren slid around his desk and right into his lap. She flipped open his laptop. "I was thinking about the dead guy— sort of." She waved a hand. "Then it hit me. He wasn't even remotely attractive while he was alive, so it should have crossed my mind immediately where I'd see his less-than-stellar face before." She called up a search engine and started looking.

Connor shifted her on his lap and shared a look with Mathias. "You know the dead guy?"

"No, I totally have never met him, but everyone I know has seen him. You probably have, too." She leaned back against his chest after picking a page. "He's ex-army. Robert Stein did a series of black-and-white pictures of vets coming back from Iraq. Justin Warner." She pointed at a picture on the screen. "That guy."

"Yeah." Connor nodded. "That guy." He looked at Mathias. "Robert Stein." He turned her on his lap so he could see her face. She gamely looped one arm over his shoulders. "Have you ever met Stein?"

"Nope, not even in passing. I saw his exhibit when it traveled to Los Angeles, but I had a private showing with the director of the gallery before the opening." She frowned at him. "I thought we agreed this wasn't about me?"

"Yeah, except Stein had all the access he could want to the town house, until he threw a big fit and threatened Mercy." Mathias frowned.

"Who said Stein sent Warner?" Lauren questioned. "He could've had his own motivations—maybe Robert Stein had something that belonged to him."

Connor shared another pointed look with Mathias. "Okay, we need to call Shawn and give him an update. Are you ready to go?"

"I need to cover the project and put up my supplies." Lauren hopped off his lap. "I'll be a few minutes."

"Take your time," Connor said as he stood. "I have a feeling I'm going to be here a while. We'll have to rethink our dinner plans."

Lauren sighed. "Man, why couldn't I have had my epiphany after I got some food and sex?"

Mathias laughed as she closed the office door behind her. "She's more than you can handle, my friend."

"Don't think I don't know it," Connor returned evenly.

8

"And you just happened to realize who this guy was?"

Lauren sighed and smiled gratefully when Connor put a cup of coffee and a bottle of water in front of her. "Yes, and since I could've kept the information to myself and let you *flail* about for weeks calling him John Doe, Detective March, you could be a little more civil toward me."

He huffed. "We would have gotten a hit on his fingerprints from the government as soon as the Forensics work was done." He tapped his pad on the conference table, clearly displeased to be out of his element. "Now, let's go over your thought process that led you to identify the victim."

Lauren frowned and turned to Jane. "You know, it's like he didn't even break into my home and attack me in the park. Since he got himself killed, he's the victim and I've got a cop treating me like a suspect."

Jane nodded. "It's like he thinks you asked this guy to attack you."

"I must have. Maybe the detective thinks that I shouldn't have worn my workout clothes so tight."

March growled. "It isn't my intention to minimize what happened to you, Ms. Evans. Would you please tell me how you came to realize the man who attacked you was named Justin Warner?"

Lauren shrugged. "I was working on a project for the gallery and Connor interrupted me. He's very distracting, and after he left, I was thinking about how I could talk him into posing for me. Then it crossed my mind that I might like to do a whole series of paintings about men and women who had a military background."

"Which made you think of the photographs that Robert Stein took?" March questioned, and glanced at his partner, who had been staring in sullen silence since they'd been led into the conference room by Shawn Trainer.

"Yeah, but mostly because I was thinking that if I wanted a project that would be popular and gain the right kind of attention, then I would have to find some very attractive ex-soldiers—unlike Stein, who had apparently gone out of his way to find people who were less attractive."

"And beauty is important to you?" Silven asked suddenly.

Lauren shrugged. "Not entirely. I've done projects with people who certainly wouldn't have fit the societal definition of physical attractiveness. My main problem with Stein's project was that he picked soldiers who had been discharged from the military in less than honorable situations. Justin Warner was dishonorably discharged from the army for theft, if I remember his bio correctly. There is a Web site dedicated to the project, with extensive profiles on the people he used."

"You found this offensive?" March questioned.

"That was the point—Stein meant to be offensive. It was his way of protesting the war in Iraq. The entire project was his way of giving the military the finger, and yes, I found that offensive."

"Your father was in the U.S. Army."

"Yes, he died several years ago." Lauren gratefully took a container from Jane, who had gone out with Mathias to get food for everyone.

"Did you ever have any contact with Justin Warner while he was in the army?"

"No, I haven't lived on a military base since before I went to college. My father retired a few years before he died, and I was visiting him when he passed, but he hadn't lived on base in years himself. He said it didn't give him enough privacy—something he desperately wanted after my mother died." Lauren pulled the paper lid off the container and turned it over carefully on the table.

Connor pulled a small bottle of hand sanitizer out of his pocket and set it beside her. "It's not your brand."

Lauren smiled. "That's okay." She picked up the bottle, removed all of her rings, and set about sanitizing her hands thoroughly. She handed the bottle back to him. "So, I'm thinking about painting soldiers, and Stein's picture of Warner just pops into my head and I went and told Connor."

"What do you think he wanted with you, Ms. Evans?"

"It's hardly my job to speculate about such things, but I don't think he wanted anything to do with me. He wanted in the town house, and I'm sure he was more comfortable trying to get my code than he would going against someone in security." Lauren pulled her plastic fork out of its wrapper and surveyed her food critically.

Connor passed a folder across the table. "This is all the information I could get on Justin Warner from my contacts. You won't get much more from the government. The U.S. Army doesn't like to go into a lot of detail when it comes to their personnel, especially the ones they let get away with theft to avoid scandal."

Detective Silven opened the file. "What kind of scandal?"

"He was caught trying to fence high-dollar items and artwork out of Iraq. A lot of wealthy people abandoned homes in Iraq during the invasion. Most of the assets were secured, but there were times when the military or civilian contractors over there would stumble across a hidden cache, and Justin Warner decided to keep and sell what he found."

"Did you spend any time in Iraq, Mr. Grant?"

Connor sat back in his chair and his jaw tightened. "You'll have to ask my government, Detective March. As I've already explained to your partner, I can't discuss it."

"You're not a citizen of this country, Mr. Grant. Are you aware that your immigration status could be endangered by your current circumstances?"

Connor lifted an eyebrow at March. "I'm not concerned about my immigration status, Detective March. Your government has always been very kind to me and given me all that I could need in the way of support—including citizenship, if I ever wish it. You really can't threaten me, and this new information does not change the fact that I had nothing to do with this man's unfortunate death. Even if I had caught up with him, I wouldn't have killed him."

"He attacked your girlfriend and you wouldn't react violently to him?" Silven asked dryly.

"I didn't say that. I just said I wouldn't have killed him." Connor accepted a container of food. He arranged his food and utensils and then sanitized his hands. "There are plenty of ways to make someone suffer horribly without killing them, Detective."

Silven stared at the Connor and Lauren in silence for a few seconds. "How long did you say the two of you have been dating?"

"A week or so," Lauren answered, and glanced at Connor's food and then her own. They'd both arranged their plates, plasticware, and water bottle in the exact same position. "He picked me up on OCDGIRL-dot-com."

Connor laughed and uncapped his water bottle. "Any other questions?"

"Ms. Evans, I find your casual attitude in this situation a source of concern," March said. "A man was murdered behind your home—he was shot twice in the stomach."

Lauren frowned. "It isn't like I found the body. Trust me, if I'd found the body, I would be a nervous wreck right now. I mean, really. I don't do well with dead bodies."

"You've been around dead bodies before?" Silven asked.

"Well, funerals." Lauren frowned. "I really don't like death rituals as a rule—they seem so pretentious and unnecessary. Most of the people who attended my father's funeral barely knew him. They just attended because they felt they should." She sighed. "Also, two in the stomach? That's rather unprofessional, isn't it?"

March leaned forward. "I don't follow."

"What she means," Mathias started, drawing their attention to him and Jane, who had demanded to be in on the conversation but had remained silent as requested, "is that a man with Connor's military training wouldn't put two bullets in someone's stomach. It's not a clean or even immediate kill. Was the body moved or disturbed prior to discovery? If it wasn't, that means the shooter took his or her two shots and then walked away from the body."

"Not something a person trained to kill would do," March summed up icily. "Is that what you're saying?"

"Are you willing to discuss the murder weapon? You haven't served a warrant for the guns registered in my name, so I can only assume you don't have enough cause." Connor glanced toward Shawn, who was silent at the end of the table with his own food.

"You don't have a registered weapon that would fit the crime," Silven admitted roughly. "We're done here, Ron. We'll let these people get back to their meal."

Lauren said nothing until the door shut behind the two cops, and then she looked at Shawn. "Do you get a lot of grief at the police station because of your relationships here?"

Shawn shrugged. "At times. Brooks throws his weight around when he's pissed, and people who don't like to do their jobs really have a problem with him when they end up in his crosshairs. That being said, I outrank those two jackasses, so the most they get to do is glare at me and make snide comments about quotas and affirmative action behind my back."

Lauren frowned. "I can totally sue them for defaming my character if it would make you feel better."

Shawn grinned. "You're too much fun." He glanced at her plate and then Grant's. "But that is bizarre—it's like fate that the two of you met."

"There is nothing wrong with things being orderly." Lauren straightened her napkin. "It's nice to meet someone who appreciates that." She reached out and snagged a white paper bag full of bread sticks. "You know, I'm absolutely starving."

"That's because you skipped lunch," Jane pointed out. "I tried to get you to leave the building and have lunch with me."

Lauren frowned. "Yes, well, I really don't relish going around the city with a four-man security team." She shot Connor a look. He shrugged. "It's ridiculous."

"Dead guy two feet from your back door," Connor said. "You'll just have to deal with it."

"I wasn't even there when it happened," Lauren protested.

"Oh, we all know where you were," Jane offered with a bright smile.

Lauren figured that deserved a vicious response, but all she had the energy for was a foul hand gesture. Since that seemed juvenile, she opted to glare pointedly at Jane and then concentrate on her food.

"Is this place off-limits now that you've set up your stuff?"

Lauren looked up and found Connor leaning against the large open doorway of the barn. "No, not at all. Lisa has a great setup out here, by the way. All of the windows are great for natural light, and she has an impressive lighting system as well for artificial shadow work." Lauren grinned. "Want to take off your clothes for me?"

"Only if there is sex involved," Connor returned dryly.

"Eventually," Lauren promised.

He laughed and walked into the barn, pulling off his T-shirt. "I don't know how I feel about people seeing me naked forever in paint, lass."

Lauren paused. "Do you remember the faces of any of my other models for this project?"

Connor paused and considered that. Then he tossed aside his shirt and unbuttoned his jeans. "As a matter of fact, no."

"Their faces are in shadow on purpose. The project isn't about that." Lauren waved a hand. "That doesn't mean that I wouldn't want to do an entire study on your face, but this project is about the body—both strong and weak. The human physical condition."

"How do you want me, lass?"

Lauren cleared her throat and flushed a little at the question. "You can't ask me questions like that when I'm trying to work." She picked up her drawing pad and a case of pencils.

Connor just grinned and slid out of his jeans. He curled his bare toes against the glossy hardwood floor and walked toward the window she silently motioned to. He said nothing as she ran her hands down his back and shifted his body so that he was half-facing the window.

"Though it's difficult to imagine considering all the sex I've already had today, if you don't stop touching me, I'm going to get hard again." He put his gun down on the ledge of the windowsill and dropped his holster at his feet.

Lauren grinned and took a step back. "You're gorgeous that way, too." She inclined her head. "Curl your hand over the top of the window frame and look outward." She arranged a light a few feet from him and shifted it so it cast most of his body in shadow. "That's excellent. I won't make you stay in one position long."

"I was a sniper, lass. I can stay in the same position for hours."

Lauren nodded. "I figured something like that, actually." She shifted the light again and hummed under her breath. "Beautiful. We have a few hours before Jane and Mathias get here for dinner."

Connor nodded. "The security panel will alert us when they come through the gate."

He watched her out of the corner of his eye as she settled in on the floor. Within minutes, she was completely lost in her work. He'd watched her do the same thing with the project at the gallery on the security cameras. To be honest with himself, he'd spent far too much time in the last week and a half watching Lauren Evans on security cameras.

If he'd caught one of his men giving that kind of attention to a female employee, he would've probably fired them. Since Casey, he had a zero-tolerance policy on that kind of thing.

She shifted him slightly after an hour and changed the lighting completely. When she sat back down, he had an excellent view of her. Her expressive face was almost still as she worked. Within a few minutes, she'd pulled four sheets of paper off her pad and spread them around on the floor in front of her. A brief glance at them confirmed they were all basic line drawings of his body with areas shadowed differently on each one.

She looked up suddenly and met his gaze. "What can you tell me about the scar on your leg?"

He glanced down at the three-inch scar on his upper left thigh. "The physical injury itself? It's a knife wound. I got it in a fight in a country that no longer even exists on a map. He stuck his knife in my leg, and I made him pay for it."

She grinned. "I just bet you did." After a few seconds, she went back to her drawing. "Does it hurt?"

"It hurt like a bitch at the time, but now not at all. I had good medical care, and it was a small blade." Connor watched her face and was pleased when she didn't seem to find the discussion stressful. "The one on my shoulder is a bullet wound."

"I know." She looked up from her pad. "Two inches lower and we wouldn't be having a conversation."

"No, we wouldn't," Connor acknowledged. "I made that guy pay for it, too."

She grinned. "I can just imagine."

"You don't want to tie me up?"

Lauren frowned and shook her head. "No, it would look false if I did. There is nothing submissive about you, and there is no use pretending otherwise."

"In your model interviews, you warned them all that there would be extreme bondage."

She smirked. "It was my way of scaring off the ones who weren't serious, and if I'd picked one of them, I probably would've tied him up."

Connor laughed. "Lass, what are you doing?"

She looked up from the pad and grinned. "Drawing you."

"My dick, you mean," Connor corrected, his tone dry. "Seriously?"

"It's very pretty," Lauren said primly. "And to be honest, it's absolutely my most favorite part of your body."

Connor snorted softly but said nothing else as she pulled off another sheet of paper and started another drawing. "How long does it take you to paint a single painting?"

"Well, the painting itself can take weeks if the subject is complicated, and I can be something of a perfectionist." She blushed when he laughed. "But I normally do no less than a hundred line drawings for each pose before I'm ready to paint."

"No photographs?"

"Not of you," Lauren murmured. "At least none of you naked."

Lauren put away the last of the groceries Jane had made Mathias and Connor haul into the house. "You know, we're not enduring a siege out here."

"Yes, well." Jane shrugged. "It sort of feels like we're all under siege. I haven't had a personal security escort in a couple of years. When that stuff got rough with Casey, Mathias had me shadowed for a solid month. It was annoying as fuck."

Lauren snickered and pulled a beer out. She grabbed Jane one, too, and handed it over. "Don't act so put out. You love his attention."

Jane snorted. "Fuck you. I thought we were at that stage in our friendship where we are cautiously nice to each other."

Lauren wiggled an eyebrow and drank deeply from her beer. "Nah, we're at that stage where we are insultingly honest with each other and plot world domination in our spare time. The 'cautiously nice' stage definitely comes before shopping for panties and sex toys together."

Jane laughed and pulled out a chair. "So what were you guys doing in the barn when we arrived?"

"I talked Connor into posing for me."

"Jesus. Really?"

"Really." Lauren sighed. "The problem is that I'm not sure I could ever part with a painting I did of him."

"Shamus normally does a single piece for himself when he has Mercy pose for him. So there is always one sculpture in his collection that isn't for sale."

Lauren nodded. "Maybe." She glanced around the large, airy kitchen. "I saw that you and Mathias brought an overnight bag."

"Mathias figured Connor could use some downtime," Jane admitted. "Time to relax his guard a little and let someone else handle things for a while. He hasn't been sleeping a lot, has he?"

Lauren shook her head. She hadn't, either. Every time Connor left the bed, she'd eventually followed him. "No, not really. Especially not since the body was discovered."

"You either."

She shrugged. "It's difficult to sleep when he's pacing the house like a caged animal."

Jane nodded. "Yeah, okay, so we're going to stay the weekend and give him some downtime—whether he wants it or not."

Lauren blew out a breath. "There goes the sex marathon I had planned for this table." She tapped the kitchen table in question, and Jane burst out laughing. "What?"

"I was just sitting here wondering how much time Brooks and Lisa spend on this table."

Lauren quirked an eyebrow. "He's really hot. I mean, you know, like Thomas Crown *hot*."

"No doubt," Jane responded, and sighed when her cell phone rang. She pulled it off her hip. "Jane Tilwell, Goddess of All Things Amazing and Perfect speaking." She grinned and winked.

Lauren laughed softly and stood up from the table. She figured it had to be Mercy on the phone, as Jane had a habit of answering her phone with grandiose titles attached to her name whenever it was Mercy.

"Should I come? I mean, I should be there." Jane stood up. "Well, you know we can't count on James Brooks to maintain a cool head under these circumstances." She huffed and sat back down. "Okay, no. Is she okay? Do you have any news?"

Lauren leaned against the counter and took in Jane's bright eyes but relaxed body and decided that nothing horrible had happened.

Mathias appeared in the doorway at that point on his own phone. "No, Dare, I want you on Brooks's ass as much as the medical personnel will allow. And have Mark pick up Ryan Brooks from his dorm. I don't want that kid driving while he's excited." Mathias looked at his fiancée and found her nodding her agreement. "He's not a careful driver on the best of days. Get Cassandra out of the gallery and put her in the delivery room with Brooks—she's to follow and monitor the babies as their personal security. Make sure the hospital staff cooperates. I don't want James Brooks having a stroke on the day his wife gives birth because people won't deal." He held the phone away from his ear. "Jane, has anyone called requesting a statement from the Foundation?"

Jane shook her head. "Mercy is at the hospital, and she's passed all of that to Casey. I don't think the press has found out yet, but they will. Also, I think it would be best if the hospital is reminded of the restraining order that Lisa has against her ex-husband. I wouldn't put it past him to make an appearance on a day like today—he might even try to see the babies."

Mathias nodded abruptly and left the room. "Understood."

Lauren left the kitchen and walked into the living room. She quickly found a local TV station airing the evening news. Jane came out of the kitchen a few minutes later and sat down beside her on the couch with a frustrated huff.

"I thought they were going to do a C-section next week?"

"That was the plan," Jane admitted softly. "Except her water broke today. She delivered the boy in the ambulance and the girl in the emergency room before they could get her upstairs to delivery. They're all three fine, but they're all in intensive care because it was considered a high-risk pregnancy and her doctor hadn't wanted her to deliver them. She sure as hell didn't want them delivered naturally."

"Jesus." Lauren sighed. "James must have been scared out of his mind."

"He caught his son," Jane whispered. "Literally." She turned her head on the sofa and stared at Lauren. "That just happens on TV, right? I mean, women delivering in the back of ambulances."

Lauren grinned. "I think it probably happens more than we think. It's her first pregnancy. We'll just put you in the hospital a couple of weeks before you're due to prevent any such problems."

Jane nodded. "Thanks, that's good. Because that would suck. I want drugs. I mean, it's a modern world. It's barbaric that a woman should have to push something that size out her hooha without drugs."

Lauren sputtered and then grinned. "Yeah, it is." She motioned to the TV. "Nothing on the news, so everyone at the hospital is keeping their mouths shut."

"Well, invading James Brooks's privacy is a lawsuit waiting to happen," Connor said dryly from the doorway. He moved into the room and plucked Lauren off the couch. He sat down in a chair and settled her on his lap and offered her his phone. "Dare is sending pictures."

"Oh." Lauren sighed. "Look at that." The baby looked sort

of like an alien but cute all the same. "You know, I think my biological clock is broken."

Jane laughed and took Mathias's phone when he offered it as he sat down. She threw her feet over his lap as she thumbed through them. "They're so sweet, though."

Lauren scrunched up her nose. "Yeah, sweet and a sincerely hot mess." She smiled as she clicked to a new picture. "They look like him. Lisa is totally outnumbered for life." Another picture buzzed in, and she accepted the download as she relaxed in Connor's lap. "Wow, who's the hottie?"

Connor pinched her. "That's Ryan Brooks. He's twenty-five."

"He's pretty like his daddy," Jane offered. "I bet you could get him to model for you, Lauren."

Lauren shook her head. "Nah, the families of other artists are sort of off-limits for me. Though I wouldn't mind doing a family portrait for them all if they wanted. James Brooks is a very lucky man."

"Yeah," Connor murmured. "He is." He looked at Mathias. "News on their health?"

"The kids were almost to term, so they seem to be in good shape. They have their own doctor. Dare says he was told that Lisa will spend the next six hours in ICU and then be moved into the room with twins that's already set up. Cassandra is on task with the babies and Ryan. Dare is moving back and forth between the front doors of the ICU and the babies' private room." Mathias sighed and let his head rest on the back of the couch.

"Why don't you go up there?" Lauren asked with a frown. "You obviously want to."

"Brooks told me to stay here," Mathias finally said. "Mercy and Shamus are at the hospital with him, and I've got six people with them. He doesn't want to have to worry about this situation and the one he has with Lisa."

Lauren flushed. "That's . . . we could all go?"

"No." Mathias lifted his head. "Sorry, I don't have the personnel in place to take you anywhere near Lisa Brooks and her babies right now. The kill on Warner might look unprofessional, but we can't take the risk that there is a hired gun in town working something none of us have an angle on yet. I can't find Robert Stein, and I've got a guy looking for him that makes me look like an amateur. He's nowhere to be found, and that is worrisome."

"The local police haven't had any luck?"

"They don't have the resources to conduct an international search, and Stein isn't in this city. He hasn't been in this city since Brooks fired him and locked him out of the town house."

Lauren frowned. "You know, I was all over that place when I first moved in. I never saw anything that could . . ." She took a deep breath. "I never went into the safe room."

"So?" Jane asked. She looked up from her own phone, which had been buzzing steadily during the entire conversation. "The vandalism was pretty extensive. Walls were torn open, furniture was cut . . ." She paused. "Jesus, someone was looking for something."

"Yeah." Lauren nodded. "And they didn't find it. Well, if they were in the house, the only place they couldn't have had access to was probably the safe room, which requires a code for entry and exit."

Connor urged her off his lap. "Let's go check it out."

"Seriously?" Mathias asked with a frown.

"Seriously," Connor responded. "If there is something in the safe room that is putting her in danger, I want to know what the fuck it is."

* * *

153

The ride back into the city had been tense, mostly because Connor and Mathias had argued out of their hearing for nearly twenty minutes before they'd all piled into Connor's SUV for the trip. Lauren figured that it was the first time the two men had argued in a very long time. She didn't know what Connor had finally said to convince Mathias to do what he wanted, but the argument had ended abruptly and Mathias had taken a gun out of his own vehicle and armed his fiancée without another word.

Jane, for her part, had taken the 9 mm handgun without hesitation. Both women had watched but not listened to the argument that had taken place between the two men on the small gravel path between the house and the barn.

Lauren had been concerned that they'd gone outside to "talk" to avoid breaking furniture if things got physical. She'd been relieved when they'd both kept their distance in the vehement conversation.

She didn't say a word as she and Jane were maneuvered into the town house quickly and the door was locked behind them. "I take it I don't have to mention the two undercover cops camped out across the street?"

Connor snorted. "It wasn't Silven or March. I wonder which shift they are working?" He turned and looked at her. "Did you notice our men?"

"Homeless guy near the bus stop and the black sedan three cars down from the cops?" Lauren questioned with a raised eyebrow. "They aren't really trying to hide, are they?"

"No," Connor admitted. "I'm mostly just doing it to piss off the cops."

Mathias laughed and walked toward the basement door. "Let's check this thing out."

Lauren and Jane followed. "And if there is nothing in there?"

"I'm going to have this place gutted," Jane returned evenly. "All of the walls, the floors—everything. If Stein hid something in here, I'm going to find it and shove it up his ass."

Mathias grinned as he went through the quick procedure to open the unoccupied safe room and frowned when it didn't respond. "Connor."

"Yeah." Connor pulled his weapon. "Lauren, behind me, please."

Lauren did as requested without a word and watched Mathias activate the biosensors to open the safe room. It scanned his entire palm and his left eye. A second numerical pad rolled over where the hand pad had been, and he entered a twenty-digit code. "It's like a bank vault."

"Better than a bank vault," Connor admitted roughly, and then leveled his weapon at the door as the hydraulics engaged and the door swung open.

It was *almost* empty, which was interesting, because Lauren was positive Jane had told her that a small cot had been placed in the safe room in case a two- or three-hour stay was required. There was a small security panel to one side and a laptop on a small table. Leaning back against the far wall was a wrapped canvas.

"Oh." Lauren and Jane exchanged a look. "You said Justin Warner was discharged for stealing art and stuff from Iraq?"

"Yeah." Connor eyed the covered painting critically and pulled a pair of latex gloves from his front pocket. "Check it out, if you will?"

Lauren glanced at Jane, who nodded and pulled a small knife from her purse and a pair of gloves. "Okay."

Lauren carefully lifted it off the floor, and Jane cut away the packing string wrapped around it. The paper sliced away easily under Jane's careful attention, and they folded it back.

"Jesus fucking Christ."

Connor raised an eyebrow. "So, you know what it is?"

Lauren nodded numbly as she took in the painting of two women in a formal music room performing for a man. She snatched Connor's hand when he started to touch it. "No. Don't touch it. Jesus."

"Talk to me, lass, what is this?"

"This is the *Concert* by Johannes Vermeer. It is believed to be the most valuable painting *ever* stolen." Lauren quickly refolded the brown paper wrapping around it. "It was stolen from a museum here in Boston in 1990."

Jane took a deep breath. "Okay. Let's think."

"Yes, let's think," Lauren snapped. "A fifty-million-dollar painting is in the safe room of a town house that James Brooks owns. Christ, Jane, the scandal . . ."

"Yeah." Jane closed her eyes.

"Fifty million dollars?" Connor demanded. "Are you serious?"

"On the low end," Lauren whispered as she retied what was left of the string with shaking hands. "It's been missing for nearly twenty years. Most believed it would never be recovered. It's insanely fragile—we need a special case to move it."

"One of those environmental cases from the gallery?" Mathias asked as he pulled out his phone. "Are you sure it's the real thing?"

"If it's a fake, it's an insanely good fake," Lauren responded neutrally. "I'm not in a position to judge that."

Jane nodded her agreement. "This is so not good."

9

Connor blinked in surprise as he watched Mercy Montgomery's eyes well up with tears. They fell down her face before she could get control of herself, and she wiped hastily at her cheeks. "I've never seen it. I wasn't in Boston when it was stolen."

Shamus pulled his wife close to him and let his face rest against the side of hers. "We need an expert in here, but this is the real deal or the person who reproduced it was in the room with the real thing."

"How do you know?" Connor asked.

"It's not framed," Mercy said as she took a deep breath. "Paintings like this never appear in public without a frame. The edges are protected from public viewing for insurance purposes, so a fake can be more easily identified. The fakes . . . the edges never match up or the artist doesn't bother to even try to. He or she just paints what is visible for the reproduction. The edges look very natural and on par with the rest of Vermeer's brushstrokes. It's not as easy to make a fake as many would believe, but it's possible. It'll need to be tested thoroughly."

"So it's a very good fake or a fifty-million-dollar painting," Mathias summed up. "Okay, let's pack it back up and get it in the safe. I need to make some phone calls, and then we need Brooks to make some decisions." He paused and looked around the room. "Connor, why don't you take Lauren upstairs to the private suite behind James's office. I don't think we need to separate until it's public knowledge that the painting has been recovered. Hopefully, whoever killed Warner will cut his losses and run."

"You know Robert Stein is probably dead, too."

Mathias nodded. "Yeah, I agree." He sighed. "Just get some sleep. This is going to suck wide for a while." He pointed at the painting. "No one touch that thing without gloves—not even the packing material."

Lauren had crawled up onto the king-sized bed in the small private suite and promptly fallen asleep. He wasn't surprised—it had been a stupidly stressful day.

He pulled off her shoes and put a blanket over her before setting his computer up on a small desk near the bed. Brooks had been surprisingly resigned to the discovery of the painting. It had been quickly decided that the best course of action was to anonymously return the painting to the museum where it had been stolen and let them sort out whether it was real.

To that end, Mathias had gone about getting a transport case that couldn't be traced back to Holman while Jane and Mercy had wrapped it in fresh packing material. The task of returning the painting to the museum had fallen to Dare.

Connor checked his watch. He imagined that Dare had breached the security of the museum already and was putting the case on the museum director's desk. The anonymous return of the painting would, of course, fuel the imaginations of people for years, but it was better than James Brooks admitting to the public that somehow a priceless work of art had ended up in his town house.

"Come to bed."

Connor turned to look at Lauren and found her sitting up, her hair beautifully tousled over her shoulders. "I have a few hours of work left, lass. I want to be awake when Dare returns."

"I wasn't asking you to sleep." Lauren pulled her blouse over her head and tossed it aside. "In fact, sleep is really overrated."

Connor groaned as she pulled off her bra, and it joined her blouse on the floor. "Lass."

She took off her socks and shimmied out of her jeans and panties. "Well, I could play by myself, but I sort of figured I didn't have to do that when I had you around."

"You're hell on my good intentions," Connor informed her with a small glare. He stood up as he dialed Mathias's phone number. "I'm going to take a nap unless you need me?"

Mathias laughed in his ear. "An hour, Grant. Just an hour. Don't make me come up there and get you."

"An hour," Connor agreed, and turned off the phone. He tossed it on the desk beside his computer and undressed quickly. He tore open a condom as he walked to the bed. "Tell me what you want."

Lauren watched him wrap one hand around his half-hard cock and jack it slowly as he put one knee on the bed. "Jesus, that's got so much potential."

Connor smirked and rolled the condom on with practiced ease. "I don't have enough time in the world to do what I want to you."

She grinned and spread her legs shamelessly. "We haven't even made a dent in my list."

He hummed a little under his breath as he ran his hands

159

down her legs and spread her farther. Her breath caught as he lowered his head and swiped his tongue across her clit. She jerked under him and lifted off the bed in blatant demand.

It occurred to him then that he'd had more sex with Lauren in the time since they'd met than he had in the entire past year. The realization was startling, as he hadn't exactly been living like a monk, but he'd set aside sex more often than not. There hadn't been a woman who really interested him in a while.

He dipped his tongue into her clenching entrance, and she moaned so softly and sweetly that he took pity on her. With ease, he slid up her body and pushed his cock right into her.

Lauren shuddered at the invasion and wrapped her long legs around him eagerly. "Yes, yes."

He slid one arm under her and settled more of his weight on her, pressing her firmly into the mattress as he started to thrust deep and hard into her. "Relax, love, and just take it."

Lauren buried her face against his neck and sucked in a harsh breath. "Connor."

"Shhh, just take it." He pushed in deep and ground against her. "Take my cock."

Lauren moaned and arched in his arms. "God, you're... fuck, Connor."

"This is how you want it," he told her. "Hard, deep, and slow."

"Yes," she agreed, and clenched her hands on his back. "Yes. Fuck me! Fuck me!" She relaxed into his thrusts and let her legs fall open wide. Her hands drifted down his back to cup his ass.

"You're mine," Connor whispered. "All mine. This pussy belongs to me."

"Yes," Lauren whispered, her eyes bright with arousal and affection. "All yours."

Connor took her in a brutal kiss, branding her with his mouth as his hands slid over her body possessively. He lifted his head, and their gazes met and held. "Mine." He matched the claim with a hard thrust and then another.

"Yes, Connor. All yours." She arched under him languidly and offered him her neck in a primitive show of submission so profound that he groaned and came.

"Fuck, Lauren!" He bowed into her briefly and clenched his teeth against her shoulder as he shuddered through an intense orgasm. "Fuck."

Connor pulled out of her and slid down. He spread her legs with his shoulders, shoved two fingers deep into her cunt, and sucked her clit so hard she screamed. She jerked against him and came, sobbing his name.

He dropped on the bed beside her and took a deep, ragged breath. "I think we'll kill each other eventually."

"Totally agreed." Lauren waved a hand nonchalantly in the air. "You're the fuck of the century."

"Nah, that's definitely you." Connor rubbed his stomach and then with a sigh rolled from the bed. "I need a shower before I meet with Mathias."

Mathias Montgomery was situated at the head of the conference table. Dare was sprawled on one side with a bottle of water. Connor took the seat across from him and accepted the bottle of water that Dare rolled his way.

Mathias cleared his throat. "It might interest you to know that the alarm in Brooks's office is in fine working order. Including the noise sensors."

Connor sighed. "Fuck me."

"Oh, that's exactly what I heard," Mathias said with an amused grin. "It just wasn't you . . . screaming it."

"My sex life is entirely too public lately," Connor responded idly, and drank half of his water in one greedy gulp.

"I don't disagree." Mathias closed his laptop. "Well, Dare?"

"Their security is a joke, and that's saying something considering they're the site of the most expensive art theft in history." Dare shrugged. "I was tempted to leave them a note saying so. I put the case right in the middle of the director's desk. No one followed me to or from the location, so if there is someone in the city with their eye on the town house or the painting, they probably don't suspect you've moved it."

"They won't until it's announced to the public that the painting has been returned anonymously," Mathias pointed out. "What did we get back on William Trent?"

"He was in Iraq until six months ago," Mathias informed them. "He was honorably discharged but with a little bit of taint. There was an investigation by the army CID regarding a theft, but nothing bore out. He chose not to sign up for another tour."

"Did he serve with Warner?"

"He was his CO," Mathias responded, his tone entirely too neutral. "He definitely had to have recognized one of his own men, so he knew who attacked Lauren in the park."

"How did a barely trained reservist end up under the command of an army ranger?" Dare asked with a frown. "I mean, Warner had zero special-ops training and did only six weeks of basic before he went into the reserves."

"Iraq is something of a clusterfuck," Mathias finally said. "They threw a lot of men and women into the mix over there, because they were running out of bodies to run the war machine. It's not ideal. Warner was probably a weekend warrior who geared up because he was a patriot. Maybe he even believed in the war to begin with, but then he got over and had to start fighting. A war where children wear bombs can change a man—and not always for the better. We all know that."

"You think Trent is involved?" Connor asked.

"I think it's a pretty damn odd coincidence that he's here in Boston, stopped an attack on Lauren, and didn't recognize a man he served with for six months," Mathias responded. "Let's keep this between us for now. I don't want to alarm Jane or Lauren."

"Agreed." Connor rubbed his head, clearly frustrated, and sucked in a deep breath. "I want a vacation after this is over."

Mathias laughed. "Too bad the school session starts in two weeks."

Connor dropped back in his chair at the reminder. There was no way in hell he'd get a vacation until after the session ended. While he didn't personally oversee any security assets at the school, Lauren would be needed, and lounging naked on a beach in Bermuda without her just didn't seem like all that much fun.

"So Chicago is out," Dare said out of the blue.

Connor frowned and looked at the table. "It's . . . the plan."

"Yeah, but plans can be changed," Dare responded easily. "You're both putting down roots in Boston, and I'm a New York boy at heart. So we don't spread out to Chicago now. Maybe we can do it later."

"Maybe." Connor sighed. "Yeah, maybe. There are a few firms in Chicago that we could probably buy into or outright purchase. That would require some trips—on-site assessments but no moving if we're careful about who and what we invest in."

"Agreed." Mathias closed his computer. "I've put out a few feelers in that direction, so we'll see what we get."

Connor sighed. "You know, I sort of figured that when I got old, I'd be that mean soldier living by himself in the middle of nowhere with a lot of weapons."

Mathias laughed aloud and shook his head. "Not you— you're entirely too social to be an old hermit."

"I think I could pull it off," Connor protested but ruined it with a smile. "As it is, I might not survive to old age."

Dare tilted his water in salute. "May we all be so beautifully exhausted, Connor."

Connor just grinned briefly and then sobered. "So, I need to go out for a while. Lauren is asleep."

"I'll set up my computer in Brooks's office and get some work done." Dare stood up and stretched. "I'm too old to skulk around like a cat burglar. Just so you two know."

"You're younger than both of us," Mathias pointed out with a frown.

Dare laughed. "Which makes you both *way* too old to skulk around." He looked pointedly at Connor and then raised an eyebrow.

"I don't intend to skulk," Connor responded evenly.

Connor relaxed in the chair and lit the cigar he'd pulled out of a box from Trent's luggage. The man shifted in the bed. "You needn't bother—I've already removed the gun."

Trent grunted. "They said I'd need to watch my ass with you."

"It's not your ass on the line here, Trent." Connor turned on the lamp beside him and blew smoke. "Nice cigar, by the way. Did you come home through Gitmo?"

"I debriefed there," Trent admitted roughly. "Are you going to kill me?"

"I really should," Connor said. "Because you let Warner attack my lass, and I have a real problem with that. Is Stein dead?"

Trent snorted. "No, that bastard ran when I realized he was trying to fuck us over."

"Don't bother trying to find him. He doesn't have the painting." Connor flicked ashes on the carpet and took another drag. "Great fucking cigar. I haven't had one this nice in years—maybe since my old man got me drunk on my first leave home after I joined the marines."

"I paid a pretty penny for them," Trent muttered. "Twice over since I had to bribe half the goddamned army to get them out of Cuba."

Connor nodded. "Okay, so here's the deal. We found the painting and you have no hope whatsoever of getting it at this point. You have one hour to leave Boston and never come back. If I ever see you near Lauren again, I will gut you."

"I haven't gone near her since the thing at the park, and I didn't authorize Warner to do that." Trent sighed. "He was out of hand."

"So you put him down in the alley behind the town house? Pretty sloppy kill."

"I figured if it was sloppy, I could blame it on Stein later if things went south," Trent admitted. "It isn't like that twit even knows how to fire a weapon. He wouldn't have accomplished anything like a clean kill."

"No, agreed." Connor glanced around the room and then refocused on the man who had wisely remained on the bed. "Was it you at the town house that night?"

"Yeah, we came back to Boston when Warner lost track of Stein. He was convinced the painting was in the house, but we didn't find it in our search. Of course, we couldn't get into the safe room."

"Then I moved Lauren in and you knew she'd have access."

"Yeah, something like that." Trent shrugged. "I don't hurt women, Grant. I was never going to touch her."

"But Warner was another matter."

"He had a reputation for hitting women in Iraq. I never left him alone with female prisoners." Trent sighed. "Can I get up and get some pants?"

"Nope." Connor flicked away some more ash. "And, really, you should know better than to sleep bare assed in the middle of an operation. It's just stupid."

"Fuck you," Trent said. "So, I'll leave Boston. Deal. It's just money, and I've got a lot already since Warner is out of the picture."

"Tell me about the painting."

"We found it in a safe in Baghdad. There was a lot of artwork, but this one was the only painting in a special airtight case. I figured it was pretty damn valuable. We fenced most of what we found before we even left Iraq. The painting was all we had left. Warner knew Stein from high school and figured he'd be able to help us determine out what it was."

"And he lied to you?"

"Not exactly—he told us what it was, but he underestimated the value. He figured neither one of us would bother looking it up. He was mistaken."

Connor snorted. "So, you realized you had a painting worth at least fifty million dollars and ..."

"Stein said he would get it authenticated and then set up a buyer. He offered Warner and me six million dollars to walk away. I told him he was out of his mind, but he hid the painting and wouldn't tell me where it was. Then he got fired from the Holman Foundation and locked out of the town house. He ran like a bitch."

Connor sighed. "He was pretty pissed when I wouldn't let him back in the town house that day. I had no idea why. I figured that's why it was vandalized before we could put the new security system in. But that was you."

"Yeah, that was me and that asshole Warner." Trent shrugged. "Is it real, Grant?"

"The director of the Holman Gallery cried when she saw it," Connor admitted roughly. "That's all the confirmation I really need at this point." He stood up, holstered his weapon, and walked toward the door. "One hour, Trent. I have a few men waiting downstairs to drive you to the airport. Don't give them a hard time—they'd just as soon kill you and put you in a hole as drive you to the airport."

"What about Warner and the cops?"

"Murders go unsolved in this city every day, and eventually the cops' captain will make them move on to more viable cases. They'll never have any evidence against me—at least you weren't stupid enough to frame me."

Lauren rolled over and curled into him as he slipped into the bed. "Yuck, have you been smoking?"

Connor sighed. "I don't think a Cuban cigar is worthy of a 'yuck.' "

She snorted and pushed at him. "Go shower, that's disgusting."

He flipped her on her back and crawled on top of her. "You're very lucky, lass, that I like you more than is remotely reasonable."

She grinned. "If you want me to shower with you, Grant, all you have to do is ask."

He nuzzled against her neck. "Come shower with me, then." He rolled off her and grabbed a condom from the nightstand as he walked toward the bathroom.

Lauren scrambled out of the bed after him but managed to walk instead of run into the bathroom. He was already in the large stall adjusting the water by the time she stripped out of her panties and his T-shirt.

She stood outside the all-glass stall and watched him under the water for nearly a minute before he turned to look at her. He raised an eyebrow in question and held out his hand. She blushed and took it.

"You left the gallery," Lauren whispered as he shifted her under the water.

"Yeah," he admitted, and reached out for the shampoo. "I want to wash your hair."

"I never turn that down." She turned and braced one hand against the wall. His cock, half-hard, brushed against her ass as he started to work shampoo into her hair. "What did you do?"

"I paid someone a visit."

"William Trent?"

Connor sighed. "Yeah, you know, I don't enjoy ignorant women, but it would be nice if you weren't always so *quick*."

"He was in the service with Warner, right?"

"Yeah." Connor rubbed the tips of his fingers over her scalp and she groaned. "He won't ever bother you again."

"Is he dead?"

"No, but he is on a plane out of town as we speak. He won't return to Boston unless he's put his affairs in order," Connor promised, and turned her gently under the water. "You wouldn't really cut your hair, would you?"

She laughed. "Never more than an inch or so—my daddy liked my hair long. I wear it this way because it reminds me of him. Sometimes I hate it, but I wouldn't part with it."

Lauren reached out for a small bottle of conditioner. "This, too, or I won't be able to get a comb through it without pulling myself bald."

Connor gamely accepted the bottle. "So I'm a man."

She shot him a look over her shoulder and shifted her ass against his cock, which was enticingly hard. "I took note of that early on."

He laughed and shook his head. "Well, you know, as a man, the last thing I ever want to discuss is my stupid feelings or anything remotely related to them."

"I'm well aware of your gender's failings on the 'stupid feelings' front," Lauren declared. She bit down on her lip and sighed as his fingers moved through her hair carefully. "You could write me a note, and I could check the box that best fits my general feelings toward you."

Connor laughed and set aside the conditioner. He turned her so they were face-to-face. "You make me want things, Lauren. Things I never thought I'd want, and I need to know if I'm alone in this."

She huffed out a breath. "I would totally go without hand sanitizer if you were allergic to it." She leaned into him and placed a soft kiss over his heart. "And later, when we're both certain we like where this is going, I would love to hear about all those things you want. I might even have a list or two of my own."

"I think we should get through your sex list first," Connor said as he prodded her under the water to rinse her hair.

"Excellent idea."

"This is really unnecessary," Lauren protested as Dare McBain checked her seat belt and shut the door on her protests. She frowned at him as he rounded the SUV and waited until he'd settled behind the wheel to continue. "I'm a grown-up, you know. I don't need babysitting, and the guy is gone. You guys made sure."

Dare nodded. "Sure, Trent is gone. We've got an asset sitting on a beach in Maui three feet from him right now. If I get one more picture of a beautiful beach full of naked women sent to my phone, I'm going to go down there and kick Jordan's ass for the bloody bragging. But the painting hasn't been announced to the public yet, which means your risk assessment is still kind of high."

"I can drive myself to the supply store. It's six blocks away."

"Lady, you're not going anywhere without a security escort.

I've known Connor since he was barely old enough to drive, and I've never seen him so taken with anyone." He shot her a look as they pulled into traffic. "So, just relax and enjoy the ride."

Lauren sighed but chose not to say anything else. It was sort of thrilling that the oldest friend Connor had seemed to think that what they had was serious. She wanted it to be serious. Her mind drifted back to the shower they'd shared the night before. A little shiver ran down her back as she thought about the way he'd met her gaze as he'd pushed his cock into her. His hands had tightened on her ass as he'd pressed her against the wall and fucked her so hard she'd come twice.

"I'd never want to hurt him," she finally whispered.

"Then let us take care of you until this situation is resolved, because the man is *gone* on you," Dare responded roughly. "So gone that I don't even feel comfortable flirting with you just to fuck with him."

Lauren laughed and blushed. "How do you like Boston?"

"I prefer New York," Dare admitted. "But it's a good city. I've always enjoyed visiting here but I was glad when Mathias chose to come here to set up our office. I wouldn't have wanted to move here permanently."

"And Connor? Why is Connor here? It seems that it would make sense for your business to spread out to another city. Three partners, three cities."

Dare shrugged. "When Mathias asked us to invest in his idea, he put up the most money because of the risk. He didn't want to put either of us in a bad place if things didn't pan out the way we'd hoped. So, Connor and I both decided that since most of the money was Mathias's, he'd make the big decisions. There can only be one leader, and it wasn't the first time we'd both chosen to follow Mathias."

"That's not answering my question."

Dare grinned. "No, I see that. So, we had a plan that involved New York, Boston, and Chicago. Mathias chose Boston because his brother is here. Connor came along to help get things settled. The Holman contract turned out to be *huge,* as you can imagine."

"But Connor is supposed to go to Chicago eventually."

"Plans change," Dare answered with a small smile. "Connections get made and people have to adjust. We're all adjusting and perfectly fine with making different choices for the company."

"That sounded suspiciously like you were telling me not to worry my pretty little head about it," Lauren said darkly.

"I'd never speak to a woman that way. My mother would never let me forget it," Dare answered. "I'm serious. Plans get changed, and the three of us are on the same page. I'd storm hell with a bucket of water and a bad attitude if that's what Connor wanted to do. Mathias would, too."

"So, I shouldn't worry?"

"Ask Connor, sweetheart." Dare pulled into a parking spot directly in front of the art supply store. "You're a good-luck charm. I never get parking like this in New York." He cut the engine and unfastened his seat belt. "Do me a favor and let me get your door."

Lauren nodded. "I can do that." She used the few seconds to pull out her supply list for the gallery project and unfasten her seat belt.

Dare took her elbow carefully as he helped her from the vehicle and shut the door. "A lot of stuff?"

"Yes, actually. Shamus and I decided on how we'd seal the panels and an adhesive for the glass pieces. We want to do some test runs for it while I'm finishing up the design. We figured we'd expose a test piece to extreme temperatures to see how it holds up."

It happened in seconds. Dare turned her and pulled his weapon seconds before the first *pop*. He jerked against her and fired in return. A man fell on the sidewalk three feet away, and Dare stumbled against her.

"Dare!" Lauren caught him, but they both stumbled under his weight. Blood was blossoming across his chest as they hit the sidewalk.

"Run," Dare hissed as he scanned the area, his gun still raised.

She pressed against the wound. "No, I can't leave you."

He grabbed a fistful of her hair and jerked her toward him. Face-to-face, he growled, "Run, goddamn it. He might not be alone." He released her and pulled out his cell phone. "Right fucking now, Lauren! Toward Connor. Now!"

Lauren scrambled away from him with a half sob and left her purse spilled on the ground around him. She hurried through the crowd toward the gallery as police sirens sounded in the distance. As she ran, it was hard to ignore the people asking if she needed help, if she was hurt. She pushed off well-meaning hands, unwilling to let some stranger get in the way of what could be chasing after her.

She saw Connor before he saw her, which wasn't a surprise since the crowd was parting like the Red Sea around him. He caught her, both of them breathless, and for a second they were both still. Then he lifted her off her feet and strode out into traffic. The door to a black SUV swung open, and he entered quickly.

It was pulling away from the curb in seconds. Lauren buried her face against his neck and clutched at him. "Sorry. I'm so sorry."

"Shhh, lass, you don't need to apologize."

"I left him."

Connor sighed. "You did the right thing. He's fine. He's already in an ambulance and on the way to a hospital. Mathias will be in the emergency room when he arrives."

"Where we heading, boss?"

Lauren took a deep breath. "The hospital. We need to go to the hospital."

"Are you hit?" Connor demanded, and started running his hands over her body. "Lauren! Are you hit?"

"No, this is all Dare's blood." Lauren curled into him. "We just have to be there, Connor. Please. This is all my fault."

"No, lass, it isn't." Connor turned his attention to the driver. "Find out where they are taking him, Zeke, and get us there as quickly as possible."

"Not a problem, sir."

"Dare said that Trent guy is on a beach somewhere," Lauren whispered.

"He is." Connor swallowed hard. "At least, he was. Now he's in a hotel room getting his ass handed to him just in case he's involved in this. I'll know for certain within the hour. If he left a team here in Boston to take you out, there isn't a place on Earth he can hide from me."

"The shooter wasn't aiming at me," Lauren whispered. "He hit Dare on purpose. Dare just moved—ruined his shot and fired back."

"Did you see anyone else?"

"No, I just ran like Dare told me to." Lauren hesitated. "But I argued a little."

Connor huffed out a breath. "I just bet you did." He pressed a kiss against her temple and closed his eyes. "I'll let Dare decide how you should be punished for it. I should warn you—his mother was one of those vicious school teachers who hit students with a ruler before it was deemed cruel, and sometimes she even did it after that."

Lauren laughed softly and relaxed against him. "That's a great big lie, Grant."

"Maybe," Connor acknowledged. "She is vicious, though. Dare gets *all* of his badassness from her."

Lauren closed her eyes and tried to push from her mind the image of Dare McBain bleeding. "He'll be okay, right?"

"He was bitching at me and giving orders as he was being worked on by the paramedics," Zeke offered from the front seat. "They had to confiscate his phone, which surely pissed him off. He can't exist if he can't text message."

Detectives March and Silven were already waiting for them at the hospital. Connor glanced around the small waiting room he and Lauren had been led to after they'd successfully pushed past a few medical personnel who'd wanted to evaluate Lauren. Jane and Mathias were sitting side by side, both on the phone.

"Detectives."

"Mr. Grant." Silven took a deep breath. "Looks like we owe you an apology."

"What?" Lauren demanded snidely. "You aren't going to accuse him of hiring someone to shoot his best friend?"

March flushed and looked away while Silven merely sighed and continued. "The dead man is a hired gun. He's got a pretty long rap sheet and was actually wanted in connection with a few federal crimes. He's a low-end guy, so he's got some money behind him."

"He probably isn't alone," Connor said. "Money implies something pretty organized and big."

"He had a motel key on him. We traced back to the room and found it empty. We're doing a search to figure out when he came into the city and find out if he traveled with any known associates."

"That's pretty fast work, Detective," Connor admitted, and

then prodded Lauren toward a chair. "Can we sit? I'm crashing on the adrenline buzz, and she's covered in blood."

"We can arrange to pick her up some clothes," Silven offered.

"I have a man on it," Mathias said from his place. "You, too, Grant." He glanced at Connor's clothes. Blood was smeared across his shirt. "I figured the cops would want both of your clothes for evidence purposes."

"Thanks," Lauren whispered. "Have you found Robert Stein?"

Mathias shook his head. "Nope. Detectives?"

"No. We traced him on a flight out of the city but nothing after that. If he hired mercenaries, we'll probably find some kind of paper trail. Even if it's just large cash withdrawals." Silven walked away from them with his phone. "I'll call a forensics investigator to come get the clothes."

March sat down in a chair in front of Lauren. "Since Mr. McBain is in surgery, it would help if we could get a statement from you, Ms. Evans."

Lauren nodded and took a breath. "Yeah, okay. Did someone pick up my things off the sidewalk?"

"Yes, they are being processed with the rest of the crime scene. We'll return everything we can as soon as possible."

"Okay." She rubbed her hands on her jeans. "Dare and I were walking into the supply store, and he must have seen something because he grabbed my arm, pulled his gun, and then the guy fired. Dare fired back. Then they were both on the ground bleeding. Dare ordered me to run, and after I argued, I did as he demanded."

"Do you think the man meant to hit you?"

"No, I think he meant to shoot my security so he could take me. He just wasn't a very good shot." Lauren smiled gratefully when Jane pressed a large cup of coffee into her less-than-steady hand. "I ran toward the gallery and Connor found me. Then we came here." She took a deep drink of coffee and was silent for a few seconds. Then she made a face. "I really hate hospital coffee."

"It sucks," Jane agreed, and then drank from her own cup. "I'll have someone bring us some good stuff."

Silven sat down in a chair beside March. "At this point, Mr. Grant, we'd like permission to search the town house that Ms. Evans was staying in."

Connor pulled out his phone. "I'll have to ask James Brooks. If he says no, you'll have to get a court order."

"Understood." Silven made a note in his book. "The dead guy isn't ex-military, but he apparently tried to join the marines when he was younger. He was rejected."

"You suddenly have a lot of resources, Detective." Connor's fingers drifted through Lauren's hair.

"Yes, well, Dare McBain turned a city street into the O.K. Corral," Silven returned dryly. "Trust me—that gets attention. The chief is concerned that we'll get some flack about not taking the threats against Ms. Evans seriously."

"I'd be the first to say you've taken this entire matter very seriously," Connor responded dryly. "And hardly the O.K. Corral—there is only one dead guy instead of three."

Silven grinned a little. "I wouldn't think a Brit would be all that interested in American history."

"What kid doesn't want to be Wyatt Earp?" Connor asked softly as Lauren leaned into him.

March stood and stared at Lauren. "Ms. Evans, do you have any idea what could be in the town house that someone would be willing to kill for?"

Lauren shook her head. "No, but then I don't understand how a kid can die on the street for a pair of shoes." Her fingers tightened against Connor's shirt. "Shouldn't we be hearing something by now?"

"I'll check," Jane said with a half smile. "He was totally bitching about his phone when they wheeled him up from the emergency room. The paramedics gave it to me." She patted her pocket. "I promised to return it after his surgery."

Connor shifted in what he was sure was the hardest chair in North America and leaned forward into his hands. He rubbed his face briskly and stared at his best friend with a mild fury swirling in his gut. "I promised your mother that I wouldn't let you get yourself killed, Dare."

Dare stirred and turned his head. "Stupid thing to promise," he muttered, and then coughed. "But you were always about promising the impossible to women, laddie."

Connor huffed and looked at Lauren, who was sound asleep on the second bed in the room. "I was a vain, stupid son of a bitch for thinking this was over."

"What's Trent saying?"

"Oh." Connor smirked. "I sent Deacon down there because Jordan wasn't getting anywhere."

Dare snorted and then groaned. "Did you tell him to leave the man in one piece?"

"Mostly," Connor conceded. "The locals have identified the shooter, and you're a national hero."

Dare glared at him. "That is not fucking funny, Connor."

"It hit CNN about an hour ago. I called your mum and updated her so she wouldn't get on a plane. I had to spend twenty-five minutes hearing *the story* about your evil American father and how he seduced her with his stupid accent and foreign ways. Then she went into this diatribe about how dangerous New York is, which did not stop even when I pointed out you were shot in Boston."

Dare sighed. "She's not coming, right?"

"I made her promise not to. I might've implied that it would be dangerous if she did." Connor shrugged when Dare glared at him. "What? Did you want your mother here? Really?"

"No." Dare sighed. "With her attitude, she'd get stopped coming into the country and held indefinitely. I'd have to visit her in Gitmo."

"I don't think they're sending suspected members of the IRA to Cuba," Connor consoled.

Dare thumped his head back against his pillow. "You utter bastard, my mother is not a member of the IRA. She has a fucking sewing circle, for Christ's sake!"

"And a stockpile of semiautomatic weapons," Connor added. "It's okay—I'd stockpile weapons, too, if I'd been seduced by an evil American."

"What? You don't think I'm evil?" Lauren laughed softly. "What are you guys talking about?" She rolled off the bed and stretched leisurely, then offered a glare in Dare's direction. "Hey, you suck."

"I do not," Dare said. "I got shot, lass. You're supposed to be nice to me."

Lauren nodded solemnly and leaned in. She kissed him softly on the mouth. "That's from me for getting shot." She kissed him again. "And that's from Mercy." She patted his cheek. "Jane insists on delivering her own."

He looked over her face. "You're going to get me shot again."

Lauren grinned. "I got your six."

10

"So, at some point I'd like you to talk about your feelings and stuff." Connor glanced her way. "You know, be a *girl*."

"My feelings about running through the streets of Boston covered in your best friend's blood *or* my feelings about the shooting part *or* my feelings about you and all the hot sex we're having?"

Connor huffed. "Just any or all of that would be great. I don't want to pressure you or anything, but I also don't want you to have a stroke from suppressing the general crappiness of the past week."

"I was thinking that I'd just repress it instead." Lauren browsed through the contents of her purse, which had been returned. "The cops kept my condoms *and* my new lipstick." She sighed. "Is this city just full of thieves or what?"

Connor chuckled. "Maybe they had trace evidence on them."

"Sure, sure," Lauren muttered, and checked all of her credit cards in her wallet. "And maybe they just want their lips to be all shiny and sparkly."

"Oh, that sucks. I liked that shiny lipstick." Connor sighed and pulled on her hair. "It looked especially interesting on my dick."

Lauren sputtered. "You're such a freak, Connor. I swear."

"It's great that we met, because I was despairing over the fact that I'd never meet a woman who was as equally perverted as myself. You've really put me at ease."

Lauren set her purse on the floor between her feet and dropped her head back against the headrest. "Do we know anything about the painting?"

"I heard through a source this morning that a heavy hitter in insurance investigation came in this morning on a private charter. He brought two experts with him. So, I think there will be an announcement sometime in the next two days."

"And what have you learned from Trent?"

Connor glanced her way. "What do you mean?"

"Oh, don't even try to play innocent with me." Lauren rolled her eyes. "I know you have someone down there doing more than *questioning* him."

"I made a mistake with him," Connor admitted. "During the conversation I had with him, he said 'they said I'd need to watch my ass around you.'" He shook his head. "I didn't catch it until today, when I was trying to find you. He all but told me he wasn't alone and I missed it."

"Well, don't kick your ass too much." Lauren closed her eyes. "It isn't like Mathias and Dare weren't listening to your entire conversation, right?"

Connor laughed. "As a matter of fact, they were. I think they thought I might do more than scare the shit out of him."

"You are terribly proud of your badassness," Lauren responded dryly, and then turned her head to stare at him. "Dare's going to be okay, right?"

"Yeah, he is. They had to operate to pull the bullet out because it didn't go through. It didn't hit anything major, and he'll probably be released before Lisa Brooks. We'll hire him a mean physical therapist, and he'll be in flirting shape in no time."

Lauren smiled softly. "He said he thought you were so gone on me that he didn't even feel comfortable pretending to flirt with me."

"It's lucky for him that he's in the hospital with a hole in him or I would kick his ass," Connor muttered.

"So you're not *gone* on me?" Lauren asked, amused.

"I'm completely gone on you, but that's not any of your business." He picked up her hand and kissed her palm. "You need something to eat and then some serious sleep. You haven't slept a full night in more days than I can even remember. I certainly haven't helped on that front."

"Yeah," Lauren agreed. "You can't keep your cock to yourself. Not that I'm complaining or anything."

Connor laughed. "Burgers?"

"That works," Lauren said.

"So dead guy number two in our parade of bad dead guys is named Cole Shelly. He's a low-end merc who failed the psych exam when he tried to join the marines. He tried the police academy but was dismissed before he could graduate." Mathias settled at the table. "Where is Lauren?"

"We ate and then she went to sleep," Connor said. "She's in the bedroom down the hall." He went to the coffeepot and filled his cup and then brought the pot over to the table to fill Mathias's. "What else do we have?"

"He arrived two days after Lauren. Within hours of his arrival, two more mercs of his *caliber* also flew into the city. Shelly checked into a motel downtown. Unfortunately, the locals have already cornered the market on that little bit of investigation. I haven't gotten anything from it that you don't already know."

"The other two?" Connor asked.

"It crossed my mind to visit them both, but I decided to pass the information to Detective Silven." Mathias shrugged when Connor lifted an eyebrow in surprise. "We've stepped on their toes a lot, and it didn't help that your government scared the shit out of the chief of police. The man was three shades of white when he came out of that phone call."

"Shut up," Connor said. "That was not my fault. I didn't call them. I'm surprised I haven't heard from the State Department over that bullshit. I'm supposed to be keeping a low profile. Dare has dual citizenship, so they don't ask much of him."

"They haven't asked much of you, either, lately."

"I don't go a day when I don't expect a phone call. I agreed to *consult* when I came over."

"The citizenship process?"

"In very good shape," Connor admitted. "I got some grief from home on that front but nothing I didn't expect. They really don't like it when their tools go off and make themselves at home in other countries."

Mathias nodded. "How is Lauren holding up?"

"She's tired and a little off her stride but..." Connor trailed off. "She's strong and capable. I would've loved to have met the man who raised her, because he did a superior job preparing her for the world." He smiled then. "It's too bad he didn't take the time to prepare us all for her."

Mathias laughed. "Or maybe just you?"

"A few tips would've been nice," Connor admitted. "I don't even know what to do with myself. When Dare and I joined the marines right out of school, we had this thing between us, this ideal that we should fight for queen and country because it was the just and moral thing to do."

He waved his hand in the air in front of him. "I can't say I still don't feel that way, but war did things to us both that made us what we are today."

"So you're wondering what sort of events in her life shaped her?" Mathias asked. "She grew up on an American military base with a high-ranking military officer for a parent. She was probably indulged far more than strictly necessary and should be a spoiled little princess."

"Yeah, she should be." Connor shrugged. "A diva artist with a bad attitude and a haughty little manner. You know, the kind you could cheerfully strangle. Except, she isn't like that at all."

"Jane said she's going to be a rock star in the art world in the next ten years," Mathias said. "Mercy has a pretty good eye for that kind of thing, too. So, it's pretty cool that she has a hardy personality that isn't influenced by other people and money. She won't end up being one of those bitches who gives Jane a headache."

The female laughter startled both men, and they swung around to find Lauren standing the doorway of the kitchen. "It's a good thing you guys are both retired from the service. I can't believe I snuck up on you."

Connor eyed her critically. At least she didn't have bags under her eyes anymore. "You didn't get enough sleep."

"Jane called me. She's halfway here and ready to shoot her security escort. I figured I'd give you fair warning." Lauren went to the coffeepot and poured herself a full cup. "Besides, I woke up when you put the fresh pot on. Who could sleep through that?"

Connor figured he could with no problem and was grateful that he hadn't developed the near-psychotic desire for coffee that he endured with most of the guys who worked for them. "Hungry?"

"Yeah, Jane stopped to get some sandwiches since neither of us is particularly handy in the kitchen." Lauren slid into a kitchen chair and pulled her legs up to her chest. "I should warn you, if she brings only one roast beef sandwich, I'm prepared to fight to the death for it."

Connor grinned. "I think I'll survive without it."

Lauren eyed him critically. "So you say, Mr. Grant, so you say."

"You eat like a trucker," Jane complained.

Lauren shot her a look. "You're lucky I like mean-spirited women or I'd punch you for that." She glanced around the barn where they'd camped out for lunch, leaving the men to their *talk* in the kitchen. "Wanna see the prep work I've done with Connor?"

"God, yes. How can you even think I wouldn't?" Jane scrambled to her feet and followed Lauren across the barn to a large table.

Lauren had most of the drawings she'd already done spread out over the table. "He's raw and perfect." She plucked one full-body rendering out of the collection and put it down in front of Jane. "This is what I'm going to paint first. The light and the shadow across his body."

Jane blew out a breath and reached out. She stopped just short of touching the drawing. "I don't even know how you can work with him standing there looking like that."

Lauren grinned. "Yeah, I know. It's like an exercise in martyrdom. He has all of this physical power, and you know how some men look diminished naked?"

Jane nodded. "Clothes make the man sort of thing?"

"Something like that," Lauren agreed. "He doesn't have that problem at all." She pulled another drawing forward. "It's just stunning really. He was right about one thing—the thing about war being a man's business."

Jane frowned as she picked up a drawing. "Mean scar on his leg."

"Yeah, knife." Lauren took the drawing and put it back in its place with a small smile at Jane's blush. "No touching. You'll mess up my order."

"Sorry." Jane shoved her hands into her pockets. "So, you'll do five of him?"

"I think so."

"And be ready for a show by April?"

"Absolutely," Lauren agreed, and then rearranged the drawings to the order they'd been in when she'd brought Jane over to look. "I don't know that I'll be able to part with the ones of him, but we'll cross that bridge when we come to it."

"It won't be a problem if they aren't for sale. We'll want to let the show travel for at least a year. You'll be expected to make appearances on opening nights. It'll conflict some with your teaching schedule, but we'll plan ahead and get all of that arranged. Shamus and Lisa have both stepped in for the artist in residence before when it comes to the academy."

Lauren nodded and chewed her bottom lip as she considered the drawings. "Any news on the painting?"

"Nothing, but Mathias heard that another expert is being flown in. There are a few rumors going around town about chemical tests and stuff like that, so they are working through the tests to check to see how old the canvas is, which isn't a great tell as you know. And then they'll start analyzing paint chips, brushstrokes, cracking." Jane shrugged. "I think once they get another person in to say yes, they are going to make some kind of announcement."

"What kind of announcement would you make?"

"Something supremely vague about the possible recovery of a highly valued painting and ongoing tests to confirm the origin of the painting. It would be enough to get a buzz going in the art world—increase traffic in the museum and get speculation going. It wouldn't take long for someone to start speculating about the stolen artwork from twenty years ago."

"Then a big reveal when it's discovered to be real."

"Yeah, something like that." Jane shrugged. "It would be good business that way and would create a stir the museum could ride for *years*. If they play it right, it will bring in crowds from all over the world to see it. Donations will increase, memberships will triple in size, and so on."

She wasn't really surprised to find Connor asleep in the bed they'd been sharing. It wasn't like he'd gotten a lot of sleep since they'd met. Between her emergencies and all of the sex, the man must have been entirely worn thin.

Lauren pulled the door closed and tiptoed into the room. She was half a second from arranging his blanket when his hand snagged her wrist, and she was unceremoniously hauled into the bed. Her abrupt scream ended in laughter as he tipped her over onto her back and climbed on top of her.

"Sorry, I didn't mean to wake you." She touched his face and rubbed his mouth with her thumb. "You need your sleep."

"So do you." Connor slid off of her and rolled so he could tuck her against his chest. "I'll sleep better if I know where you are, so how about you stay put?"

She shifted and rested her chin on his chest. "Do I get a prize when you wake up?"

"I think I can arrange something." He slid his fingers through her hair.

* * *

186

Lauren woke with a hand sliding down her belly and teasing at the edge of her panties. She sighed and opened her eyes. "Don't be a clit-tease, Grant, or you'll learn the true depth of *my* badassness."

Connor laughed softly against the side of her neck and slid his hand right into her panties. He cupped her sex with his hand and teased her entrance with the tips of two fingers. He moved slightly and covered her mouth with his own, his tongue plunging into her mouth as his finger pressed into her pussy.

She groaned against the dual invasion, and a shiver ran down her body. His fingers delved confidently into her hole again and again until she was lifting her hips in time with his penetration.

He lifted his head and stared intently at her face. "We still have guests, you know."

Lauren groaned softly. "They suck."

"Yeah," Connor murmured in agreement. "They really do. You're going to have to be quiet. I don't want them to hear you getting off—that's for me. All for me."

Lauren closed her eyes and exhaled sharply. "That's . . . yeah . . . I can be quiet."

"Are you sure?" he asked silkily. "I'll spank your ass if you make any noise."

"That's hardly an encouragement to behave," Lauren retorted. "I'm pretty sure I'd love it if you spanked my ass."

Connor laughed and pulled his hand free from her panties. "Strip."

He took care of his own clothes while she shimmied out of her panties and tossed her T-shirt aside. Connor relaxed back on the bed and rolled the condom into place under her intent gaze.

"Sit on my cock."

Lauren huffed. "Christ, you're an evil bastard." She gamely rolled to her knees and slid astride his hips. "You expect me to be quiet on top?"

"What? You can't follow instructions?" Connor demanded roughly as he cupped her ass.

Lauren slid one hand down between them, positioned his cock, and slid right down on him. He choked back a groan and she smirked. "Shhh. We wouldn't want Jane and Mathias to know what we're doing in here."

Connor arched on the bed as she started to move. "The damn bed is going to give that away."

It did squeak and groan very nicely, Lauren thought as she braced herself on his chest and started to rock up and down on his cock in earnest. He let her control the pace for less than a minute before he cupped her breasts with his big, rough hands. Then he snapped his hips up against her, and she nearly bit her tongue to keep from screaming.

Blunt, thick fingers plucked and pinched at her nipples mercilessly as he thrust up against her, pushing his cock in so deep and hard that it was as much pain as it was pleasure.

Lauren arched and stilled against his body, her back bowing as she came hard and sharply. She took a shuddering breath. "Jesus. Fuck."

Connor rolled them over and braced himself on the bed. "You're gorgeous when you come." He ground his cock into her. "So fucking beautiful." He started to thrust deep in and out of her and laughed softly when she spread her legs for him and arched into him. "That's my lass—just take it." He buried his face against her neck and groaned softly. "You were made for my cock."

Lauren pressed her heels against the mattress and took each

punishing thrust with a shudder of relief. "Yes, fuck, yes," she whispered fiercely, and dragged her nails down his back.

"No, I'm not remotely interested in doing an interview right now." Lauren rummaged around the dresser and started dumping various things into the small purse she'd dug out of a box. "Look, Rachel, I realize you have a press *plan* but right now? Right now I'm a little preoccupied with a few things, including starting this new job. I'm still working on lesson plans, and I was sort of almost kidnapped twice in the past week, which I'm absolutely not ever discussing with a member of the press."

Connor watched her from the corner of his eye while he finished dressing. She made even mundane things seem like an *event*. They were currently preparing to go to his place to pick up some more clothes for him, and apparently that had required she change purses and call her agent. He pinched her ass as he moved past her, and she just smirked at him and dropped a miniature bottle of hand sanitizer into her purse.

"And then there is the truly astronomical amount of sex I'm having. I couldn't work magazine interviews into my day if I wanted to."

Connor laughed and walked out of the bedroom with a shake of his head. Mathias was at the kitchen table with Jane in his lap. They were having a quiet conversation, which stopped the moment he entered the room. He glanced their way as he went to the teapot Lauren told him she had prepared while she was making coffee for herself. "Good morning."

Jane wiggled her eyebrows and looped her arms around Mathias's neck. "We voted and we figure if they ever add sex to the Olympics, you guys could take the gold in Heterosexual-Couples Copulation."

Connor poured his tea with a small grin. "Americans spend

entirely too much time talking about sex and not nearly enough time actually shagging."

Lauren laughed as she entered the kitchen with an empty coffee cup. She refilled and leaned on the counter near coffee-maker. "I have a rule about discussing sex before I've had breakfast."

"You have a list of rules about sex?" Jane asked with a grin.

"I have a list of rules for *life,* and discussing sex on an empty stomach is just"—she waved a hand—"wrong." Frowning into her cup, she opened a cabinet near her and pulled out a small bottle of honey, which she slid down the counter in Connor's direction as he pushed a small tin of sugar in hers.

He shot honey into his tea while she split a bagel for the toaster. "We can get something substantial in town. Maybe hit that diner down from my apartment."

Lauren hummed as she shoved the bagel into the toaster. "That sounds like a total plan. You want butter or cream cheese?"

"Whatever you're having is fine," Connor responded. "There are some travel mugs over the stove if you want to take your coffee with you."

"Water for you?" Lauren asked as he started to leave the kitchen.

"Yeah, thanks."

Lauren pulled a bottle of water out of the refrigerator and a small tub of cream cheese. "So, what are you two planning today?"

"I'm making him take me to see the babies, and then I'm going to meet with Casey about a press release concerning the twins. There was a leak to the media, but no real information has been released. James wants to cut them off at the pass so to speak." Jane slid off Mathias's lap and rummaged through her purse for her phone. "I synced my schedule with our virtual office so you'll know where I am most of the day, and I'll send a text if I make any changes."

Lauren nodded. "I have my phone." She glanced up as Connor came back into the kitchen pulling on his holster. "A man with a gun and my own personal brand of bad attitude. I'm all set for the day."

"Well, as long as you have a plan," Jane said with a grin.

Three minutes later, Lauren was settled in the SUV with her coffee and the bagel she figured she would have to force-feed him. She didn't offer him a piece until they were out of the gate and only raised an eyebrow when he took it without question. "Did you hit your head in the shower or does morning sex make you agreeable?"

Connor glanced at her briefly. "The sex certainly did a lot for my general disposition." He grinned. "What did Jane say when she caught you quartering that bagel?"

"Nothing, she just rolled her eyes at me." She passed him another section and then popped one into her mouth. "It's easier to eat this way, and I watched you cut your toast into four pieces yesterday, so don't even try to tease me about it."

He laughed. "I'd never tease you about something so fundamental as good organization."

Lauren sort of figured he was perfect. "The last man I seriously dated made fun of me a little about my *stuff*."

Connor snagged her hand and threaded their fingers together carefully. "I'm willing to go kick his ass."

She grinned and leaned toward him. He met the kiss halfway, one eye on the road. "I'm completely charmed by you, Mr. Grant."

Connor leaned in the doorway and watched Dare McBain ineffectively try to push off the nurse who was trying to help him get dressed. "I'll take over, lass. Scotsmen aren't known for their gratitude."

The young nurse blushed and stepped back. "Thank you. I'll be back with the discharge papers shortly."

Dare glared at her until she was out of the room. "She made me piss in a bottle."

Connor grinned and shook his head. "Well, lad, you got shot."

"In the shoulder," Dare muttered, and picked up his shirt. "Come help me with this so that little girl doesn't come back in to help. I'm hurting like a motherfucker, and I don't want to be cruel to her."

"Oh, but you can be cruel to me?" Connor asked with a grin. "I see."

"Yeah, well, I've been your best mate since we were twelve. You can take it."

Connor smirked but gamely helped Dare with the T-shirt and then a casual button-down shirt. "Sling?"

"Yeah, God help me," Dare muttered. "Where's your lass?"

"Upstairs staring at babies," Connor said with a sigh. "I just hope it doesn't make her biological clock explode or something."

"You're going to keep her, right?"

Connor flushed and fastened the sling a little more roughly that was required. "Shit, sorry."

"Don't be sorry—just be honest," Dare said, and patted him on the cheek with his free hand. "My mum will be pleased."

"I wouldn't go telling her if I were you," Connor responded. "She'll be after you to make a permanent connection of your own." He grinned when Dare dropped down on the bed. "Shoes?"

"I have some trainers." Dare motioned toward the bag near the end of the bed. "That silly girl wanted me to wear *slippers*."

Connor swallowed back a laugh and unzipped the bag. "It

would be easier on you later, but I'm more than willing to play Prince Charming for you."

"Wanker," Dare muttered.

Lauren hated coffee machines on general principle, so she'd made her way down to a coffee shop on the first floor of the hospital. It was contrary to the very strict instructions she'd been given when Connor had pushed her off the elevator on the maternity ward floor, but she figured she'd be back up before anyone was the wiser. Which made her current circumstances a little embarrassing. She'd never met Robert Stein, *but* she'd seen a ridiculously vain spread on him in a magazine earlier in the year.

The gun pressed into her side was something of an annoyance and a curiosity. He didn't hold it confidently, probably couldn't even hit the broad side of a barn, but she didn't doubt his ability to be lethal at such a close range. The walk out of the hospital was pretty quick, but he was far more careful than she would expect from an amateur. He didn't rush, didn't stumble, and made sure she didn't meet anyone's eye as they moved through the large lobby and toward the parking garage.

They were in the car before he even spoke to her. "Slide down. I don't want anyone to see you."

Lauren huffed but obligingly slid down in the seat. "This is a stupid thing to do."

"Just shut up," he spat. "This would have been over already if you hadn't started fucking that security guard. Christ, why the hell would you waste your time on a man like him?"

Lauren glared at Stein and turned her face away so she wouldn't have to look at the gun. Connor was going to be so pissed at her. She wasn't a stupid woman by any means, but she'd acted without thinking about the consequences, and for a man like Connor, that was a *sin*.

"You'd better hope that your code still works."

She considered telling him the painting wasn't in the town house anymore, but she needed to give Connor time to realize she was missing, to realize that she needed him. Stein had made a few stupid moves—he hadn't made her dump her purse, which meant she was still carrying the cell phone that the Foundation had given her. She figured it had a GPS locator in it but hadn't bothered to investigate it thoroughly. To avoid having him dump the purse and the phone, she didn't make any move to pull it out.

There wasn't a single fucking cop on the street, and Connor had apparently pulled the security team from the town house as well. It was a relief when the door opened easily with her code. She couldn't fool him on the security panel—the man had lived in the town house, so she didn't try to fuck up her code to alert security. Hopefully they'd be alerted that she was even entering the town house to begin with.

Stein snorted. "I see they redecorated for you."

"Wasn't much choice. The place was vandalized after you moved out. Someone ripped up the furniture and the walls." Lauren crossed her arms over her chest. "So, what do you want?"

"What do I want?" Stein demanded. He shoved her toward the basement door. "Let's go downstairs."

"There is nothing down there but the laundry room and that stupid safe room." She rubbed her shoulder and stumbled toward the door when he shoved her again. "You know, nowhere in your magazine interview did you bother to mention that you liked to hit women."

He glared at her and raised the gun. "Downstairs, right now."

The basement was cold but well lit. Stein shoved her toward the large silver door that led to the panic room, and her stomach clenched in anger. She felt so stupid for letting the situation happen at all. He hadn't tried to hide who he was, hadn't tried to bargain with her. No money had been offered. It was because he planned to kill her.

"Open it."

"No." Lauren took a few steps back from him and looked around the room for something she could use as a weapon.

He cocked the revolver far more confidently than she'd expected he'd be capable of. "Open the fucking door."

"No. You're going to kill me when I open it." Lauren shifted on her feet and glanced toward the stairs. Exactly how many minutes was she supposed to wait for rescue?

"If you don't open it, I'm going to kill you."

"Which means you won't ever get in to it," Lauren reasoned. "Think about this, Stein. You're screwed. You shouldn't have come back. The police are looking for you. They think you killed someone already. They found all of those guys you hired to do your work for you. I think they should charge you with criminally negligent laziness."

"Open the goddamned door!"

Lauren flinched and then took a deep breath at the sound of the front door security panel beeping. Stein shoved her abruptly away from the stairs just as the basement door opened and Connor came down the short flight of stairs.

"Don't move, Grant. I'll shoot this bitch. Don't test me."

Connor looked from Lauren to Stein as he made room for Mathias to finish coming down the stairs. "Did he touch you, lass?"

"I have a few bruises. He shoved me around a bit," Lauren admitted, and crossed her arms over her chest. "Sorry."

"Oh, we'll talk later," Connor promised darkly. He focused on Stein. "Do you want to live?"

Stein blinked in surprise, and his hand wavered a little. Lauren flinched because he still had that stupid gun pointed at her. "Yes."

"Then put down your gun. The police will be here shortly, and we can end this in a civilized manner."

"And if I don't? What if I just shoot her instead?"

"I'll kill you," Connor responded evenly. "I'm sure it would upset Boston's finest to come down here and find me covered in your blood, but it won't stop me from gutting you. If you want to survive, you'll put down your gun, because I won't hesitate to end you." He chambered a round, and Stein dropped to his knees. The revolver skidded across the floor when he threw it.

Lauren snorted her disgust and skirted around the man. She squeaked just a little when Connor grabbed her and jerked her close. "Okay, so your badassness is awesome."

"I'm going to spank your ass," Connor muttered against her hair, his gun still leveled at Stein.

"Do not talk about our sex life in front of him," Lauren hissed, and blushed when Mathias started laughing.

Mathias slid in front of Connor. "Take her upstairs and I'll keep Stein company while we wait for the cavalry."

"Don't trust me?" Connor asked.

Mathias shot him a look. "I trust you to want to do *exactly* what I'd want to do in your place. Take your lady upstairs and update Dare before he gets himself too excited and tears his stitches."

Connor figured that James Brooks was the best liar he'd ever met in his life. He watched the man calmly and without a single hesitation open the safe room door. A covered painting was leaning against the wall in the back.

He casually went in, picked it up, and sat it on a table in the middle of the basement. "It's a Monet," James offered as he cut the string and unwrapped it. "It's a gift for my wife."

"Your wife?" Detective Silven questioned. "How much is this painting worth?"

"I paid twenty-seven million for it," Brooks admitted with a tone so bored Connor almost laughed. Mouths dropped open around the room. "It's a present and an apology."

"A present for your wife," Silven repeated with a raised eyebrow. "How did Robert Stein know about the painting?"

"I'm not entirely sure," James said. "I did purchase it while he was in my employ, but I didn't put it in the safe room in the town house until after he was fired." James shrugged. "My wife has *spies,* gentlemen. I had to hide it to keep it a secret. As far as I knew, only the auction house where I bought it—and of course our security people—knew it was here. It's the reason we moved Ms. Evans as soon as we realized someone was trying to use her to gain entry to the town house."

"You never mentioned it," Silven said with a mild air of frustration he was vainly trying to bury.

James looked him over. "You didn't ask and Ms. Evans didn't know it was here. She probably would've tattled to my wife."

"A present and an apology?" Lauren questioned as she looked at the painting.

"Well, she just made me a father again. The apology part is for the twins thing." James winked at her. "We didn't plan for that."

Lauren grinned and carefully started wrapping the painting back up. "It's gorgeous. She'll be thrilled, and I'll endeavor to keep my mouth shut as to not ruin her surprise."

"That would be appreciated." James looked expectantly at the cops. "You'll, of course, be charging Mr. Stein for kidnapping or whatever legal term applies for his treatment of Ms. Evans today?"

"Yes, sir."

"Good." James passed the painting to Connor, who slid it into a large case for travel. "I'll be going home to my wife and children if we're finished."

Lauren sighed when Silven turned to her. "Can I come in tomorrow and make a statement? I mean, I'm sort of tired and bitchy at this point. I try not to be that way in public if I can help it."

Silven laughed and relaxed. "Yeah, first thing in the morning." He glanced toward Connor. "You, too. Stein said you threatened to gut him, by the way."

"I'll be sure to remember my exact words for my statement," Connor promised.

Lauren managed to hold in her questions until they were in the SUV on the way back to the farmhouse. "Where did he get the Monet?"

"He bought it six months ago. It really is a present for his wife." Connor shrugged. "We figured we might have to produce some kind of explanation, so we pulled it out of his office safe and put it in the safe room as a replacement."

"What if Stein confesses?"

"Stein has a four-hundred-dollar-an-hour lawyer and a lot to worry about. The less he says the better off he is, and he knows it. They'll try to pin him down for Dare's shooting and the murder. He sure as hell isn't going to admit he was trying to fence a fifty-million-dollar piece of art that was smuggled out of Iraq."

Lauren nodded and glanced out the window. "Are you going to spank me?"

He laughed softly. "No, because you'd like it too much. You scared the fuck out of me, Lauren." Connor picked up her hand and exhaled. "And I'm getting used to the idea that I might keep you."

Lauren flushed with pleasure and smiled. "Yeah, I'm okay with that."

"Yeah?" Connor shook his head. "You know, women are normally a little more forthright in discussing their feelings."

"Want me to tell you that when I was holding the babies this morning it made me want to have yours? Because it did—my biological clock went all *boom* and shit. I'm surprised you didn't hear it." Lauren rested back in her seat and looked out the window. "I have this rule about saying I love you before the six-week mark."

Connor grinned. "Good rule." He paused. "Six weeks from our first date or six weeks from our first sexual encounter?"

"Did we date?" Lauren demanded with a frown. "Because I think I missed that."

"Well, we had breakfast that one morning," Connor reminded her with a grin. "I think that counts."

Lauren huffed. She was pretty damn sure it didn't count at all, but it did add a few more days to their six-week mark. "Yeah, let's go with that breakfast."

"I thought you might agree." He brought her hand to his mouth and kissed it gently. "If you ever ditch my security guys again to feed your caffeine habit, I will berate you for a *decade*."

"I'd prefer a spanking," Lauren muttered.

"Exactly why you won't be getting it," Connor shot back. "You took years off my life. It's bad enough I fell in love with you against my will, but you keep trying to get yourself killed on top of it."

Lauren turned to stare at him and then laughed. "Against your will?"

"Well, you're definitely not in my ten-year plan. Though when I think on it, I don't know how on Earth I could've planned for you." He grinned when she frowned at him. "That's a compliment."

She lifted one eyebrow at him and looked him over. "I'm going to have to think about that for a while." Lauren exhaled and then turned to stare out the window.

"I'm a very patient man," Connor promised.

She grinned and rubbed her thumb over the top of his hand.

Connor sighed as Lauren sprawled out on the bed in front of him, her legs spread wantonly. He rolled on the condom and shifted on his knees to get comfortable. "I don't even know where to start."

She lifted one leg and brushed her toes over one of his nipples. "Just come down here and be my man."

"Yours," Connor repeated softly as he moved forward and settled on top of her, his cock brushing against the wet flesh of her pussy.

"All mine." She touched his face with shaking fingers. "If you break my heart, Mr. Grant, I'm going to make your life *miserable*."

"I'll keep your heart safe," he promised against her mouth. "I'll keep all of you safe." He shifted and slowly pressed his cock into her. Her eyes widened and darkened as she accepted his physical invasion with a soft sigh. "I love how you take me, lass."

Lauren slid her legs around his waist as he started to rock in and out of her. "God, Connor." She shuddered and arched as he pushed in deep and then stilled. "Fuck."

He lifted away slightly and braced himself with one arm so he could slide one hand between them. His fingers teased over her mound and dipped between the spread lips of her sex to tease at her clit. Lauren shuddered under the stimulation and clutched at the sheets beneath him as he started to move into her with strong, deep thrusts.

"Come for me," Connor ordered, his voice soft but demanding. "Come."

Lauren arched against his hand and trembled through an orgasm, startled by his demand and her ability to meet it. Connor ground against her, watching her eyes glaze over as pleasure surged and ebbed between them.

"So lovely," Connor whispered, and pressed soft kisses against her mouth and then down her jaw. He urged her hands over her head, and she obligingly curled them around the bars in the headboard. "Brace your feet on the mattress."

Lauren tightened her grip on the headboard and did as instructed with a soft, pleased sound. She strained up against him as he started to work his cock deep and hard into her. Connor clenched his teeth and sucked in a deep breath with every little needy movement of her body.

"Fuck me," Lauren demanded softly. "Please, Connor."

He buried his face briefly against her neck before lifting off her and pulling his cock from her body with a groan of frustration. "Get on your knees, lass."

Lauren pulled her legs up, wincing only slightly as she shifted to her knees. She turned around and laughed softly when he pulled her to him and kissed the back of her neck. She rested back against him when he cupped her breasts with both hands. He pinched her nipples mercilessly and bit down on her shoulder when she groaned.

"Brace yourself on the headboard," Connor murmured as he released her.

He picked up the tube of lube from the nightstand. Connor rubbed the small of her back in a small circle and uncapped the lube. "Have you had a man this way before?"

Lauren shifted backward against him and huffed a little. "Once—a few years ago."

"Did you enjoy it?"

"Not as much as I enjoy playing on my own," Lauren admitted. "He wasn't all that good at it."

Connor hummed under his breath and nudged her thighs farther apart. "You can trust that this will be a different experience."

Lauren laughed softly and shifted under his hands. She took a deep breath and forced herself to relax as he breached her ass with one slick finger. Her whole body clenched briefly in anticipation, and she rocked back against the invasion. "More."

"Greedy girl," Connor whispered as he added a second finger. "We're going to be the death of each other."

"Going out naked and screaming has so much appeal," Lauren whispered as she rocked back against his invading fingers. "Please."

"Relax, lass," Connor admonished, and leaned down to press a kiss against the small of her back. "Just relax, sweetheart. We have all night to get there."

Lauren grabbed one of the pillows and buried her face in it to keep from screaming in frustration as he slowly added a third finger. There was some small part of her that enjoyed the care he was taking with her, but mostly she was frustrated. She knew, however, that demonstrating that wouldn't get her what she wanted from him.

He added a little more lube and laughed softly when she wiggled her ass a little. "You're so pretty, lass."

"Eager, too."

"Yes, I took note of that," Connor murmured, and pulled his fingers from her.

Lauren glared at him over her shoulder and actually sighed with relief when she realized he was slicking up his cock. "No rushing you, huh?"

Connor smirked and casually stroked his cock. "Nah, not so much. You'll thank me tomorrow."

She'd like to thank him right now and certainly would if he would stop teasing her. Lauren shivered slightly as he pressed the head of his cock against her asshole and hissed as he pushed into her with one steady, relentless thrust.

"Jesus. Fuck."

Connor gripped her hips to keep her from moving. "Take it easy."

"Please." Lauren took a deep, shuddering breath, her voice catching in a soft sob.

Connor lifted her away from the headboard. "Brace yourself on my thighs, lass." He cupped her pussy with one big hand and pressed two fingers into her hole as he ground against her clit.

Slowly, he started to move, timing the strokes of his cock into her ass to match the deep but even breaths Lauren was taking. Her fingers bit into his thighs, nails scraping against his skin as he fucked her with his cock and his fingers.

Lauren arched against him, her body tightening around him as she fought her way through one intense climax only to tumble into another. She scrambled against him, seeking purchase and respite from the deepest pleasure she'd ever known in her life.

"Connor!"

"Easy, little one," he whispered against the back of her neck. "I've got you. Just relax and take it."

Her body dampened with sweat as he continued to push into her, and a chill ran over her skin as he pressed against her clit with the heel of his hand. "Fuck."

"That's my girl," Connor whispered as she relaxed against him. "So fucking gorgeous." He sucked in a deep breath and groaned when she clenched down on his cock. "You're going to make me come."

"Yes," Lauren whispered. "Come for me." Her fingers clenched on his thighs.

Connor groaned softly and fucked deep into her ass one

more time before he gave in to her demand. She turned her head and offered her mouth with a sigh. He pressed a series of kisses on her lips and then carefully pulled out.

Lauren collapsed onto the bed with a contented sigh as Connor left to dispose of the condom. "You're right. We're totally going to be the death of each other."

Connor snorted softly as he returned to the bed with a washcloth. He cleaned her thoroughly and then tossed the cloth aside in favor of climbing back into bed with her. Once she was settled against his chest and they were under a thin, cool sheet, he responded.

"I'm quite okay with that. I always kind of figured a woman would end me, anyway."

Lauren grinned and pressed a kiss against the center of his chest. "I fell in love with you against my will, too."

"Oh, yeah?"

"Yeah, I'm kind of pissed about it, but I figure it's not really your fault. You can't help being perfect for me."

Connor laughed and ran his fingers through her hair. "It was the hand sanitizer, right?"

Lauren laughed. "Shut up or I'm not going to be your green-card wife."

He pressed a kiss to her forehead. "You're the only green-card wife I could ever imagine wanting."

Lauren closed her eyes with a soft sigh. "It's romance like this that will see us through our golden years."

She screamed only a little when he flipped her over and crawled on top of her. Hell, she thought, sleep was really overrated, anyway.

Author's Note

The Concert, by Johannes Vermeer, was stolen from the Isabella Stewart Gardner Museum in Boston on March 18, 1990. Thirteen works of art were taken from the museum, including works by Édouard Manet and Rembrandt van Rijn. The works were worth an estimated $500 million; it remains the largest art theft in American history. The crime remains unsolved.

The Concert is considered to be the most valuable painting ever stolen. The original frame hangs empty in the Isabella Stewart Gardner Museum.

Turn the page
for a preview of
Tawny Taylor's
DARKEST FIRE.

On sale now!

1

Sin in stilettos hunted him.

In Drako Alexandre's lifetime, lust had worn many masks—fair and sweet, dark and exotic, male and female—but whatever form it took, it always, without fail, seized its prey. There was no escape. Yet, like the quail in Drako's favorite sutta, "The Hawk," Drako knew he would eventually break free from the predator's grip...and shatter its heart.

Tonight, the hunting ground was one of Drako's favorite haunts and lust was a redhead in an itty-bitty fuck-me dress, her mile-long legs bared to *there,* her full tits a sigh away from tumbling out of her dress, and a dozen erotic promises glittering in her eyes. She didn't know it yet, but the hunter would soon be the hunted.

Drako acknowledged her with a hard, piercing stare. In response, lush lips pursed in a seductive pout.

Yes, he'd have this one. But on his terms.

Let the games begin.

Eyes on the prize, expression guarded to keep her guessing, Drako tipped his beer back, pulling a mouthful of bitter ale from the bottle. As he swallowed, the heavy bass of the music thrummed through his body, pounding along nerves pulled tight with erotic need. Red and blue lights blinked on and off, casting everybody in the nightclub, male and female, in an alternating crimson and deep indigo glow.

Her gaze shifted.

His body tightened.

Oh, yeah. He liked this place. A lot. He slowly swept the crowded room again with his eyes. Writhing, sweaty bodies, mostly female, packed the small dance floor. Groups of people crowded around tables, the flickering red tips of their burning cigarettes dancing in the shadows.

"I've got the redhead," he announced.

"That's just as well." His brother, Talen, set his empty glass on the bar's polished top and shoved his fingers through his spiked platinum hair. "I'm not in the mood for this tonight."

"Not in the mood? Are you kidding me? Look around, baby brother." Sitting on the other side of Drako, Malek shot Talen a bewildered glance. About a dozen women gaped as his shaggy blond surfer-punk waves danced on a breeze.

Drako slid his quarry, a heated glance, then twisted to flag down the bartender. "Yeah, well, if you spent half as much time working as you do playing, Malek, we'd—"

"Yeah, yeah, I've heard it before, big brother." Malek ordered another beer for Drako, then clapped him on the shoulder. "But like I say, life is short. You gotta live while you can." He slipped from the stool, peeled off a twenty, and handed it to the bartender. "Do either of you have a bad feeling about tomorrow's meeting with the old man...?" Malek stood a little taller, tipped up his chin. "Ohhhh, yes. Talk to you later." Not waiting for them to answer his question, he headed toward the nearest flock of admirers.

"I think I'm calling it a night," Talen said, watching Malek gather a small herd of women around him.

"Okay, bro. See you at home." Drako checked his redhead again. She was still sitting at the table with her friend, but she was looking a little less certain of herself now. One hand was wrapped around a wineglass, the other nervously tugged at a lock of hair.

That was better. An aggressive woman did nothing for him.

Letting the corners of his mouth curl slightly, he lifted his fresh beer to his mouth and waited for their gazes to meet again.

Uh-huh. Much, much better.

He held her gaze, and everyone and everything else in the crowded bar seemed to slowly drift away, until nobody but his redhead existed to him. Electricity sizzled between their bodies, like lightning arcing between storm clouds.

Her tongue darted out, swept across her plump lip, then slipped back inside. She set her glass down and, breaking eye contact, leaned over to her friend sitting next to her. They both glanced his way. The friend smiled and nodded, and then the pair of them stood.

Their arms linked at the elbow, their gazes flitting back and forth between him and the back of the bar, they hurried in the opposite direction, toward the bathroom.

That was an interesting reaction. Nothing like what he'd expected. Was she playing him? Were they both?

Mmmm. Both. Maybe he'd have two women tonight. Two was always better than one.

He dropped a fifty on the bar. And with his beer clutched in one fist, he walked around the far side of the room, taking the scenic route to the dark corridor at the rear. He'd catch them out there, where it was quieter, more intimate.

His timing was perfect. Just as he rounded the corner, they clacked out of the bathroom on a breeze of sweetly perfumed air. They halted instantly, eyes widening, one pair a soft gray-blue, the other a deep brown.

Up close, the redhead lost a little of her charm. It was her friend who demanded his attention now. Her features were different—her almond-shaped eyes tipped up at the outer corners, the uncreased eyelids hinting at her Asian ancestry. Her full lips were plump and freshly coated in shimmering gloss. Her carefully applied makeup emphasized a set of picture-perfect cheekbones, and her slightly mussed hairstyle lengthened a slender neck, a tumble of silky blue-black waves cascading over her shoulders.

He'd seen her before. Where?

"Hi," the redhead said, her voice a deep and sultry siren's call.

He turned toward her again, catching once more the sensual promise glimmering in her cool blue gaze. Despite the invitation he read on her face—or maybe because of it—he found himself tiring of her already. His attention snapped back to the quiet woman next to him. An old David Bowie song, "China Girl," echoed in his head. "I know this is the world's worst line, but don't I know you from somewhere?"

"I'm not sure." His China Girl stared at the tattoo on his neck, following the curved line up to his jaw. "I think I recognize the tattoo."

"My brothers and I have the identical design, a griffin. It's kind of a family thing. Our mother did the work."

"Your mother? How interesting." The redhead inched closer to get a better look, or so he assumed. "It's very sexy. I'm not crazy about tattoos, at least not most of the ones I've seen. This one's very different. All black and gray and sorta...what's the word I'm looking for?"

"Celtic?" the brunette offered.

That brunette was spot-on. Their mother had been 100 percent Irish. There could never be any doubt, with her mane of copper-colored hair and freckles. And the design she'd created for her three sons was as Irish as her maiden name, O'Sullivan.

The redhead scowled. "No, that's not it. I mean, yeah, it is Celtic, but that's not what I'm trying to say. Men with tattoos are a little...dangerous."

"Wicked." Something darkened the brunette's expression.

"Yes, wicked." The redhead's white teeth sank into her lower lip. "That's a good word."

Yeah, that was a good word.

He was feeling a little wicked something going on. And he could tell at least one woman was feeling it too. "Can I buy you ladies a drink?"

"Actually"—the brunette shot the redhead a nervous glance— "we were getting ready to leave—"

"But one more drink wouldn't hurt," the redhead finished, slanting a smile his way. "Thank you. By the way, my name's Andi and this is Rin."

"Good to meet you, Andi and Rin. I'm Drako. Let's find a table." He motioned for them to precede him out of the dark corridor. He followed them back into the crowded heat of the bar. As they shuffled and wound their way through the throng, his gaze meandered down the back of Rin's body, from the bouncing curls that tumbled down her back to a nicely rounded ass hugged in a snug black skirt. When she stopped to let a couple pass by, he leaned over her shoulder and whispered, "Maybe we can figure out where we've seen each other before."

A delicate fragrance drifted to his nose. Jasmine. It was refreshing compared to the cloying blend of cigarette smoke and cheap cologne hanging heavy in the air and making his nose burn.

"Sure. Maybe." She hurried around a couple clawing at each other like bears in heat.

He smiled at her expression as she shuffled past them, her lips parting, cheeks flushing a pretty pink.

Damn, this was a hot place, in more ways than one. It sure put him in the mood to fuck, with all the gyrating bodies and hard, thumping music. A song he recognized started playing, a slow, sexy number, and taking advantage of the moment, he caught Rin's slender wrist.

She glanced over her shoulder.

"Dance with me." He didn't wait for her to respond, just tugged her gently until her body was flush with his. He looped one arm around her back, splaying his fingers over the base of her spine. He felt her stiffen against him, then relax.

She was petite, the top of her head hitting his chest at about nipple level. He liked how small and fragile she felt in his arms, how her little body fit against his.

And how she worked those hips of hers. Damn.

Sparks of erotic hunger zapped and sizzled through his body with every sway. He tucked his leg between hers and rocked his hips from side to side, melting at the feeling of her hips working perfectly with his. Her feminine curves conformed to his hard angles as she pressed tighter against him. He cupped her chin and lifted, coaxing her to look at him, to let him see that beautiful face, to maybe taste her lush mouth.

A second female body crowded against him from behind. A woman's hands glided down his tight thighs. Breasts flattened against his back. Within a second, his prick was hard enough to bust through brick, his balls tight, his blood burning like acid.

Rin's eyes lifted to his, and her lips parted in a natural pout, so different from the practiced expression her friend had donned for him.

That was it; he had to kiss her.

He tipped his head, his entire body tight and hard and ready. But just before his mouth claimed hers, she lurched away. He opened his eyes to catch the redhead slipping into her place as the music changed.

He twisted to find his delicate Rin, but she'd disappeared into the crowd.

"She's my friend," Andi shouted over the music as she undulated against him. "I won't say anything bad about her. But she's just not into this. She's so shy. Sorry." She smoothed her hands up his torso.

He was sorry too.

There was something about her. A quiet sensuality that didn't need to be forced. He hadn't been that intrigued by a woman in a long time. "No need to apologize for her."

"I'm guessing you like your women a little less aggressive?"

"Yeah."

"Got it." Her expression softened. "If you want to be the predator, I can be the prey. Let's play." Giggling, Andi slipped out of his arms and dashed into the crowd.

Now this was getting interesting.

Rin all but forgotten, he set out to hunt down his redheaded quarry in the black fuck-me dress.

Hunter. Prey. It looked like both of them would get what they were after tonight.

The next morning, Drako headed down to the library with a satisfied smile on his face and memories of one lush redhead strapped spread-eagle on his Saint Andrew's Cross.

Damn, that had been one of the best nights he'd had in a long time. Andi wasn't just a slut; she was a pain slut. The more he gave her, the more she begged. And that insatiability had applied to *everything*.

By the time they were through, both his single-tail whip and his cock had gotten a thorough workout.

He'd sent her home less than an hour ago, had taken a shower to wash away the lingering scents of sex from his skin, and was ready to face whatever news their father was about to deliver.

Whatever it was, Drako knew it would be major. The old man had said his good-byes ten years ago, after his brothers and his wife had been buried. He hadn't called, written, or even e-mailed his three sons since. Not that any of them could blame him. He'd paid his dues; he'd earned his freedom. Someday, they'd earn theirs too.

Until then, duty was duty. It wasn't like they had it bad.

When he entered the room, he found the old man sitting behind the desk—the one Drako considered his—hands clasped, waiting, silent, gaze sharp. It was damn good to see that face.

Malek was slumped in a chair next to the fireplace, looking like he'd had a long night—which he probably had. Talen was looking bright-eyed and alert, no doubt because he'd turned in early, like usual.

Drako knew he looked like Talen, but inside he felt like Malek. Dead-dog tired.

The old man lifted his cool gray eyes to Drako and cleared his throat. "We can begin."

"Sorry I'm late." Drako snagged the closest seat and braced himself for what was coming.

Their father stood, hands on the desktop. "All three of you men know how vital your duty is. You've served well, protecting The Secret faithfully since my brothers and I stepped down over ten years ago. For that, you have earned my respect." He straightened up, crossing his arms over his chest. "But now it's time to prepare for the future." His assessing gaze turned to Drako. "Son, you're my oldest. The leader of your generation of Black Gryffons. You've proven to be an excellent leader—fearless, loyal, responsible, and yet sensitive. I admire the man you've become."

Drako didn't know how to respond to his father's words. It had been a decade since the old man had paid him any compliment, let alone one so great. "As I admire you, Father. You set a fine example, as the firstborn of your generation."

The old man smiled. After a beat, he said, "You've just celebrated your thirty-first birthday. In order to assure your retirement by your fiftieth, all three of you must father sons within the next twelve months. Which means you must take wives. Immediately."

Wives. Children.

Drako had understood this day would come, since shortly after taking his father's place as the leader of the Black Gryffons. Thus, he'd accepted it long ago. It was their fate, their duty, their honor.

But, gauging from Malek's barely stifled groan, at least one of his younger siblings hadn't been mentally prepared for the responsibility of wife and child yet.

"*Must* we all take a bride?" Malek asked. "If Drako conceives three sons, there would be no need for the rest of us to father children."

"Of course," their father said. "There's no guarantee he'll produce one, let alone three."

Malek's shoulders sank a tiny bit. "Okay, but today, marriage and children don't always have to come hand in hand—"

"No bastard child will ever be a Black Gryffon." Their father shook his head. "That's the law."

"I think the law's antiquated," Malek grumbled.

"Doesn't matter what we think." Drako stood, giving his scowling younger sibling a clap on the shoulder. "So what? You have to take a wife. It's not the end of the world."

"Depends on your perspective."

"Hey." Drako glanced at his father. "There's no law that says we have to be monogamous, right? I mean, if our wives know beforehand that we have no intention of limiting ourselves to having sex with just them, then we're good, right?"

Their father shrugged, his eyes glimmering with an unexpectedly playful sparkle. "If you can find yourselves wives who are willing to live with that kind of arrangement, then more power to you. Your mother wouldn't. It was hell, giving up certain things, but I could never deny that woman anything." He sighed. "There are some sacrifices that are worth making."

"I hear you," Drako said, knowing fully well what kind of agony it had to have been. "Discomfort" was an understatement, but he respected the old man, more than he could ever say, for his commitment to their mother. Since at least the early eighteenth century every Black Gryffon had practiced some form of D/s, and many of them had taken multiple lovers. His father had done neither.

In the silent moment that followed, Drako studied the man he had emulated his entire life. The old man's once-dark brown hair was now all silver, and lines fanned from the corners of his eyes, but otherwise in Drako's eyes this man would always be the powerful guardian leader he had respected and admired. His father's body was still heavily muscled, his mind as sharp as a blade. Drako guessed retirement hadn't slowed him down a bit.

Only the deep shadow in the old man's eyes hinted at how close he was to passing from their world to the next.

"I miss her, son," their father said. "Your mother loved like nobody I've ever known. The last ten years have been so empty without her."

Drako touched the side of his neck. He could almost swear his tattoo—which had been, ironically, his mother's final gift to him before she died—was tingling "I miss her too." Knowing somehow this would be the last time he'd see his father alive, Drako gave the old man a hug, then watched as his brothers did the same. It wouldn't be much longer, he guessed, before their father would be reunited with the woman he missed so dearly.

Their father left with a final wave and a smile, and Drako shoved aside the deep sorrow tugging at his heart and forced his mind to the next task he faced as leader of the Black Gryffons.

It was his duty to help his brothers find brides, women who would be willing to live with husbands who, in Malek's case, wouldn't be faithful and, who would, in Drako's case, accept his lifestyle. It had to be this way, even if it meant it would take longer to find the right brides.

He had to be honest with his future wife, and he expected his brothers to do the same. He would never be able to live with the guilt of hiding the truth. The pain those secrets would cause.

His wife. His bride. Who would she be?

It was a matter of choosing the right woman. A special woman.

A certain set of deep brown-black eyes and sculpted cheekbones flashed in his mind, and it was then that he remembered where he'd first seen his quiet little Rin.

It couldn't be. But it was.

The supposedly shy Rin wasn't who her friend believed. Quite the opposite.

His lips curled into a smile and his heavy heart lifted.

He knew exactly where to find his bride. Rin was one very special woman, and he had a good feeling she'd be willing to listen to his proposal.

In general, people tried too hard to simplify issues. Life wasn't comprised only of black, white, sane, insane, good, bad. There were an infinite number of shades of gray in between.

He had gone to great lengths to find people who saw a full spectrum of gray in the world. Only they could appreciate him, could share his vision.

Someday, every man, woman, and child on the earth would thank him. They would finally appreciate the truth he'd tried to share with them so many times. The simplemindedness that had blinded them wouldn't matter anymore. The truth would be too big and dazzling to deny.

That someday would be soon.

Smiling, he signed the document, ending his voluntary stay at the hospital. He gathered his prescriptions and personal possessions and stepped out into the warm, sunny day. The antipsychotic medication left his mind a little fogged and suppressed his emotions, but even with a full dose of Haldol still coursing through his bloodstream, he was ready.

So much work to do, so little time to do it.

A sleek black Mercedes-Benz crawled down the driveway and rolled to a stop in front of the hospital's entry. He waited, unsure whether it was his ride or not. The window rolled down, and a hand waved at him.

When he approached, the passenger handed him a card with no name, no phone number, only a gray-scale image of a chimera.

"Enter," the passenger said, his or her head turned so he couldn't see the face.

Without questioning the passenger or the driver, he got in the car.

2

"Fifty thousand."

Rin Mitchell's heart slammed to her toes.

Fifty thousand. Those two words echoed in her ears as she stared at the scumbag sitting across from her, sipping coffee in the cheerful Coney Island restaurant.

Why so much? Dammit!

She'd known the price would be high, maybe as much as ten thousand dollars. She'd managed to scrape together almost half that much by starving herself, living in a dump, working in a pit, and selling her car.

But fifty thousand? Why?

There hadn't been any of the normal expenses associated with smuggling a sex slave across an ocean or over international borders. Rin's sister Lei had been born and raised in the United States. And although Lei was pretty, and exotic—she was half-Japanese and therefore could work in brothels catering to men who liked Asian women—Rin saw no reason why she'd command such an unbelievable price.

Fifty thousand was unreasonable.

Impossible.

"Your price is too high." Rin shook her head, trying her best to hide the sense of defeat eating away at her confidence. The image of Lei's hollow-eyed stare flashed through Rin's mind. She had to buy Lei's freedom, whatever the price.

Five thousand. Ten thousand. Whatever. It was worth every penny if it meant her shy, innocent sister would be released. She could only imagine what kind of hell Lei had already lived through. Their mother had sold Lei into slavery over twelve months ago, then lied and told Rin she'd been kidnapped. When Rin had learned the truth, she'd vomited in the middle of the kitchen and then spit in their mother's face.

How could she do such a thing? To her own child? And who would have ever guessed that a young woman could be sold into slavery? In the twenty-first century. And in the United States.

What made it that much harder to swallow was the pittance the bastard had paid. No human being was worth so little. Not even the woman who'd sold her child into slavery.

"Too high?" The man poured some more cream into his coffee, stirred it, and lifted it to his mouth for another sip. "Name your price, and perhaps we can come to an agreement."

Holding her breath, she locked her gaze to his. "Ten thousand."

"You insult me." He set down his coffee cup and leaned closer. "She is priced fairly. That girl is very special, and you know it. For ten thousand, you can go buy yourself a common whore." He stood, turned away, and headed toward the door.

"No, wait!" Rin could hardly believe months of hard, disgusting, demeaning work had led to this. Months of starving herself. Sacrificing everything.

For what? Failure? No!

Trying not to cause a scene, she hurried to her feet and followed the man to the restaurant's exit. He pulled open the door, but she caught his wrist before he left the building. In her peripheral vision she watched the waitress dashing over to a coworker and thrusting a finger toward the door, no doubt thinking she was running out on the check.

"Please," she whispered, waving at the waitress. "Fifty thousand dollars is a lot of money. Give me a week."

"A day is all I can wait."

"Five days. Please. I'll get the money. Somehow."

His gaze slid down to her hand, still gripping his wrist. "Three days."

She unfurled her fingers. "Okay. Three."

"Call me when you have the money."

Defeated and desperate, Rin nodded and watched the bastard walk away. Calling him every name in the book, she rushed back to the table, slapped down a ten-dollar bill, and headed back outside. The second the door swung shut behind her, the dam broke loose and the pent-up tears burst from her throat in painful sobs.

This was so freaking unfair.

The average person would probably tell her to go to the police. But she'd done that the minute she'd learned her sister had been sold, and they'd given her no help.

A month later, she decided she'd have to search for her sister herself. Over the months, as she travelled through some of the most god-awful places in the United States, she'd learned a few things. First, that the sex slave industry was huge business. Second, that sex slave traders were slick and had more connections than she'd ever have guessed. And third, that they protected their property fiercely and hid their identities behind successful-business-owner masks.

Twice, she went to the police after she'd located her sister—

in New York and Chicago—and twice her captors smuggled her away again.

Going to the police meant certain failure.

She was so close, once again, and now nothing.

No doubt, after this meeting, Lei would be moved again.

Fifty thousand dollars.

That was the price she would have to pay for her sister's freedom. Fifty freaking thousand. It might as well be a million. Ten million. Where could she get that kind of money? Where? How?

A scream of frustration sat at the back of her throat. Rin swallowed hard, over and over, struggling to keep it from sliding over her tongue and through her lips as she made the long walk home.

To think she had to work tonight too. Even though she wasn't a masseuse—thank God!—she was not in the mood to deal with a bunch of leering suburbanites buying sensual massages. Buying sex.

Call her jaded, but it seemed there was a price attached to everything nowadays. Sex. People. Morals. Power. Freedom. You name it.

Her pessimistic mood followed her home, accompanied her through her getting-ready-for-work ritual, and shadowed her as she walked to work, growing heavier and darker as she turned toward the massage parlor's grimy back door.

She'd hated every minute she'd spent in this building. Every second. But knowing she was getting closer to finding Lei, to freeing her, had made it at least tolerable. But now, she felt Lei slipping from her grasp, her hopes slowly evaporating. Her stomach turned at even the thought of spending five minutes in the filthy dump.

The men and their hungry eyes and grabby hands.

She shuddered and nearly gagged. There was no way she could do this. None.

Doing a one-eighty, she headed back outside, into the trash-strewn alley. Hoping no one inside had seen her yet, she hurried back around the side of the building, her head down, her gaze fixed on the littered sidewalk. Up ahead, a pair of men's feet were approaching. Probably a customer. Walking, she slowly lifted her gaze while stepping to the side so he could pass.

No. She halted midstride, and her heart practically jumped up her throat.

It was *him.* The guy from the bar. And the only man she'd ever seen at Magic Touch Massage that she might actually be tempted to do something with—other than rub his back.

Drako. Drako Alexandre. He was a man no girl could forget. Especially after that dance last night.

Instantly, memories of his hands gliding over her skin filled her mind. Her face burned hot. Her nerves sizzled and zapped. At the same time, a chill prickled her nape.

It couldn't be a coincidence that he was here now. He recognized her last night. Obviously, it had simply taken him a while to remember where he'd seen her.

He smiled as he moved closer. The expression was as friendly as it got, coming from a man so large and darkly sexy. "Hello, Rin." He stopped within reaching distance. "Are you heading into work? Or leaving?"

Nervous, she glanced over her shoulder. "Um, leaving."

"Good. Care to get some coffee with me?" His hand slid under her elbow, and his fingers curled around it, tugging gently.

"Actually, I…" *What? Need to get home to plan a bank robbery?*

"There's something important I want to talk to you about." He tipped his head and gave her arm another little pull.

Talk to me? Important?

She stood there for a second, until her curiosity got the better of her. *Important?*

She gave him a quick up-and-down glance, then concentrated on his face. Such a stunning face it was too. All sharp angles and hard planes. He wasn't a pretty man; he was magnificent. His features were formed like a man's should be, his body thick and hard and powerful.

And looking at his clothes, their fit, their quality. His shoes. If they were any indicator, he wasn't just financially comfortable, he was rich.

What did he want?

Unlike last night, the guy wasn't looking like 100 percent predator-on-the-prowl. More like 50 percent. The other half of him appeared to be just a man who wanted to talk to her. A man who wasn't out to hurt her, or take advantage of her, or throw some lame line at her to get into her pants. Only sit down and share a cup of coffee.

And talk. About *something important.*

"Okay, let's go talk." She let him lead her back down the street. They had to walk a couple blocks to find the nearest restaurant, past dilapidated brick buildings housing tattoo parlors and party stores. As she walked beside him, her curiosity grew. Her imagination ran wild, drumming up one bizarre scenario after another to explain why he'd tracked her down and what he wanted to talk about. Most of them revolved around her friend Andi.

Finally, they reached the restaurant, a greasy mom-and-pop diner. A cowbell clanked over her head as they entered. *Charming.* Her nose burned with the oily odor of fried meat and the cloying stench of cigarette smoke. Her escort led her to a booth in the back, resting a hand on the tattered, red vinyl-covered seat. "This isn't my first choice of places. I'd rather go somewhere else—"

"It's fine." She slid into the booth and watched him take a seat across from her.

The waitress, a tired-looking woman with her silver hair scraped flat against her skull and knotted into a tight ball at the back of her head, shuffled over, took their orders, and left.

"So...?" Rin curled her paper napkin around her fork, wondering what a man like Drako could want with someone like her. This never happened—a rich, powerful man from the right side of the tracks hunting her down and asking her out on some kind of pseudodate.

Granted, she was decent to look at. And she was far from a dummy. And if things had been different, a guy like Drako might have been interested in dating her. But they weren't. Not yet.

Someday they would be, she hoped.

She'd had a very humble start in life, but she'd worked hard to drag herself out of the gutter. She'd waitressed and phone-solicited her way through four years of college and two years of grad school. But he didn't know that. All he knew was that she worked at the massage parlor his brother frequented. One that was known for illicit activity.

A couple of times, Drako had come inside with Malek. But he'd always declined a massage. Another reason to admire him.

Finally, when he didn't say anything, she glanced his way.

He was staring out the grime-streaked window, a muscle in his jaw clenched so tightly it looked like it might snap.

Was he angry? No. Couldn't be.

He visibly inhaled. Exhaled. His gaze jerked to her face. His ears reddened.

Ohmygod, was he nervous?

Now, more than ever, she wanted to know why he'd come looking for her.

He cleared his throat.

The waitress returned, carrying a cup of coffee for him and a glass of diet cola for her. He thanked the waitress, asked Rin if she wanted anything else, and then scooped up a handful of sugar packets and emptied them into his coffee.

"Like a little coffee with your sugar?" she teased, watching him tear open a couple more.

One side of his mouth lifted into a lopsided smile that nearly stopped her heart. "I have a sweet tooth."

"I see that."

He stirred, the spoon clanking against the ceramic. "Thanks for coming."

"Sure." She took a sip of her cola. Lukewarm and watered down, just the way she liked it—*not*. "You said you wanted to talk to me about something?"

"Yes, I did." He curled his hands around either side of his cup. He had nice hands. Long, tapered fingers. Neatly trimmed fingernails. A little spark of heat buzzed up her spine at the memory of those hands, touching, holding her. Arms pulling her close. Music thrumming. Bodies swaying. Nice memory. "I wanted to discuss a proposition with you."

Proposition. Her mood dimmed, all thoughts of dancing fled her mind. That word called one particular activity to mind—sex. He thought she was a whore, a semilogical deduction, considering where she worked. But if he wanted to buy sex, why was he going to so much trouble? Why not just head down to the massage parlor, like his brother did?

She wanted to get up and walk out, to let him know she was not for sale, and then suggest he take his *proposition* to Magic Touch and offer it to one of the girls who wouldn't be insulted.

But something made her say, "What kind of 'proposition'?" instead.

His expression changed, and some emotion she couldn't name flashed in his eyes. "Actually, it's more of a proposal. One that involves marriage."

It took at least a heartbeat or two for his words to register in her head. Her hands flew to her mouth, slamming over it just as an expletive of disbelief tumbled over her tongue.

What the hell? Marriage? No. This was a joke. A bizarre, sick prank.

Finally, she trusted herself not to say something rude or embarrassing—for some reason, she wasn't ready to tell Drako to fuck off yet. "You're asking me to *marry* you?" she asked, exaggerating the disbelief in her voice. "Marry? As in church, flowers, dresses, veils. *Vows?*"

"Yes, marry. Vows, sure."

"You? A guy who could have any woman you want?"

Dammit, she thought he was an idiot. Or desperate. Or both. He wasn't either.

Before his intriguing Rin could shoot him down, he fought to explain, "Yes, me. I know this isn't the way things normally go between a man and a woman, but I just thought..." What? That she was desperate, since she fucked men for money. For very little money, as he had been told.

He couldn't say that. She'd probably cry.

"Thought what?" she shot back, scowling.

He sighed, shoved his fingers through his hair and looked at her. What an ass he was making of himself. It was easy hooking up with a woman. He had that routine down pat. But this was new territory. He wasn't looking for a quick fuck. This woman was going to be his wife. He couldn't be his usual guy-on-the-hunt self. Dammit, he didn't know how to be anything else with a woman. "Look. I'm the last guy who should judge anyone. I'll admit, I've fucked more women than I can count. But you and I both know what you so-called masseuses do in Magic Touch for your money. You're not giving therapeutic massages."

Her mouth tightened and she turned away from him.

Shit! He'd hurt her feelings.

He swallowed a growl of frustration. It wasn't supposed to go this way. She was supposed to be squealing with glee, her little arms wrapped around his neck, and those lovely eyes filled with tears of joy.

All the way into the city, he'd told himself how easy this would be. Rin—as lovely as she was—was a sex worker. Thanks to his brother, who lacked principles and thus had friends in low places, he'd met many sex workers. Dancers. Prostitutes. Actresses in adult films. He may not know any of them intimately, but he knew one thing—to a sex worker, everything had a price, even her body. Especially her body.

Rin should be glad to walk away from the life she had now. She couldn't love it, right?

Right. Rin was just doing a job because she had to.

Like all the others, she'd found herself trapped in a life she despised. She didn't know how to get herself out. Whether she'd admit it or not, she needed the kind of opportunity he was about to offer. Yes, she did.

All he had to do to convince her to accept his proposal was tell her how great she'd have it with him—tell her about the money, the clothes, the shoes, the lifestyle—and she'd gladly kiss that life good-bye and scamper down the aisle with him.

He just had to determine what her price was. No problem. Cash talked, he reminded himself.

He reached into his pocket, pulled out his wallet, and lifted out a Grover Cleveland. Because he used cash only, for everything, he always had a pocket full of large-currency bills. He quietly laid the thousand-dollar bill on the table in front of her.

She glanced down. Her eyes narrowed to slits. Her pretty lips thinned even more. But she didn't shove the money away. Or cuss him out for making any presumptions. Nor did she snatch it up and stuff it in her pocket either. She didn't make any move.

Weighing her options.

Maybe he needed to sweeten the deal.

Dipping into his wallet again, he pulled out a second Cleveland. He set it on top of the first.

Still nothing from her.

He added a third, fourth, and fifth.

Finally, she looked at him. "Why do you need to buy a wife, Drako? Maybe years ago men like you would buy a wife. But anymore? Come on. Guys with money buy whores and collect trophy wives."

Drako slid his wallet back into his pocket. "I won't disagree with that—for the average guy like me." Hell, if it weren't for the fact that his duty as a Black Gryffon called for him taking a wife for more reasons than appearances, he would've found himself a woman who was content to call herself his wife in public while living separate lives in private. "But my situation is a little unique."

"Unique? How?"

They were straying from the topic at hand. And more than ever, he was determined to convince her to accept.

She was lovely. Delicate and small. Her voice was sweet and smooth. He sensed a spark of intelligence. And the memories of their dance made him hard and tight. He pulled out his wallet again, added another thousand dollar bill to the pile. On top of that, he placed a ring box and lifted the lid.

Her eyes flared with some unreadable emotion as they tracked his movements.

"You'll have a very good life. A nice home. Clothes. Jewelry. Art. A very generous sum of money to spend any way you like. As my wife, you'll have every comfort you can imagine."

After a beat she asked, "How generous?"

Yes, even this stubborn beauty had her price. Now, he felt like he was on solid footing. Negotiating a deal, he could handle. Tiptoeing through a woman's emotional minefield was an entirely different matter.

He measured her reaction to the money, the ring. She hadn't reacted as he'd hoped, leading him to believe she might have very high expectations. Her manner of speaking, the way she carried herself, and her cool demeanor spoke of culture and refinement she shouldn't possess. "Twenty thousand a month."

Her eyes revealed nothing. "What's the catch? There's always something. What do you expect from a wife you'd buy versus one you'd meet, fall in love with, and then marry?"

He felt the smile spread over his face, "See, that's just it. If I wanted love from a wife, I wouldn't need to buy one."

"No love?"

"No love."

"Can I ask, why?"

Shit, he'd hoped she wouldn't ask that question. "Well, because I'm trying to avoid some very serious complications in my life."

She set her elbows on the table and plunked her chin on her fists. "So, you've had some bad experiences?"

"Yes and no."

Rin placed one hand on his. "I'm not judging you. I'm just trying to understand."

Feeling like things weren't going the way he'd hoped, and anxious to get the conversation back on track, he searched for the right words. "I've watched men fall in love and then fall apart. I can't allow myself to be weak. Too many people count on me."

"I think I understand." She stared down at the ring. "Kind of." She touched the stone, a brief, hesitant contact with one fingertip. "Will there be sex?"

"Yes. That would be part of the marriage."

"Children?"

"Most definitely. That's the most important reason for my taking a wife."

"But no love. Not ever."

"Not ever. I can't let myself fall in love. I won't. I'm trying to be honest, lay everything on the table upfront." He slid the stack of bills closer to her. "And it may go without saying, but I don't want any misunderstandings. Divorce is not an option. So, now you understand why I'd rather buy a wife than find one by more traditional methods. I want my wife to understand and accept my limitations ahead of time. It's my hope you can approach our marriage like a business partnership, or a friendship, rather than an emotion-driven relationship. That's not to say there won't be some tender feelings. Respect. Admiration. Loyalty. Even affection."

"I see. Will you be...?" She sipped her cola and set down her glass. "Will you still go to the dungeons? Do the bondage stuff?" After a beat, she added, "My friend Andi told me."

"Yes, I will," he answered, making sure to keep his voice free of any guilt or apology. "D/s is a part of who I am. But if it's not something you're interested in, I respect that. I would never ask you to do anything just for me, my pleasure."

"Then you'll do those things with someone else?"

"Yes. But I promise I won't have intercourse with another partner. I won't put your health or mine in jeopardy. My activities in the dungeon will be strictly nonsexual."

Again, he could read nothing in her eyes.

"I need time. To think. One day?"

He nodded. "One day. Should we meet here?"

"No. This is the worst dump ever. There's a nicer restaurant on Main and Seventh. Riley's. How about we meet there tomorrow at noon?"

"Tomorrow at twelve o'clock, at Riley's." As he watched her stand, he palmed the ring box, then pushed the money toward her. "This is yours to keep, regardless of your decision."

This time, as her eyes met his, he did read something in them, something that looked a lot like gratitude.

"Okay." She gathered the bills into her fist and tucked them into her purse.

Confident he'd found his bride, he smiled. "I hope next time you'll let me buy you a meal."

For the first time in a long, tense stretch, she returned his smile. "I'll think about it."

He'd just walked out. Nobody had stopped him; nobody had known they needed to. According to the United States Constitution John Dale Oram, head of a clandestine group called the Chimera, had every right to sign those papers, releasing himself from the hospital. For the past ten years, he'd been in and out of halfway houses and hospitals, but he'd never been violent, never hurt anyone. His diagnosis: hebephrenic schizophrenia. Just a month ago, he'd voluntarily committed himself again, but his "condition" was under control. And he was no longer viewed as a threat to himself or others.

Drako knew better.

Oram wasn't delusional and his thoughts were far from disorganized. He was calculating, intelligent, and his seeming preoccupation with religion and philosophy had a purpose.

Nobody suspected the truth.

Oram was a bigger danger than anyone had ever guessed—not to himself, not to a few people, but to millions.

Drako had put out a call to a few close friends, hoping he'd get a bead on the man, but Drako had found out too late that Oram had checked out. Within minutes of being released, the man, and the vehicle he'd left in, had vanished.

The timing of Oram's vanishing act was too convenient to be accidental.

Within moments of learning his father had taken his last breath, Drako had been told that the man his father had nearly executed was out walking the streets, the shroud of a fake psychiatric condition cast aside.

When his brothers entered the library, Drako didn't wait to tell them the news. He started with, "Father's dead," and ended with, "Oram's on the move and he already shook our tail."

Malek was the first of the two to find his tongue. "Damn."

Talen shook his head. "I knew it would be soon, but...shit. I'll miss him."

"Me too." Standing at his desk, Drako flattened his hands on the top and leaned forward. "Unfortunately, there's no time for grieving. It'll be a quick burial. Nothing complicated. And for obvious reasons, we can't attend. We've got to keep focused; it's our duty." Drako straightened. "Oram has had ten years to plan for today. We have to be ready, to be aware of everyone and everything around us. He doesn't know what we look like or our aliases. And he might not know how to find us yet, but already it's obvious he's been using the time wisely. If he launches an attack before we're ready, we're fucked."

"And so is most of humanity," Talen added.

"Yeah," Drako and Malek agreed.

The three shared a silent moment, a thought, a prayer, for

their father's peace. None of them said it, but Drako imagined they all thought it, he was finally with their mother again, in a better place.

When his brothers both met his gaze, letting him know they were ready to move on, Drako pulled a file from his drawer. "We need eyes and ears. But we need to be careful who we hire. We don't want to risk tipping off the enemy." Drako pointed at Talen. "I'm thinking two good men should do it."

Talen nodded. "I'm on it."

"Malek, if Oram finds out who we are, we want to divert him to another location, not here. We need another house, somewhere far enough from here to keep us safe."

"Got it."

Satisfied they were on the right track, Drako sat. "I'm going to—"

"Get married," Malek interrupted. "As soon as possible. You can't put it off now. Not with father gone. There's nobody but us. Father's brothers died years ago, and they left no sons to take our places. If we die without sons, there isn't a man, woman, or child alive that won't suffer the consequences."

"You're right." Drako drew in a deep breath, released it. "A wedding is the last thing I want to think about right now, but it's my duty. It will be done."